Tempting Disaster

Edited by
John Edward Lawson

RAW DOG
SCREAMING
PRESS

Published by Two Backed Books, an imprint of Raw Dog Screaming Press
Hyattsville, MD

First Paperback Edition

Cover image: "Deadly Dance by Dina Lenkovic, www.dina-lenkovic.com
Interior illustrations by Cake Earthhead
Book design: John Edward Lawson

Printed in the United States of America

ISBN 1-933293-00-4

Library of Congress Control Number: 2005900533

www.twobackedbooks.com

Acknowledgements

"Junkyard Fetish" by Darren Speegle is from the collection *A Dirge for the Temporal*

"Broken by Love" by Mark Howard Jones first published in *Unknown Pleasures*

"Painstation" by Ronald Damien Malfi first published in *Peep Show*

"N is For..." by J.M. Heluk first published in *Horrorfind Fiction*

"Andrea Gives Good Head" by Wendy Brewer is from the collection *Beyond Damnation*

"The Doll, or: What the Dead Think About at the Very End of the World" by Lance Olsen is from the collection *Hideous Beauties*

"Black Wings" by Jeffrey Thomas first published in *Unkown Pleasures*

Contents

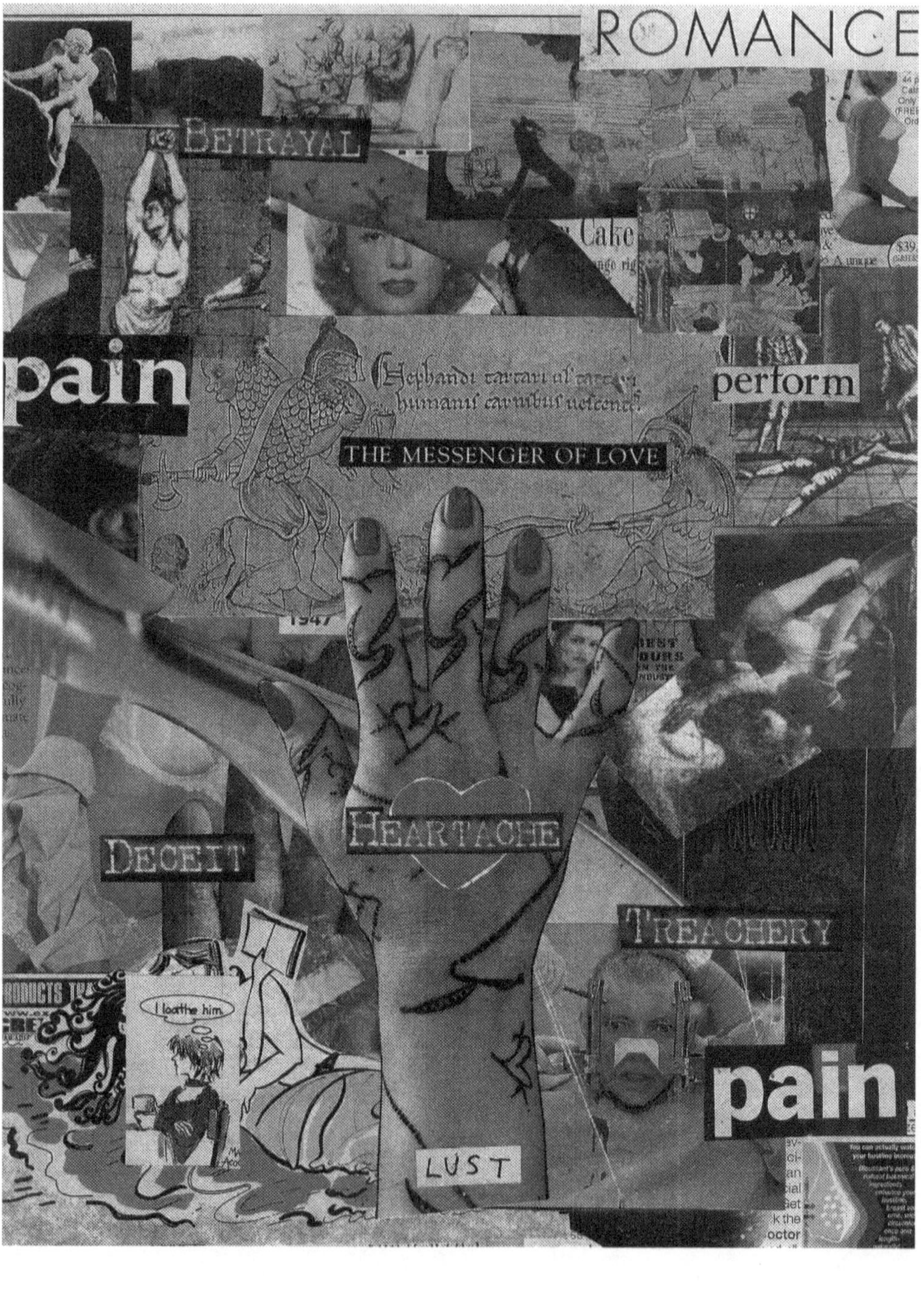
ROMANCE
BETRAYAL
pain
perform
THE MESSENGER OF LOVE
HEARTACHE
DECEIT
TREACHERY
I loathe him.
pain
LUST

Love, Loathing, Lust

Junkyard Fetish

by Darren Speegle

OOH, *had his sex*, unh, *had his body,*
Had him beggin' for my honey,
Had him chained and screamin' mercy,
Quench my hunger, suck my thirsty…

The *ooh* and the *unh* got him, as always. He didn't give a damn if he was on the freeway, he was unzipping. Alice helped him get it out, but when she bent down to do more, he pulled her away by the hair.

"What?"

He didn't answer. He had seized his nobility in his hands and was stroking, hard.

Ooh, *shared his lust*, unh, *shared his naughty,*
We were bathin' in the honey…

He was swollen to bursting already, and the song was still in its opening verse; the blood part hadn't even come yet.

"Save some for me, won't you?" Alice said.

"Shut up!" he panted.

Fucking Alice. She would never be the woman Amy was. Never.

"You're gonna get us killed, Ricky. Here, let me have the wheel."

He did, finding leverage with his free hand, giving it all he had with the other.

When he went, he went with a bang. Just like Amy, who had left him

9

chained to the door of the Mercury.

Untwisting the wire that held the flaps of the torn fence together, they made their way among the wrecks to the same heap of mangled metal they always did. Alice was more eager than him today, maybe because of what she had witnessed on their way here. He remembered a time when he literally had to pin her down. An erstwhile stripper, having worked in one of the seediest spots in the city, she had encountered all sorts. But she had never played what he and Amy had always referred to as blood games until he introduced her. He didn't know where one went to find such sport; he and Amy had discovered it on their own, with a little unintended help from Amy's dad.

The rear door on the driver's side hung askew, open enough to slip a heavy chain around each side of the window frame, but little more. Bits of safety glass clung to rotting rubber, and in place of the vehicle's one shattered window was a thick piece of plywood, bolted in place, ragged from the claws of hounds, particularly around the holes the chains fed through. Dried blood still stained the area where the door had once molded with the car's body. The place where the damage had occurred, where the impact of the truck had been absorbed, was rusted almost through. Buck, Amy's dad, said the driver and two passengers were killed. Having been hired on at the junkyard long after the Mercury was dragged onto the lot, Ricky took the old man's word for it.

The appeal of the Merc went beyond its history, though. The car was back in the corner of the yard, about as far from the office as possible. It had a huge back seat, everything two starry-eyed bloodlovers could ask for in an afternoon escape. But most attractive was the element of danger, pungent like old oil, shrill like stripped metal on the tongue.

Each day at closing time, the old man took a ride around the lot in a forklift, satisfying himself that everyone was gone before he let loose the dogs. He couldn't see back in the niche where the Merc had been laid to rest, but they could hear him as he drove past. They knew they had minutes to attain the peak they had been teasing at for the last half hour or so, unlock the chains that bound whichever one was slab that day, and slip back through the rip in the fence. They had cut it close so many times, the old man thought nothing of his hounds racing off in that direction, howling their heads off. He assumed it was to do with the punks who lived on the next block, always pitching back tall boys and flipping people off.

The stupid old man probably never realized those were the very boys his daughter had formed her pop band with, went to fame and fortune with, leaving junkyard games to Daddy and Ricky and whomever else might want to experiment.

The visible links of chain worked at Ricky's nerves and appetites as he approached in the company of his inferior replacement partner. He hated Alice and supposed eventually the game would go too far and he would kill her, leave her body for the hounds. The old man didn't come back here any more, no need to worry about him finding what was left. And if he did, he wouldn't be able to tell her from the bones of the woman who started the whole cycle.

It was all cyclic. Ricky had watched the afternoon shows enough to know it was all fucking cyclic. TV was all he had to do before he found Alice at the strip bar; he had quit the junkyard when Amy left.

He looked at Alice and wondered why he hadn't told her everything—not through the casual remark, but in credible detail. In theory it would only enhance the experience. Maybe it was impatience. He'd virtually had to force her the first few times, before she finally admitted she had begun to crave their afternoons. He didn't have the wait power to let her come to terms with the fact that Amy, as a teen, had witnessed the old man in the Merc with his secretary. Amy had not just gotten her eyes' fill of their kinky backseat amusements—the plywood had no doubt been installed to keep out the gnashing, maniacal dogs, which the old man clearly liked to have about when he drilled the woman—she had watched the old man kill her.

From the lot's chain-link perimeter, Amy had looked on. It was night, no less than the fourth in a row that her father had made her let out the dogs. Terrified of them and their insanely possessive loyalty to their owner, she carried out his wishes from outside the fence, using a long rod to shove aside the beam that held the double doors of the ramshackle structure which contained the beasts. The fourth night she had dared to see what the hell was going on in the back of the lot.

The way the old man did it was an image that screwed itself in permanently; he had pushed his secretary's head into the crack of the askew door, where the dogs could get at it.

Ricky saw it in his mind's eye as he led Alice around to the passenger side rear, opening the door on screechy hinges and shoving her inside.

The tools were on the floor, scattered among the safety glass, screaming at him as always to be picked up and used in one fell, double-fisted stroke. He didn't. He wouldn't. Dead blood was no good to anybody. Besides, it was his turn slab. Alice got to work the instruments this afternoon.

"God, I loved watching you in the car," she breathed on his neck as she closed the locks.

Per routine, he tried the locks, remembering how he had tried them then, that last day with Amy. As always they were secure; he was bound; he was slab.

Alice removed her shirt, revealing the scarred mounds of her once beautiful breasts. She placed one nipple against the mutilated tissue at the top of his scalp, where the hair no longer grew. She thought the area a product of the game from the past, which indeed it was, only in a different way. That particular experience he would never share, in detail or otherwise. It wouldn't shrug off like Alice's electing not to believe him about his former blood partner being the same Amy who was known in the world of pop music as *Honeygirl*. Funny, if she only bothered to look outside the blood-tainted windows of her little dollhouse occasionally, she would eventually come across the former-junkyard-girl-rises-to-the-top-of-the-charts story. He'd seen it himself on a couple talk shows.

Yeah, he understood how an old man could grow sick of his dull, unimaginative partner. He could understand how one person might want to feed another to the dogs. This was why he did not hate Amy. He had forgiven her even before the unleashed beasts came howling and slinging their bloodthirst. He had loved her even as their snarling, salivating muzzles squeezed through the crack of the door, tearing at his head, which, thanks to her enviable, textbook expertise with the chain, she had rendered virtually immobile. He had delighted in her even as his fingers madly worked to get around the key, which she had left in the lock for him, like a last demented amusement. God did he love her.

Ooh. Unh.

"Come on," he said through his teeth. "Come on, Amy."

Alice was used to being Amy. She didn't care. She liked the song too. She wouldn't have cared if she had been presented proof that the Top Ten hit, *The Games We Played*, was silently dedicated to Ricky. Bloodlust just didn't fucking care.

Ricky had long since fixed it so the old cassette player could be turned on via a direct link to the battery. The recorded tape came on now, somewhere between *The Games We Played*, *The Games We Played* and *The Games We Played*, the constantly recycled song of songs stolen from her debut CD.

"What do you want from Amy, huh?" said Alice. "A little of the cut love?"

"Yeah, Honeygirl. Come on with the cut love. Bleed me, you twisted bitch."

She held a fillet knife with a flimsy blade. It had come from a tool or tackle box in the trunk of one of the wrecks. Ricky used to go around with Amy looking through the cars, hoping not to run into any customers lest the compulsion to contribute to the bones in the back of the lot come over them. Alice didn't know that, and didn't care. Her addiction had sucked all the superfluousness that plagues the unseasoned right out of her. Not that she wanted any blood but his. Ricky was the dealer. Ricky's was the best. No one detested her like Ricky.

Ooh, *had his sex*, unh, *had his body,*
Had him beggin' for my honey...

"Open your mouth, Ricky, stick out your tongue." She liked the tongue because it healed so well, so fast. He had always thought it weak of her, but admittedly enjoyed it himself.

Had him chained and screamin' mercy,
Quench my hunger, "SUCK MY THIRSTY…"

"What the hell?" It was Alice who spoke, reacting to Ricky's start as well as to the voice that had intruded on their game. He watched her eyes dart from window to window, back down at his amazed, inspired face.

"Yeah the taste buds, mmm the tickle
Yeah the taste buds, mmm the trickle
Of the blood
Our married blood
Ooh, the blood
That is the honey…"

"Hello, Amy!" he announced, rising against the chains.

"You've taken a whore," she said, still invisible to them.

"Tired of waiting for the old one," he said, laughing. "Get in here, you. Where are you?"

He was looking at Alice as he spoke, pasting her with it…this confused child, sorry excuse for a lover.

Still Amy did not show. She was a voice. That voice that had titillated the world…

Quench my hunger, suck my thirsty…

"If I was the whore, I'd run," the voice said, "'cause my dad's coming and he's *mean*."

Sufficiently frightened, Alice grabbed her shirt, backing off him. "Save some for me," she spat. "For me, you fucker." Then she was shoving open the door, and dodging wreckage as she ran away.

"Get in here, you!" repeated Ricky. "I've missed—"

Then he heard the barking. Her face flashed in the window, made-up like MTV, and the *ooh* and the *unh* and a tire tool in her hand.

As it came crashing through the window, the noise of the dogs rose to a not altogether alien crescendo of bloodlust.

Broken By Love

by Mark Howard Jones

THE MECHANIZED CURL of her head was proving almost irresistible to me. Her scalp, like a prehensile tongue, tasting the air for clues. "Do yu expec' me to tch-tch-tch-trust yu?"

I swallowed hard. My penis grew hard.

"I...I...I...," I began, then stopped. Her carapace flicked open and closed quickly.

I remember thinking, in the middle of it all—*Right now, if I met God, I'd thank him for not existing.*

The melding of terror and arousal was like...nothing describable.

I thought at first she might be attracted by my piercings and markings (mostly self-created), but when a huge drop of oil splashed onto my shoulder from of the huge wheels as they passed over us, I realized the truth.

My skin was covered in a green-black film. Perhaps it reminded her of a Klektchst male. Maybe she'd never seen a living specimen of the other half of her species and didn't know what to look for.

The gaze of her luminous amber and green eyes lay fixed on me beneath her dark brow.

I could not read her expression.

She stood just short of five feet tall with slender multi-jointed limbs, sleek and shining and dark.

I had been drawn to the specimen I had seen previously in an exhibition case. It possessed an elegance and allure no human female could come close to matching.

I'd gazed for hours at the line of flesh where the carapace joined the body. Upon leaving the exhibition, I had struggled to hide my erection beneath my clothes. I went back every spare minute when I was not on shift.

Now that a live Klektchst female stood before me, my arousal was almost agony. The dead flesh I had seen before had caused me problems. A breathing female generated an unbearable degree of attraction. The folds of flesh that held the carapace puckered and stretched sweetly in a way that made me groan with exhilaration and frustration. I prayed that she did not know what the sound meant.

The glistening, green-black curves of her naked torso gave an impression of unknown strength and suppleness. No woman had ever or could ever...

A soft whirring escaped her mouth as she moved closer to me. I felt electrified, my nerves on fire.

A thin, fast rain began to fall as a muffled thud sounded from the docks behind us. No doubt it was blasting away more precious Klektchst carvings to make way for extra cargo space.

The sound hadn't been particularly loud but she seemed to think it was a threat. Almost before I had realized it, she was gone. Small clouds of dust followed her to the tensed alloy fence of the compound, which she negotiated in seconds.

I ran to the fence, freezing the shout I had ready in my throat—that would be useless, I knew. She crouched, staring back at me for a few seconds. Then I watched as she disappeared swiftly into the dry, dead space beyond the wire.

It took me 10 minutes to find the nearest exit in the fence—there was no way I could climb something that high. Securing it behind me with my ID, I began to follow her tracks out into the barrens. She had made no effort to hide the evidence of her progress. I couldn't think why she wasn't using her wings.

♋

Little was known of their mating ritual. When we arrived their numbers were low and they were written off as another extinction event waiting to happen—we'd seen it so many times before. (It terrified me to think that the

16

human race was the only vital, expanding species left).

I'd been here six months before I even heard the rumors. They'd interested me so I started digging.

Appropriately enough, the first mention I found was hidden under multitudinous layers of boring data in the Archaeological Guild's core dump. There wasn't much beyond a supposition that the mating lasted nearly two days (36 hours) and hints that it may have involved ritual incisions or piercing. Even those scant details would have been inaccessible to me without the cinnabar-level clearance afforded me by my position as on-world information architect with the Transport Guild.

The only other reference was some ticketing orders relating to three individuals—one man, two women—who were being transferred to the Geo-cartographic Guild's private lazaret for treatment. There was a suggestion that the nature of their injuries was unusual.

Within a few days of their transfer off-world, the exhibition space near the harbor obtained its first specimen of a Klektchst female. She had died (or been killed) only a few days previously, I discovered. When I finally saw her, I was dismayed to see she was displayed in a seated position.

♋

I'd first seen her lurking near the ritual harbor at Tkunactekctest, with its curving carved jetties and withered monoliths—the aliens' love of carving natural features into haunting forms still shone through the heavy veil of time. Perhaps she was drawn there by the part it had played in her race's history.

We were assured by our archaeologists that the Klektchst had used it as a place to receive their emperors ashore after an enforced two-year absence on one of the small offshore islands. The reasons for this were a mystery, we were told.

Now the harbor was used for the more mundane task of shipping minerals out to the offshore launch sites and receiving goods from the most recent landings.

Whatever the reasons for her presence, I had been the one who had spotted her there and I had been the one who had fallen in love with her.

I'd tracked her for days as she hung around the loading pens, secreting herself by the enormous water vats waiting to be shipped inland to the desert towns. I had even seen her dodge between the 15-foot-high wheels of one of the constant stream of trackermeks as it departed with its liquid cargo. The drivers and the few other staff in the area either didn't see her or decided to ignore her until she became a problem. Practical people…but ignorant.

Her speed had been a revelation. It served to increase my desire for her.

On the fourth day, my clumsiness betrayed me. She had wheeled on me as I rounded the corner of a vat and half tripped over a discarded canister. Her glittering eyes seemed fascinated by me, as if trying to guess why I was following her. She evidently decided I wasn't a threat but the decision about when (or if) to announce my intentions was taken away from me.

Isamu laughed. "Yeh, yeh…very good!"

I knocked the cup against the ring in my upper lip. "I'm serious," I said in a serious, low tone.

He turned from his screen and looked at me sideways, trying to read my face. He knew I was a good actor but thought he'd known me long enough to figure out what I was really thinking.

"Nah!" He shook his head, smiling.

I put the cup down and slid across a bad image of her I'd managed to capture the previous day. "She's beautiful," I said, aware that the blurred pixel pattern showed nothing of the poise of her incredible body.

He picked it up and looked at it, putting it down almost at once."Very nice…what's her name?"

"Yes, very amusing."

"Well, what do you expect me to say when you tell me you're in love with a member of an alien species that we know almost nothing about. You need to see the doctor!" He grimaced. We'd shared quarters for almost a year. Issy and I didn't really have a lot in common (he was big on skill games—which drove me mad) but I felt I could trust him.

"I'm going to follow her—I want her."

He spun around on his chair and stared at me in horror. "What? Are you insane!!?"

Issy pulled his chair closer to where I sat. "If they find out you're talking like this, you will lose your job. You're back home quicker than they can send you—understand? They don't like it when you start playing with dangerous alien species."

I felt hurt. "She's not dangerous. Anyway, it's the worst fucking job I've ever had. I only took it to get away from Luri and her bloodhound legal bastards."

Issy ignored my reference to my wife's attempts to dissolve our marriage in the most painful way possible. He wagged a finger at me. "You don't she's not dangerous. Her sort might look on us as an addition to the menu. Or she could be carrying lethal diseases. Or you may not be able to fuck her—you may not have the right equipment. We just don't know."

I shook my head.

He looked at me with concern, which sank into frustration when he saw he hadn't got through to me. "It's been lovely knowing you," he muttered, spinning his chair back to his game.

♋

The first time she spoke, it shook me to my bones.

The Klektchst had no written literature and seemed to use words only as naming tools; the few anthropological texts available assumed they were nonverbal, assigning their sophisticated carvings the status of an infant's "sand sculptures."

As Issy had said dissuasively: "They're not animals—but they're little better than that."

Yesterday evening, I'd trailed her around the bunkers and silos for half an hour, entranced.

I lost her for a few seconds and leapt nearly 10 feet off the floor when she touched my back with her long, carved fingers.

I wheeled, my heart thumping with fear and lust.

She was a foot away, looking up into my face. "Tch-ck…w-hee…w-whyee follow?"

My tongue refused to move as I stared. Her first words had struck me dumb.

My eyes struggled to believe what they saw as she repeated her question more urgently.

When she got no reply, she seemed angered, rearing back.

In seconds she had disappeared into the gloom, an angry clicking sound snaking its way back through the darkness to me.

♋

Four hours of trekking after her in the heat underlined what a stupid move following her had been.

Thinking with my cock had got me into trouble with Luri and that's what I had come here to escape. This was a much bigger risk.

For all I knew, I might end up dead out here, despite the easily-followed trail left by my alien prey.

My hopes were dashed when I came to a deep ravine. The tracks stopped at the edge—peering across to the other side I could see that they did not resume. She was nowhere to be seen.

I panicked for a moment, dashing to the edge of the deep gash in the ground. I thought maybe she'd fallen and was lying at the bottom, injured or dead, until images of her alien agility and speed flashed into my mind.

Kneeling, I peered over the edge. There were faint traces of her progress in the wet dust. She was down there.

Panting with fatigue, I began to climb clumsily after her, relying on small outcrops to hold my weight.

By the time I had reached the only sizable ledge in the ravine, I had uncounted scrapes and bruises from my descent. To one end was an opening.

The doorway into which she had disappeared was surrounded by subtle carvings recessed into the pale rock so that they were difficult to spot from above.

A name was cut into the rock among the carvings; Itkoztanaztkt.

A soft, warm wind passed me from inside the opening.

There was no obvious light source but the whitish stone made it easy to see, perhaps Klektchst eyes had few problems with the dark.

Wide recessed galleries lay carved from the rock on either side of a broad corridor that descended slightly. Absurdly, an image of the arcades of old Paris back on Earth flashed into my mind. I doubted that the galleries had once been shops—the Klektchst didn't strike me as eager consumers.

There were no doors or openings on either side, so I assumed she must have gone straight on into the stream of warm air.

After a few hundred yards, the corridor opened into a large, light palazzo lit by an odd marine light that seemed to come from the floor.

Tiered buildings rose on all sides, carved out of the stone and meeting in a central vault above me. They had all been badly damaged by some previous seismic shift and several looked on the verge of collapse. "Our Geo-cartographers would kick themselves to death if they knew they'd missed this," I thought.

Large boulders, their natural shapes enhanced by skilled carvings, lay everywhere. They had obviously been put in place intentionally and lent the space an eerie air—as if they sensed I was intruding where I did not belong.

I groaned. She could be anywhere. I scanned the huge square.

A soft whirring sound came from a long, low building projecting into the right-hand side of the square. The tingle in all my nerves told me it must be her.

I hurried over to the building's wide doorway and peered inside. A corridor painted with bright images set high on the walls stretched away from me. I hadn't known the Klektchst painted. Perhaps I was the only one who'd ever seen them.

I followed the corridor slowly, trying to make out the paintings as I went. I had little luck and, even if the light had been better, I doubt I would have been able to understand what the bodies in the paintings were doing. Something medical, maybe.

Eventually I entered a low-ceilinged room. Arranged around the sides were a dozen long stone slabs, bifurcated at one end.

The whirring sound came again. Peering closely into the dimness, I saw her. She was crouching at the split end of one of the slabs.

Her amber and green eyes glowed at me in the gloom. Her lips parted. "Ch-c…ch-c…ch-c…come".

It was an invitation that I felt I'd come millions of cold miles to accept.

Broken By Love

I approached the slab cautiously. Did she find me as attractive as I found her? The rain had washed off much of the oil that she might have found alluring. Now to test my theory that she saw me as a mate and not as a meal.

As I reached the slab, she almost bounced to her feet, stretching forward and tapping the surface of the stone with her digits. Startled, I stopped, ready to step back.

It was only when she repeated the action that I understood that she wanted me to lie down.

The stone (or whatever material it was) was cold at first but slowly seemed to grow warm and soft. She stood at the far end of the slab, staring at me with fascination, before jumping up onto the slab, resting two of her limbs on the twin spars just below my feet.

Slowly she lowered herself, her head curling from side to side rhythmically, until she squatted before me.

I raised myself up so I had a better view of her and for the first time I saw her genitals. The smooth dark flesh of her belly led to an opening like a human vulva, except that a short tube extended downwards like a prolapsed organ. When she flexed it, I immediately began to grow hard.

She noticed the bulge and seemed puzzled by my clothes. I quickly began to struggle out of my damp garments. I wore nothing underneath.

Her scalp raised slightly as she gazed at me, fascinated by my livid erection with its pierced tip.

She sprang forward suddenly, her body pressing against me. An electric tingle ran through me as the soft, aphrodisiac whirring rose in her throat. My penis pulsed with longing.

She drew herself up off me, arching her back. Limbs raised, eyes fixed on mine, the whirring increased in intensity as small horns extended from various points on her limbs and body. I began to panic as a hard, octandrous object appeared from her flexing genital tube.

She threw herself down on me, the horns piercing my arms, shoulders and thighs. Some missed, scraping against the stone beneath me. I thrashed and yelled as the eight-pronged genital probe scratched against my lower stomach.

After a moment's shock, she began to mimic my sounds, evidently believing them to be elements of human mating.

I felt things snap and burst inside me. Even in the center of the pain, I found it exhilarating. I even managed to reason that Klektchst males must have orifices or cavities to receive the horns which were causing me such agony.

A searing pain racked me as her eight-pronged horn began to cut its way into my stomach. Now I knew: the females must take the seed from inside the males. My screams echoed off the white walls.

Suddenly, her carapace flicked open and she flew away from me on translucent vestigial wings, cawing loudly. Small chunks of flesh and torn skin fell from the barbs as they retracted inside her and a thin rain of my own blood covered me.

Landing a few feet away, she lunged towards me as her wings slid back under her carapace, seemingly ready to attack. She stood for a moment, covered in my blood and her own sexual secretions, staring at me. Panting with pain, I lay helpless. I blacked out with the agony after she had broken both my arms.

♋

When I awoke, she was cradling my head and gazing down at me.

The pain ebbed and I realized she must have given me some sort of drug. Perhaps I would still be unconscious if she hadn't.

She pulled me off the slab. I screamed as my shattered legs hit the floor, useless to support me.

Her huge strength was obvious as she pulled me upright with hardly any effort.

She dragged me, bleeding and drooling, across to a piece of polished metal set into one of the walls.

I saw her reflection first. She looked disappointed with her handiwork.

Then my eyes fell on a shape I didn't recognize. It took me several seconds to see myself in the shining surface.

I resembled a figure that I had only seen in ancient carvings until now; an uncomfortable parody of her grace and stealthy elegance. It was the nearest she could come to an adult Klektchst male—unaware she had destroyed me and that my human flesh and bone could not sustain her "rearrangement" of it.

23

Broken By Love

♋

We could not breed. There would be no young. She seemed unworried by this…or perhaps she was unaware of it. That would be unfortunate if she became aware and vented her frustrations on me. But then, what could she do to me that she hadn't already done?

I now had no choice but to turn my back on my human heritage. I knew I must accept a life lived in the shadow of her ancient culture and alien ancestry, as we lay together in the shattered shell of the last Klektchst colony, sipping the true darkness of love.

Painstation

by Ronald Damien Malfi

THERE COMES A time in every fanatic's life when he or she is confronted—inarguably—with the severity of their own psychoses. It is at that moment a decision is to be made: pursuit or disengagement? It is the mind's way of warning its host that he or she has crossed the threshold of reasonableness and has stepped foot into the muddy trenches of human decline.

Such a realization was made clear to Keanan as he crouched behind the wheel of his Civic in the dark, hidden from streetlights, and watched Casey Madigan disappear into Façade. The notion struck him like a throng—a thousand metal utensils clattering to a cement floor—and he broke out in a sweat. Evenings, he'd stay late at the office because she stayed late. Four cubicles down from his, he could adjust his computer monitor at an angle that would reflect her image. She hardly spoke to him. He didn't care. Watching was sufficient.

Keanan cracked the Civic's window. Frigid November air whistled into the car, fragrant with the stink of the East River. Across the street, dull sodium lights flooded the stone front and gold-and-white awning of Façade. He'd never been inside the club, knew nothing about it. Yet, as he watched Casey slip inside the smoked-glass doors, it quickly became a place of severe importance to him. In his mind, he watched the svelte clockwork of her buttocks shift beneath the tight fabric of her skirt; imagined himself running his hands through the breath of her hair; caught glimpses into the pursed openings between the buttons of her blouse, and at the treasures within.

25

Painstation

Pushing the car in gear, he spun around the rain-soaked alley and headed back toward his midtown apartment. Once there, he showered, masturbated bitterly, and fell asleep with his pale and knobby legs draped over one side of the bed.

One evening a full week later, as Keanan watched a collection of Mexican janitors with lazy fascination push through the office, Casey strode past his desk. The lilac scent of her perfume coupled with the swoosh of her pantyhose jerked him from his daze, and he watched her walk, stifled by fixation. Sitting up in his chair, he shuffled through the paperwork cluttering his desk until he found the Façade's dining brochure, folded it, and stuffed it into a desk drawer.

He peered around the wall of his cubicle and stared at Casey by the copy machine. His neck felt prickly and his heartbeat was racing. The back of her legs—specifically the creases at the back of her knees—caused him to shudder, and he quickly turned away. In his mind, he embraced her warmth as if she required such affection, needed it from him, and he wondered what her breath would feel like along his neck, what her mouth tasted like. With almost youthful fascination, he contemplated the color, shape, texture of her nipples. He contemplated *everything*.

The swoosh of her stockings was suddenly very close to him. Her head peered around the side of his cubicle.

"Fucking copier is jammed," she said.

He saw her face as something exclusively designed to accommodate his obsession. Eyes, mouth, nose—her perfection was something more than evident. Not for the first time, Keanan wondered how a creature of such exquisite splendor had been created: what sort of god had, in all his malevolence, felt the desire to provoke him with such unattainable magnificence?

He stood, palms sweating against the pleats in his pants. "I'll check it out. Could just be a stuck piece of paper."

When she finally left for the evening, he followed her out into the street. It was cold and the bundle of his coat would hide his face if she happened to look in his direction. She paused amidst a wedge of pedestrians before a crosswalk while waiting for a break in traffic. Vapor wafted from her mouth.

Absently, Keanan wondered what it would be like to inhale her exhalations. Would that somehow make her part of him? Almost?

She took a cab to the East Side. Keanan followed at a safe distance in his Civic. With assumed knowledge of her destination, he felt confident keeping a healthy distance behind the cab. Three out of the five nights this week she'd hopped a taxi and disappeared beneath the gold-and-white awning of Façade.

Up ahead, he saw the cab's brake lights flare in the darkness. Tapping his own brakes, he eased the Civic to a halt in the rutted, rain-swept alley. His breath jabbed at the windshield, fogged it up. He saw Casey pay the driver and vanish through the tinted glass doors as the taxi backed up, did a one-point turn, and zipped past Keanan's car. Adjusting his tie, he popped the door and hurried toward the club.

The interior of Façade was poorly lit and only moderately populated for a Friday evening. A pianist at the end of the bar tinkled the high keys. The dull murmur of conversation rose from a sparse arrangement of circular tables to his left. The air, blue and cloudy with cigar smoke, burned his eyes. He pushed alongside the bar to his right, grabbed a handful of cocktail napkins, blotted his eyes. Looking up, he saw Casey pass down a dark, narrow corridor at the back of the club and disappear. To pursue her now, he knew, would be ridiculous. Yet there was something nestled in the creases of his brain, forcing him to continue, to follow her. At that instant, nothing else seemed to matter—his surroundings had suddenly become ineffectual and without consequence.

A clean-shaven bartender in a shirt and tie materialized. "Get you something?"

Keanan shook his head. With the stealth of a drunkard, he wove between a pair of tables and slipped into the darkened corridor. The din of conversation from the bar was immediately blocked out. Sharp, acidic smells filtered into his nose. Two restroom doors stood opposite each other further down the corridor. He paused outside the women's room, absently chewing at his lower lip, a foot tapping on the linoleum. The door was open a crack, the light on. He pushed his head back against the wall and peeked inside.

Painstation

The restroom was vacant.

Where did she go? he wondered.

Continuing further down the corridor, the echo of his footfalls became more and more prevalent. The stink of acid now burned his eyes. Unable to see properly, he ran one hand along the paneled wall, wincing at the sticky feel of it.

He stopped. There was a closed door at the end of the hallway, a water-color caricature of a grinning skeleton in a top hat painted on it.

Go home, a voice in his head spoke up. *Go before you embarrass yourself.*

The voice was powerless. His mind—stronger than any voice could hope to be—summoned Casey Madigan in all her angelic grandeur, nude before him like a thousand missed opportunities suddenly united into one perfect instance, one final chance to do what he needed so badly to do.

He pushed against the door and it opened with little protest. Before him, a wooden staircase dipped into blackness. The stink of sulfur now accosted him, potent and unapologetic. Something else, too…

Lilacs, he thought. *Her perfume.*

What was at the bottom of the stairs? There was no light switch—none that he could see, anyway—and there didn't appear to be a railing to hold. Despite this, he felt he could not be swayed; he suddenly needed to see her, at least one last time, before going home. His tenement was getting darker and darker with the passage of each day. How long could he stand there in the dark, listening to the groanings of his neighbors through the walls, while his mind repeated and repeated and repeated and repeated? Eyes closed, he only saw her face. Her image: reflected on the black walls of his cramped bedroom, his cramped mind. Each morning the spray of the shower against his body was her embrace…was individual fingers poking and prodding and caressing. It got to the point where he'd wake up, his face sore and puffy from sobbing in his sleep, curled up in a ball on the bathroom floor. Or in the hall closet. Or on the kitchen counter.

It's been long enough, he thought, feeling as if he were actually talking to her. *I need to take you now. I need another look. Nothing else matters.*

He started down the steps, the planks protesting beneath his feet. The sensation of submergence—of sinking into the earth—grabbed him around the throat and he suddenly found it difficult to breathe. The stairwell emptied into a spacious, cellar-like room with a low ceiling and track lighting. The walls were cinderblock and black with moss. Faintly, he could hear the pump of industrial music vibrating the floor and in his ears. A series of bolted steel doors stood at the far end of the room. A shape shifted in the gloom, its movement giving it away.

"Hello?" Keanan's voice quaked.

The shape stepped into the light. It was a man, constructed primarily of muscle and leather, with a shaved head and deep, insect-like eyes. He acknowledged Keanan without significance, and situated himself on a barstool in front of the row of steel doors.

Keanan approached timidly. Had he been mistaken? Surely Casey had not come down here...

"Brand," the man said.

"Excuse me?"

"No brand?" The man spoke with little inflection. He had a tattoo of a spear etched into the soft well of flesh beneath his left eye. "Two hundred dollars."

"For what?"

The man frowned. "You fuckin' around, buddy?"

Keanan shook his head. "I don't understand."

"Two hundred to get in," said the man, "unless you got a brand. Which you don't, otherwise you'd know what I'm talking about. So—two hundred."

"I...I don't have..." He patted his clothes but knew he had roughly three dollars and seventy-five cents on him. "What is it?"

Irritated, the man adjusted himself on his stool. "Turn and hit it, buddy. It ain't my job to play fifty questions."

"I'm looking for someone." The words were out of his mouth before he knew he'd said them.

"Then it's two hundred."

Is she in there? he wanted to scream. *Is Casey Madigan behind one of those iron doors?*

29

Painstation

The pumping music through the walls was making his legs weak. He frowned at the large man and turned, moving back through the darkness. He spent the next hour slinking up and down the destitute streets that ran parallel to the East River, his hands stuffed into his pockets, his mind reeling. He couldn't go home—he knew this, felt it like a premonition. She would be there: on every wall, in every closet, crouched in the cover of every shadow. There…but not there. Not real. Back at home, she was nothing he could touch and taste. Only a figment bent on the destruction of his own sanity. Obsession, he was beginning to understand, was a very angry thing.

Casey Madigan, he thought. *Casey Fucking Madigan.*

In his own unconventional way, he loved her. It wasn't just about attraction or lust. He *loved* her. He could feel her absence now like a fatal wound.

He stopped inside Skiff Laundromat, pumped cash from the ATM machine, and ran back down the length of the alley like a child fleeing a schoolhouse on the first day of summer. His feet splashed through countless puddles; his tie streamed behind him like the tail of a comet. He passed a derelict man with one arm who scowled at him as he ran. As casual as he could be, he moved through the serene atmosphere of Façade and scampered down the darkened corridor like a hound fixed on the scent of a rabbit. As he had done an hour before, he descended the rickety staircase into the underground room. The tattooed hulk was still seated on his stool when he approached the mesh of steel doors.

"Round two," the hulk said.

"I need to see her." As if he owed this behemoth an explanation.

"Two hundred."

Keanan rifled through a handful of greasy bills, produced four fifties, and held them out to the man. Expressionless, the man folded the bills into his leather wristband, stood, and slid aside a steel bolt that ran the length of the two center doors.

"Only rule is to follow the rules," said the man.

"What rules?"

"Pay attention."

With a forceful yank, the behemoth pulled both doors open, filling the outer room with a surge of thick bass and heavy drums. Lights spun and glittered behind the doors. The shapes of people moved in the darkness. A blast of hot air struck Keanan, forcing him to recoil, followed by the stink of alcohol, sweat, and sandalwood.

"Welcome to Painstation," said the hulk, and gave Keanan a forceful shove through the doors.

Blinded by confusion, an army of hands groped for him, held him vehemently. He was toggled and jerked. Something wet was pushed against the top of his left hand while someone yanked his right shirtsleeve above the elbow. Someone shouted "Bovine!" and he suddenly felt a world of white-hot pain erupt along the flesh of his right arm, screaming down to the tips of his fingers and burning up to his shoulder, where it exploded in a stroke of heat and pain throughout his chest. Like an injured animal, he tossed his head back and howled. He could smell the stink of his own burning flesh.

Someone grabbed a swatch of his hair, yanked his head back until a patch of hair came out. He screamed. Music drummed through his body. Through bleary eyes, he managed to make out a black-hooded figure before him. Something was held up and glistened with iridescent light: a hypodermic needle. Moaning, he tried to struggle free of their grasp, but it was useless. A pair of hands stabilized his head. He felt the needle penetrate the flesh at the base of his neck and draw blood.

Screaming, he brought his arms up to his face, ready to fight the figures off him. But just as quickly as they had appeared, they vanished. Behind him, the steel doors slammed closed. In front of him, the darkness was criss-crossed by intermittent patchworks of light, pulsing to the droning bass-and-drum music. Shapes—human shapes—twisted and writhed in the blackness ahead of him. His heart skipped with each downbeat of the drum. Moving slowly against the wall, he made his way through the rave, his body jolted several times by fleeting shapes in the smoke.

Finally, after what seemed like an eternity, he crossed into a narrow antechamber that amplified his breathing. In pain, he curled against the stone wall and rubbed the scorched flesh of his right arm. It was swollen and tender and hurt like hell.

Painstation

What the hell is this place?

He found it difficult to summon Casey's face and body in a place such as this. Somehow, even in his mind, her perfection was corrupted by the stone walls and reams of incense smoke. He grappled with the fleeting visage of her face in his head, felt it slipping, slipping, gritted his teeth like an animal. Could he let her slide, let her get away? How could he go home then? How would he breathe?

The passageway emptied into a black, concrete room cramped with velvet sofas and ornately carved statues depicting various sexual acts. The room smelled of lighter fluid. Iron vats hung from chains in the ceiling, draped with burning oil rags. A number of people littered the floors, sofas, and walls, coupling to beat the devil. To his right, a nude couple gyrated against each other like some refined piece of machinery. Further in the room, a shirtless obese man in checkered slacks had his face buried in the crotch of an impish older woman. In ecstasy, the woman moaned and ground her hips into the fat man's face while twisting the twin bulbs of her nipples between her fingers. A third cluster of people—four or five of them in all, predominantly male—quivered against one another, their bodies accessible and erect, the amalgam of their bodies a mass of floating hands and rigid sex organs.

Head down, Keanan pushed his way through the room to the corridor at the opposite side. A redhead with bad teeth wearing a leather basque nudged past him, leading a naked older man along with a leash attached to his testicles. "Siddy is in for the shit this time," she muttered to no one in particular and grinning ear to ear.

Keanan looked ahead and caught a glimpse of Casey Madigan passing in front of the doorway at the end of the hall. His breath seized. It was like a rush of energy—enough to revivify his mental image of the woman. He'd been wrong—her perfection was still strong here, even among the living refuse. And it was enough to get him moving again.

He hurried to the end of the passageway and found himself in a small, box-shaped room that reeked of urine. A group of naked bodies had gathered in one corner and were administering electric shocks to some woman's genitals. One of her tormentors cracked a whip along the backs of the other tormentors, drawing blood and shrill cries. He turned away in repulsion.

Casey had disappeared behind yet another door.

Is this deliberate avoidance? he thought. And would he ever be able to punish Casey for any intentional mistreatment directed at him? He tried to imagine Casey with metal plugs clipped to her labia while he toggled the switch to send current into her body, to rape her with current, but the notion only caused him to grow weak. He felt his crotch tighten.

Someone bumped his shoulder, hissed at him with porcelain fangs. Shuddering, he pushed forward and slipped through the door Casey had vanished behind.

He stood in a cylindrical hallway with a grated floor and a row of folding chairs against the wall. A number of chairs were occupied, mostly by people who looked very much like—

Like me, he marveled. *They look like me.*

Suits and ties and floral-print dresses. Casey was not here. There was a second door at the other end of the room. Had she gone out the other side? Reeling, he felt like Alice chasing the white rabbit.

The small man in the chair beside him nodded timidly in his direction. "Lights are harsh."

He only stared. "Beg pardon?"

"The lights," he man repeated. He pointed to the bright fixtures just above their heads. "Very harsh. Hurts your eyes, coming in from the dark like that. I know."

"I'm okay."

"Have a seat."

"Did you see a woman just come through here?"

The man rolled his shoulders. "Seen lots of women. What's your name? I'm Craig."

Keanan looked at him. He was a slight, almost comical man, with great knobby temples and huge eyes swimming behind the lenses of his glasses. He wore a tan blazer and a crooked brown necktie, dotted with what appeared to be mustard spots.

"What *is* this place?" Keanan asked. Peering down the row of fold out chairs, he saw their occupants sitting motionless, their eyes focused on the blank tiled wall in front of them. Could they see something he could not?

"Waiting room," said Craig.

"For what?"

"Sim-Sim."

"The fuck is that?"

"Simian Simulation. Have a seat. Wait shouldn't be too long tonight."

A bit cautious, Keanan eased himself into the chair beside Craig. The small man proffered a delicate hand, as if to shake. Keanan didn't take it.

"Craig," the man repeated.

Agitated, he said, "Keanan."

"Craig's not my real name, of course. No one here uses their real name."

"Right," Keanan said.

"Oh." Craig's eyes widened, his thin lips forming a surprised circle. His skin reeked of Skin-E-Dip ointment. "That explains it."

"What does?"

"Your arm," Craig said. "The brand is new. You can tell the way the flesh puckers up like that. See the difference?"

Craig rolled up his right pant leg. He exposed a burn-mark in the shape of a gothic "P." The mark was blue-black and flush like a tattoo. Keanan examined his own mark. It was the same as Craig's, only more vivid. The skin surrounding the brand was red and inflamed, puffed out to nearly the size of a golf-ball.

"I've been coming here for a year now," Craig said. "You're obviously new. That's what I meant."

Keanan peered down the length of the room. Like zombies, the people only stared straight ahead.

"Why the hell do you come here?" he asked.

Craig offered a timorous half-smile. "I'm sorry?"

"This place."

"Painstation," Craig said.

"Painstation," Keanan repeated. In his mind, all he could see was the vague, capering form of the woman he loved—the object of his deepest obsession. In the event of a sudden romance, what would she allow him to do? Would she let him do it all? He'd want to taste, to inhale every inch of her body, every part, and to do so with no reservations. He would love her body in any presentation.

"I come here just for the simulation," Craig said. "I'm not like those others out there. I don't think I could ever be that way. But simulation is different. Let's us all be as free as we used to be, as we ever wanted to be." He chuckled nervously. "Almost like a blessing, in this crazy world run by kings and politicians."

The door at the opposite end of the room opened and a beefy-looking figure dressed in a black cloak and hood stepped inside. He tapped the closest two zombies on the shoulder and motioned them to follow him back through the door. They did without a single word.

"Who's that?" Keanan whispered. "Death?"

Craig laughed nervously, twisting his fingers in his lap. Keanan caught the slight bulge of an erection there and quickly looked away in disgust.

"You'll like it," Craig said, his voice cracking. "It's really something else. It's like nothing in the world you've ever seen. Nothing like you've ever been a part of. Ever been skydiving?"

Confused, Keanan shook his head. "You?"

"Gosh, no," said Craig. He ran a nervous tongue along the length of his upper lip and adjusted his eyeglasses. "Don't need to. This is much better."

"Sim-Sim," Keanan mused.

"It's something so special," the strange little man reiterated.

The door opened again and the man in the black cloak stepped into the room. This time, he walked the length of the row of chairs, eyeing those seated before him through the nylon veil of his hood. He paused in front of a plump woman wearing a large gold cross, pointed at her. She stood and moved toward the door, exited the room. The cloaked Goliath continued down the row and stopped between Craig and Keanan. His index finger professed itself, hung in the air like an unfinished thought, then pointed to Craig. Silently, Craig beamed. Goliath's hand rotated and the finger then fell on Keanan. In a twirl of robes, the cloaked hulk turned and advanced toward the door again.

Painstation

"Come on," Craig said, visibly excited. "It's both of us!"

Keanan stood and followed Craig through the door at the other end of the cylindrical room. Surely Casey must have passed through here. It could be the only explanation as for her disappearance. Yet, unlike the others—and himself—she hadn't taken a seat and waited to be summoned. Perhaps she'd been a member for longer than Craig. Perhaps for years.

This isn't a fucking country club, he thought.

The cloaked stranger stopped Keanan, Craig, and the plump woman outside another set of doors. Behind Keanan, built into the wall, were rows of tiny numbered lockers. With that same pointing finger, the cloaked stranger presented each of them with a number: "Seventeen," to Plump Lady; "twenty-two," to Craig; "six," to Keanan.

With a subtle jerk of his hooded head, the figure nodded in the direction of a copper plaque sealed to the wall beside the set of doors. He paraphrased the words: "Rules. Only one, and with *no exceptions*. This is an authentic simulation of simian life. You must behave in accordance to said environment. That is the only rule. Any violation of this rule, be it deliberate or otherwise, may result in punishment or revoked membership from the establishment."

Revoked membership from the establishment, Keanan thought. *What the fuck is this all about, anyway?*

"Disrobe," said the hooded stranger.

As if reacting to the crack of a starter's pistol, both Craig and the woman began tugging off their clothes. They moved as if in a frenzy, or as if to stay clothed for another second longer would result in their immediate deaths. At one point, Craig glanced in Keanan's direction. A wealth of exhilaration had blossomed across the little man's face. His breath came in quick, excited gasps. Beside Craig, the plump woman had stepped out of her pantsuit. She stood there naked except for her tremendous bra, her ample thighs pitted with dimples, the swell of her belly a network of red stretch marks. Her crotch was a wiry cloud of bristling pubic hair.

"Disrobe," Craig muttered beside Keanan. He was tugging his knobby knees out of his slacks. "Hurry."

Do it, that same prodding voice inside his head said. *Casey Madigan did this very same thing, you know. We're all a part of each other.*

With some reluctance, he began to undress and to place his clothes in Locker 6.

A moment later, the three of them were standing before the cloaked gate-keeper as naked as newborns. From the corner of his eye, Keanan could see the stirrings of an erection between Craig's legs. For some insane reason, it reminded him of childhood fishing trips to Saratoga Lake with his father.

"Twenty minutes," the cloaked figure said. He spun a combination lock on one of the doors. Keanan heard the tumblers slide. The gatekeeper grabbed the steel handle on the door, depressed it, and pushed the door open.

Again—more heat. But filled with moisture. Rain forest. A mist seemed to roll in through the doors. Eager to begin, both the plump woman and Craig hurried through the opening. Keanan tried to follow their example, but moved much slower. When he crossed the threshold, the doors were closed on his back. He heard the lock click.

Before him lay a rain forest wonderland.

For all he knew, he'd just been transported to the Amazon. Immense tropical trees, looming like towers, blotted an artificial sky. Wild ferns grew from the dirt at his feet. Before him, a slight decline in the earth led down to a carpet of lush grass and underbrush which, in turn, gave way to what looked like a mile of dense forestry. With the exception of the wall to his back, he could make out no other visible form of human construction: no walls, no ceiling, no flooring, no vents, no windows. Above him was actual sky—or so it appeared. And the light all seemed to be coming from a single simulated sun in the sky, almost as bright and as hot as the real thing. In the distance, he could hear running water and the caws of wild birds.

This is incredible, he thought, *standing in awe. There must be acres of vegetation here. It's Eden.*

Craig and the plump woman were already down the embankment. Like apes, they staggered around incommunicative, dragging themselves through the make-believe forest on all fours. And to Keanan's astonishment, Craig and the woman quickly attacked each other, dropping to the ground. Shrieking like animals, they commenced in rigorous copulation, their bodies thrusting with such audacity that it was almost frightening. Stunned, Keanan only stared.

Movement deeper in the forest caught his eye. Squinting, he could see another couple mating in a succession of quick, reflexive hip-lunges. The woman screamed, threw her head back against a tree. Her partner bent and sank his teeth into the soft flesh just above her collarbone. She cried out in pain, her hands and feet clawing at her assailant, though her face boasted a twisted suggestion of rapture.

He downed the embankment. More couples materialized the closer he got to the body of the forest. He paused once to watch a lone woman crouch, defecate on the ground, then scurry away.

Animals, he thought. *They're acting like animals.*

A man moved past him, sniffing the air, sniffing the ground. For a moment, Keanan watched him with confounded desperation. The man paused directly in front of him, sniffing Keanan's skin.

"Watch it, buddy," he warned the stranger. "The hell is going on here?"

The stranger froze, stared into Keanan's eyes for a moment. There was no intelligence in those eyes, he saw. This freak had left all semblance of humanity out in the waiting room.

The stranger struggled with a frown, then hurried off to some other corner of this make-believe world.

A cold hand gripped his forearm, spun him around. It was another cloaked gatekeeper, though this one was shorter and carried a big wooden stick.

"That's one break," the cloaked figure said. He brought the stick up and thrust it into Keanan's gut. A roiling tumult of pain blossomed in his belly. "The rule is simple, buddy. Don't break it again."

Doubled over in pain, he watched the cloaked figure retreat through teary eyes. Bending down, the cloaked figure opened a hatch in the ground—*the floor*—and descended a stairwell hidden inside it. With nothing more than a bump, the hatch closed behind him.

"Jesus," he breathed quietly. *Was that for talking? Just for talking to someone?*

A second hand fell on his back. Tense, he spun around to see the slight, pale form of Craig from the waiting room standing behind him, a meager smile playing over his lips. Craig's small erection jutted from a nest of pubic hair like a baby bird straining for its mother. Disgusted, Keanan turned away.

I got lost somewhere along the way, he told himself. *Somehow, along the way, I lost sight of Casey and wound up here, in this alternate version of reality.*

Casey...

Craig's sweaty hands gripped Keanan's waist and he felt the man's pelvis thrust toward him—felt the biting sting of Craig's cock as it nipped his tender flesh. Appalled, violated, Keanan twisted away from the little man, but Craig's grip was tight. His hips pumped against Keanan's buttocks, his slender prick struggling for access.

"Fuck!" Keanan shouted, stumbled forward, then turned around to face the little rapist. He cocked a fist and drove it into Craig's face. A spout of blood burst from Craig's nose and the little man reeled backward and slammed onto the ground. His eyelids fluttered; his hands came up to his face. His small, red shoulders hitched. His erection quickly receded.

"Rapist fuck," Keanan breathed.

Shaking, on the verge of tears, Craig surprised Keanan by hissing through a mouthful of blood and scampering off into the forest.

This is a nightmare, he thought.

Someone slammed him from behind, knocking him to the ground, a burst of agony rupturing down his spine. Wincing, eyes filling with tears, he craned his neck to see another cloaked figure with a staff standing behind him. The figure introduced the side of Keanan's head to his steel-tipped boot. Keanan felt the world spin and go gray. Faintly, as if from the far end of a corrugated pipe, the cloaked figure warned him about breaking the only rule of Painstation and the Simian Simulation: *do not break character*.

"You're not a man in here," the figure said. "Quit thinking like one."

Keanan remained crouched on the ground until the spirals and stars faded from beneath his eyelids. He brought a hand up to his temple and it came away wet with blood.

This isn't real!

Painstation

He was suddenly overcome by the urge to prove this to himself—to prove the falsity of this room, for starters. How big could the room actually be? It was all under ground, wasn't it? There had to be walls somewhere; he'd just have to run far enough to find them. And how far?

In a frenzy, he darted toward the trees, hurdling over entwined and squirming bodies and brushing past reaching, straining hands. There were walls—had to be—and he would find them and expose this horrendous landscape, this counterfeit world. How could they even keep him locked up in here like this? Anger made him run harder, faster, and it felt good—as if he could do anything he wanted at that moment. Anything at all: rape, kill, bite, fuck, scream…just as long as he did it as an animal, did it without thinking.

There were no walls. The room had to be miles in every direction. Overhead, a flock of large, colorful birds took flight.

Casey Madigan was bent naked over a simulated stream, lapping at the water with her tongue. Seeing this, Keanan froze. A collage of Technicolor images flooded his brain: every make-believe fantasy of this woman now paled to the sight of the real thing. This splendid creature, this rape fantasy. It wasn't just her nakedness that was exposed to him for the first time; it was her *baseness*, the stripped-down, untamed essence of her being in its purest form. There, crouched beside the river like a creature of folklore and myth, her body proffered and rising, sinking, rising, sinking, her aromas filling his nose, his head. He breathed her in and allowed her natural scent to occupy every cell of his body.

Trembling, his mind like a single cable pulsing with current, he advanced toward her, stiffening.

I've seen you like this so many times in my head. So many times, just like this…yet never like this, too. It's this place. We're all different here, aren't we? Here, we can be and do whatever we like until the door opens again and we have to get home. Would you even look at me tomorrow?

He came up from behind, her scent overpowering now, and mounted her. Against him, she shuddered, sighed, rolled her head back. Their eyes met briefly. He pushed into her with a sudden burst of ferocity and she cried out. His body quivered at the sound, the feeling. Her warmth engulfed him. He saw her without opening his eyes: the firm S of her back, the tender flesh of her thighs, the purse of her sex…

She bucked beneath him and a swirl of colors filtered through his mind. *I'm here I'm here I'm here I'm here I'm—*

He felt the world pull from his feet, his knees, his spine, and quake through the shaft of his body. A giant network of nerve-endings, his entire physical self convulsed as a tingling wave of excretion erupted inside him. And in the throes of passion, he cried out into the false wilderness.

"*I love you!*"

Casey stiffened beneath him and wrenched her body from his. Keanan shuddered and nearly lost his balance, slamming against the side of a tree. Before him, Casey clambered away on her hands and knees, her wide eyes glowering at him from over her shoulder. Hot with unrequited passion, he watched her crawl away, needing her now more than ever despite the abrupt conclusion of their act—his act.

"Casey…"

Behind him: the sound of creaking hinges. He spun around and saw a number of hidden doors embedded in the trunks of the trees swing open. A regiment of cloaked figures carrying heavy staffs poured out and reached for him, yanked him to unsteady feet.

"No—" he tried to protest.

One of the figures tore his shirtsleeve up the center, scrutinized the letter P seared into his flesh. "Fresh one," the figure said.

A second figure grabbed him by the hair and jerked him backward. "This is three," he barked. "You're revoked."

In a dress of arms, Keanan was dragged toward the open doorway in the body of one of the trees. As if in a dream, he watched Casey Madigan's nude, trembling form slowly grow smaller and smaller. He clenched his hands, made fists, felt the tightening of his muscles beneath the strong grip of hands.

Into the tree. And darkness. The sound of a collection of feet trampling iron steps. Eyes wide, he could see nothing in the darkness. He smelled urine again, and fear. His own.

The beatings lasted for several long minutes. They were administered with the keen practice of seasoned professionals. Several times he thought he would black out but he never did.

I'm here, his mind said, and even the voice in his head faltered.

He was taken to another room. Left on the floor. His own breathing echoed in his ears. He thought of Casey's body shifting and pumping against his own and smiled. He tasted blood. His body was a brilliant tangle of pain.

A door opened and boots clopped toward his face. He was aware of a number of people around him. He thought he heard someone spit on the floor.

"Revoked," someone breathed. "Do you understand, sir? You have violated the only rule of Painstation. You are no longer permitted within these walls."

But what about Casey? he wanted to ask. *Beautiful, beautiful Casey?*

"I love…"

He was grabbed, rolled over onto his back. Hooded silhouettes swam in and out of the light. His vision failed him. Someone grabbed his right arm, squeezed the brand. He groaned. Someone said something else, but he could hardly comprehend words now. He heard the sliding sound of an enormous knife blade…saw it gleam briefly in the sodium lights above…

"Remove the brand," one of the figures said.

Icy pain pierced the flesh of his right arm. It deepened and struck bone. Paused. Broke through. He thought he might scream. But he didn't—*couldn't*. Now, only his mind was capable of operation.

Will Casey Madigan love me with one arm? he wondered.

The Wound

by Brandi Bell

THE ONE HE screams at when he is drunk never feels like she is
the same one he holds tight to his body while trying to sleep
off the hangover, though she is.

The cock that probes her cunt does not know that she is
picturing an open wound where his mouth is. An open wound where
the hurtful words flew out. An open wound for the beer breath.

He places his mouth on her breast and she begins to cry.

The one who seems to absorb the pain that he can't handle
anymore does not feel,
she never feels,
like she is the same one who caused the pain in the first place,
though he thinks she is.

He straddles her so that the cunt is hard to get at and
impossible to see.
He forces his cock into her that way.

He whimpers.
She whimpers.

The Wound

The open wound against her breast sobs.
She wraps her arms around his head.
The friction of the cock makes her feel like a little girl:
tight and hard to penetrate; unused; unfucked; unfucked up; new.

He thrusts. She's still. In his mind of her cunt is a bear
claw trap.
He thrusts. She's still. Her hands clawing at his back   his
chest   his face.
He thrusts. She's still. Impaled on his cock and
permanently.

She wants to spread her legs,
thrust her cunt,
open up.
She wants to fuck him back.
But his legs pin her legs to the bed,
his torso weighs down her torso,
his arms trap her head.

She moans.
He moans.

The wound against her breast becomes a mouth again and bites.
The mouth whispers, slut.
The nipple puckers, hardens.

The cunt becomes wetter because of the furious friction of the
cock trying to penetrate.
The cunt does not know that mostly he wants to hurt her right
now.

She struggles a little, still wanting her legs free, still

wanting to participate in the fucking.
The cock moves faster and further.
Her cunt, becoming wetter, blooms red and gaping and wounded in
his mind.
Wounded by him.
He fucks faster.

The one who holds her so tight never feels like the one who says
he can't stand her, can't stand her need, though he is.

The cunt, still forced closed by his legs, is doing everything
it can to open and let the cock in more.

All the cunt wants is that cock.
All the cock wants is to feel the red blooming gaping w/hole.

She whimpers.
He thrusts.
She moans.
He thrusts.

She whispers, my little girl hole, and he gasps
because yes that red gaping bloom is and he still wants to hurt.

The little girl hole begins to recognize this.
She whispers, fuck my little hole, because she wants him to.

He whimpers.

When he wakes after this he will not remember feeling the way
she seems to absorb his pain, though she does.
He will instead remember how trapped he feels and the need to
force himself into her and cause a blooming red gaping in his

The Wound

mind.

He holds his face in her hands while he comes.
She whimpers like a little girl wanting to be fucked pure, new.

The Agent

by Michael Hemmingson

Y ou're at this party in Tribeca and you really don't want to be here, but…here you are. What you hate about the evening: very little, if any, business calls. You keep checking your cell to make sure it's getting reception. You strike up a conversation with a young woman with long brown hair; you really like her eyes. She touches you, you touch her back; you play with her long hair, twist it in your fingers, smell her perfume and tell her you approve of the scent. The next thing you know you're in one of the bedrooms having sex with her on a pile of coats. When this hasty act is done, you leave the room first. No one at the party seems to notice your indiscretion; you stop feeling guilty and begin to feel like the conqueror—like a Norseman who has just ravaged some princess on the high seas of a badly written Viking romance novel. You get yourself a new drink, and you need a drink; you go out to the balcony and sit down. Two minutes later, the young woman joins you. She also has a cocktail, and she appears freshly fucked—glowing and smiling.

"So," you say.

"So," she says.

"That was something else," you say.

"Oh yeah," she laughs. "Do you do this sort of thing often?"

"No," you lie.

"Me either," she goes.

You ask her name.

"Trinity."

"That's really your name?"

"Like The Matrix movies," she says.

You nod and say, "I like it."

"That's my chat room handle anyway," she says. "Do you do the Internet?"

"Only e-mail."

"And porn?"

You smile and say, "Who doesn't look at porn on the Net?"

"My husband, he looks at it all the time."

"Your husband?"

"Jacks-off to the weirdest sites."

"Husband."

"You know my husband, right? I saw you talking to him like you were old friends. William Blount."

"Holy shit," you say, "you're Bill Blount's *wife*?"

"Relax," Trinity says. "He has no idea what we just did. He never notices anything. Terrorists could fly a plane into the building down the street and he wouldn't take heed. It's *okay*."

"I didn't know you were married."

"I didn't tell you," she says, and: "Does it matter?"

You're like, "No."

"Ever do cybersex?" she asks.

"Once or twice."

"I do it all the time," she says. "It's fun. I like it."

"Good for you."

"So what do you do? And what's your name?"

You tell her your name, and tell her what you do for a living.

She says, "An agent? Like, you represent *actors*?"

"Writers."

"What?"

"Novels and screenplays," you say. Under thirty, you're the youngest and hottest mover of product at a big and well-known agency; you know how to find the stars in the piles of manuscripts. You don't tell Trinity this.

"Oh," she says.

"Your husband publishes writers," you say.

"Oh," Trinity says, "I never talk to him about his work. Have you always been an agent?"

"I used to deliver pizzas when I was a kid," you say. "I was a bike messenger in college. Then I tried my hand as a junior stockbroker."

"Stocks!" Trinity goes. "I love playing the stocks. I have an Ameritrade account," she says.

"Yeah?"

"I," she says proudly, "am a day trader."

You tell her you do a little day trading on your Schwab account.

"Sometimes I make money, sometimes I don't," she says. "Usually I do. What I like most," and her eyes get this little *something* in them, "day trading and having cybersex at the same time."

"Sounds like fun."

"So why aren't you on Wall Street anymore?"

"Stress," you say.

"There's no stress being an agent?"

"It's a different kind."

"As long as you're happy. Are you happy?"

You have to think about that. You say, "Yes." You say, "Yes, I am."

"That's good," she says, "it's good to be happy. That's all that matters, right?"

"Right."

She says, "So, who are your hot clients?"

"Right now I have two." You're more than happy to talk about this. "They're different as different can be. One is this wild fellow from Arkansas; he wrote a novel called *Sunlight Reflections on a Crushed Beer Can*. It's the ultimate tome on white trailer park trash. It's an unbearably sad work of bone-crushing genius—a 980-page monster of a book."

Trinity says, "980 pages?!" She goes, "I'll wait for the movie."

"There very well may be a movie," you tell her; "I'm talking to several producers. Now, my other precocity," you go, "has written a collection of

49

eight stories, a slim but dynamic volume, called *Sex, Drugs, General Mayhem and Death in Junior High*. The writer, by the way, is a thirteen-year-old girl."

"Junior high is the worst," Trinity says, "kids can be truly evil in those trying and awkward years."

"Yes, that's what my young author claims."

"Uh-oh," Trinity says, "William is looking at us."

"He is?"

"It's okay. I better go to him."

"Okay."

"It was fun."

"Yeah."

She leaves. You stand there on the balcony. Your cell rings. The caller sounds far away—and he is. He's a publisher you know in Osaka.

"Takayuki-san," you say. "How goes it?"

"Let us talk dinero," Takayuki says.

He wants to buy the Japanese rights to four books you rep. You're ready to make a deal tonight; doing so makes you feel complete when you finally go to bed. You'll wake up feeling *right*.

♋

The next day—noon—interior: at the office—you get a phone call from Los Angeles (it's nine a.m. there, the day's just starting); it's Bernard Goldman, a producer, and he's distraught.

"Your client, man," Bernard says, "your client, Johnny Ray Thorn—"

"What about him?"

"—thought it was all an act, a ruse, you didn't tell me he was an *actual fucking hick*!"

"He wrote a novel about hicks," you say. "What did you think?"

"But, yeah," Bernard says, "I didn't know he was one!"

"What happened?"

"I invited him to this party in Bel Air. Belairbelairbelair, and who do I allow to enter the gates of the Elysian hills? I guess I should have checked him out first, but man oh man you could've given me some kind of heads up here, guy. He comes to the fucking party in smelly old overalls and no shoes! All three hundred and twenty-five pounds of him! And he proceeds to get drunk as a skunk and grab-asses every starlet in the vicinity. Mind you, some of these girls didn't mind, they found him kind of amusing, but to me it was as embarrassing as walking into a green light meeting without my prize Rolex. I mean, really, guy! I mean, I love *Sunlight Reflections on a Crushed Beer Can* and I want to get the abridged version up on the celluloid, but I'll tell you *this*—I do *not* want this hillbilly mofo on the set. I mean, he's talking like he'll be there, like he's going to be at every shoot and have say-so on all the dailies, but I declare this here and now, dude: it ain't gonna happen. No way, no how. He is not L.A. material."

"Bernard," you say sincerely, "I don't know what to tell you; I'm sorry the meet didn't go well."

"The guy can tell a story on paper, but he should be locked away for the good of all humanity."

"Nevertheless," you say, "the movie's going to be a hit."

"Let's hope so. After all, I'm *banking* on it."

"So let's sign on it."

"I can't yet. You know how it goes."

You always know how it goes.

An hour later, Johnny Ray Thorn calls from his hotel room in Century City.

"This place is weird," he says, "and the people are weird."

"Maybe it's time to go home, Johnny Ray. Arkansas is calling. Eh?"

"Arkansas can kiss my hairy ass," says Johnny Ray. "I booked a flight to New York. I'm leaving in two hours."

"New York?" you say, rubbing your forehead very hard. "Why New York?"

"Maybe I can do some book signings. I talked to the lady in publicity. She says she can set something up in a day or two. My novel is still selling, right?"

"Flying off the shelves," you say. "Flying."

"So no problem. I'm flying too."

"Well," you say, "call me when you get in."

"Isn't that little girl in New York?" Johnny Ray asks. "You represent her? The schoolgirl slut?"

You hesitate and then say, "Molli Runes. She is here doing promo stuff."

"Yeah, that's what I read. I'd like to meet her."

"She's very busy, you know."

"I wanna meet her."

♋

Molli Runes is at the SoHo Grand in a $600-a-day-room. She has a reading and signing to do at six, another reading at nine, and two talk shows in the morning. Her story collection is #5 on The List, she's going to be in *The Village Voice's* "Writers on the Verge" Issue, and you hear rumors she may be up for a PEN/Hemingway Award. Or was that the Faulkner? You can never get the two straight—and does it matter? Either way, it's sales and attention and you've been telling her to get to work on that novel; and like any teenage girl, she's stubborn to listen.

You go to see her at the SoHo, to escort her to the readings/signings; you are not prepared for this: a naked and apparently young author bouncing up and down on the bed.

She has a crack pipe in one hand, a lighter in the other. Her hair is sticking out in all directions. Her body is pale pink, her pubic hair wispy and her breasts like tiny apples (so they say).

"Hey!" she goes. "There you are!"

"Oh hell," you mutter. "Molli," you say, "please put some clothes on."

You look at the wall.

She goes, "I know you're not such a *prude*."

You're like, "Get dressed."

"What do you have against the human body?" She hops off the bed and she's next to you, looking up at your closed eyes. She smells like hotel soap and rock cocaine. "Oh," she says.

"Molli."

She says, "Will you look at me?"

You look at her.

"Why don't you get naked," she says.

"Why don't you get dressed."

"Why don't we *fuck*," she says. "I need to get royally *fucked*. I've been smoking this bad shit for an hour and I'm horny as a horny toad. My cunt is dripping, don't you see? Look, oh look. Just look. You can feel my slime if you want."

She giggles.

You are *not* Humbert Humbert; still, you cannot help yourself from checking out her nymphet form. You fear she will destroy many men when she's ten years older, if she hasn't destroyed a number of men already. In her short fiction, the "I" has slept with teachers and older men who live across the street and give the "I" marijuana and tequila.

"Where," you ask, "is your mother?"

"She's not here."

"Where did she go?"

"She didn't *come*," Molli says. "She's back at home, fucking her new boyfriend."

"She let you travel *alone*?" you say, incredulously.

"I'm a big girl," Molli says, and then looks at her breasts. "Well," she goes, "maybe I'm *not* big," and giggles, "but I can travel to The Big Ol' Apple by myself. They gave me this room. I have my own credit card, thanks to you."

"Yeah?"

"Thanks to *you*, I'm semi-rich."

"Yes, Molli," you say, "and with such things—there is a certain amount of responsibility."

"Poo on that," she goes, "let's celebrate my impending fame." She tugs at your arm and says, "Let's have a sticky quickie." She says, "Don't worry, I'll never let a biographer in on this special moment, even if you knock me up. Oh, Mr. Agent, Mr. Secret Agent, won't you please please stick your fat dick in me and fill my womb with your baby-making love seed?"

All you can do is envision the repercussions. You're reminded of the James Bond movie *For Your Eyes Only*, and the scene where a blonde underage nympho ice skater tries to entice Roger Moore into bed with her pink naked body; but Bond says, "Don't grow up too fast," and turns her down. When you saw the movie, you thought: *Oh, Mr. Bond!* because let's face it, you would've pumped that little pussy if you were 007.

And yet you are not on Her Majesty's Secret Service with Q providing lots of gadgets, so you take Molli's crack pipe away.

She goes, "*Hey.*"

You say, "There's a book to promote."

She goes, "Bummer."

You say, "This is your career."

She's like, "You have a point. It's all that matters, right?"

"Right."

♋

Molli does the Catholic schoolgirl thing: plaid skirt, white blouse, black penny loafers, off-white knee-high socks. This, you find, is more sexy than nudity. She knows what she's doing and you know she'll get far in this business, and for whatever duration (another collection, a novel, maybe a movie, then oblivion) you will get fifteen percent.

So, at the six o'clock bookstore gig, she performs well. She reads two stories from her book, thirty minutes total, and you're amazed at her delivery: the projection, the dramatic pauses, the levels in her voice, the various voices she gives to her characters. She must have had some training in drama or speech in her hometown, Seattle. There are about thirty people at the store and everyone buys books. A young man from the publisher's publicity department is there, and he says he has a limo to whisk Molli to her next gig.

"A *limo*," Molli says. "Coolness."

The limo has a fully stocked bar. Molli makes herself a vodka tonic; you know it's pointless to admonish her. You make yourself a Tom Collins, drink it fast, and make another.

"Better watch it," Molli says, "you'll get drunk."

"I never get drunk," you say, and this is true. You can drink and drink, and the best you can do is a damn fine buzz. You have never been shit-faced in your life.

"My whole family—alcoholics," she says. "Especially my Mom. Sometimes I think I *shouldn't* drink."

"You should not. You're too young."

She laughs and says in a snotty high-pitched tone, "And I'm too young to have published a book full of sex and debauchery."

She has a point.

She gives you her vodka tonic. "You finish it. I have another reading to do."

You drink her drink.

At the second reading, the one person you don't expect to see is there— you're hoping you wouldn't see him, not right now. Johnny Ray Thorn, all six-foot-five, three hundred-plus pounds of him. He's an impressive sight: barrel-chest, big belly, thick arms. His legs are very skinny. His hair is unkempt, unwashed, and he's missing several front teeth. What did the *L.A. Times* say about his author photo? *The most unattractive and scary-looking Southern writer since Harry Crews.* That's Johnny Ray Thorn, all right, and damn it all if you're not proud of the sonofabitch; you're just not prepared for him being here, here. At least he's wearing shoes. He's wearing the overalls; he's told you it's the only clothes he feels comfortable in. There are fifty, sixty people at this reading, and every one of them looks at Johnny Ray with the appropriate literary snobbish glance, one you've seen all too often, as if to say, "What is that trash doing here?" But a young fellow wearing a brown sports coat and horn-rimmed glasses says, "Aren't you John Thorn? You wrote that trailer park novel that's a bestseller, right?"

"Yeah," Johnny Ray says flatly, "that be me."

"I loved your book."

"Thank you kindly."

"Johnny," you say. "Jonathan."

"I love it when you call me that."

"You made it."

"It was a hairy flight," he says. "Hairy like a skunk's ass, and just as smelly. Lots of bumps in the air. What do they call that stuff? Turby. But I had this." He removes a flask from his overalls. "Always helps."

"And what's that?" Molli says, joining in.

"Moonshine, baby," says Johnny Ray. "Distilled it myself. My grand-papppy's original recipe."

"Wow."

"You're Miss Runes," says Johnny Ray.

"And you're Mr. Thorn," says Molli.

"Seems we have much in common."

"Yeah, our names pop up on the same bestseller lists."

"And we have this crazy man." Johnny Ray wraps a big arm around your neck. You wince. You smile. You can smell his armpit and it ain't a field of daisies.

Molli slaps you on the ass.

They both laugh.

"Well," you say.

"I read your stories," Johnny Ray says, letting you go and stepping toward Molli, looking down at her, "and I wanted to meet you."

Molli stares up at him like she would view a mountain in the desert. "I can't say I've read yours. I have it, but it's just too big for a girl like me."

"One day you'll be able to take it."

"I'm sure I will."

"Enough of this," you say. "Let's get out of here."

"Yeah," Molli says, "we have a stretch."

♋

There are five of you in the limo—the fellow in the brown jacket and a skinny clerk from the bookstore were invited by Molli and Johnny Ray; they are both aspiring writers and they want to show you their stuff, they want book deals, they want to be famous without having put in the work it takes. They are as common as nineteen-year-old porn actresses who've done one or two videos and have visions of money and underground fame. You usually tell them (on the phone) that you have too many clients right now, but since they're here in the limo and drinking martinis, you tell them, "Send me what you have, here's my card, send me your novel or story collection, let's see what you got." The bookstore clerk says she has an historical novel she's been working on since she was Molli's age; the fellow in the jacket says he's written "the new novel."

"And what's that?" Johnny Ray says. "What's that shit?"

"My novel would blow you away, man."

"It would have to be a mighty wind," Molli says, "to blow such a big guy like Johnny Ray away."

Something happens—tires screech, brakes groan, there's a thump and a smash and everyone spills their drinks on themselves. Molli yelps. The limousine has come to a stop.

Seems another limousine—a longer one—has hit the one you're in. The longer limo is filled with drunken prep school boys in blue jackets and red ties. They all have blonde hair.

Other cars honk. Cabs, mostly.

The two limo drivers yell at each other, standing in the street.

"What the fuck?" the prep school boys say. "Someone's gonna pay for screwing up our night."

Molli opens the sun roof and pops her head out. "What's with you jackasses? Can't you hire a driver who can *drive*?"

"Hey, look at the little girl."

Molli sticks out her tongue. She opens her white blouse and flashes her tits at the boys. She giggles and ducks back in the limo.

The boys—half a dozen of them—surround the limo, pound on the windows; they say they want Molli to come out.

"Step out, honey," they say, "we wanna rape you!"

"Hold this," Johnny Ray says, handing you his flask. He walks out of the limo like Godzilla emerging from the ocean. The boys all go quiet. One of them is like, "Oh shit, we're in trouble."

As your star author defends the honor of your other star author by beating the living crap out of the drunk prep school boys, you sniff the flask. Smells like gasoline. You try it; the moonshine burns your mouth and throat but it gives you an immediate buzz, the best you've ever had. So you drink more.

You wake up on a bed in the SoHo Grand. It's 6 a.m. Molli is next to you, and she's getting up. She's wearing pink pajamas. Johnny Ray is asleep on the floor. Your head is pounding and your eyes hurt. It's your first hangover. "Oh God," you say.

"Don't worry, nothing happened," Molli says. "I have to get a shower. Morning talk show, remember? Go back to sleep."

You close your eyes.

You open your eyes three hours later. Johnny Ray is talking on your cell phone. You sit up.

"He's awake," Johnny Ray says. He holds out the phone. "It's for you. Good news."

"Who is it?"

"L.A."

It's Bernard Goldman. "Hey, guy," he says. "Okay, so Thorn ain't so bad. It's all in the presentation, but the man has talent. Let's seal the deal."

You do some talking, say, "FedEx the paperwork to my office," and you go to the bathroom and piss. You almost puke. Things are still spinning. You don't like this feeling.

Johnny Ray is sitting on the bed and looking out the window. "They're really gonna make a movie of my life," he says. "Weird."

"Where's Molli?"

"She took off to her TV thing. I wanna do TV things."

"What happened last night?"

"Let's see. We got in a fender bender, I whooped some Central Park rich ass that needed a whooping, we escaped the cops, and you got drunk as a skunk, my friend."

"You didn't do anything with Molli, did you?"

"Oh, man, that's a dumb thing to ask."

"Did I?"

"We had to carry you up here."

"I've never been drunk," you say.

"Welcome to the real world."

"Drunk people do dumb things."

"Look, about Molli," he says. "She's a child. This whole wayward slut thing is an act. A ruse. We talked; she's a virgin. She knows the game. It sells books, right?"

"Right."

"And that's all that matters, right?"

"Right."

"So why don't you get washed up and let's go get us some pancakes?" he says. "Do you like pancakes?"

"Jonathan," you say, "right now I could eat a whole stack of them. Lots of butter, lots of syrup."

"Breakfast is a very, very important thing in a man's life."

You couldn't agree more.

Andrea Gives Good Head

by Wendy Brewer

THE PAIN SLAMMED into Andrea's head all at once, driving into her ear like the razor-sharp tip of an ice pick. It circled around her skull like barbed wire and *squeezed*. She dropped the piece of chicken she was breading and screamed, gripping the sides of her head with both flour-coated hands and falling to her knees. The sound was like a dentist's drill, burrowing into her head and vibrating her entire body. Tears gushed from her eyes, saturating the front of her blouse and she pulled at her hair, jerking her head from side to side, screaming through clenched teeth.

Ten minutes later, she rose shakily from the floor, an expression of confusion on her face. Her head throbbed faintly and her body was drenched in a sticky sheen of sweat. The incident was already fading from her mind and she bent down, picked up the piece of chicken from the floor and tossed it into the frying pan.

♋

James frowned as he wheeled his old Chevy into the driveway. Cars lined the road in front of his trailer on both sides of the street. He squinted against the setting sun, looking at the thick, dark forest that sat about a half an acre behind his trailer. He could see the shadowy outlines of people moving along the edge of the woods.

"What the fuck..." he muttered, frowning, his cigarette dangling loosely between his lips. He grabbed his six-pack of Bud off the seat and got out.

The smell of fried chicken hit him before he even opened the door and his stomach grumbled loudly. He took one last drag off his cigarette, then flicked it out into the yard.

"Hey hon," Andrea greeted him with a smile. "Hurry and wash up. Dinner ain't no good if it's cold."

"Yeah…what's with all them people back in the woods?" he asked as he moved across the kitchen to the refrigerator. He set the beer onto the bottom shelf then went to the kitchen sink to wash his hands. He watched through the window above the sink as the dusky silhouettes of people moved back and forth in the distance.

Andrea placed a large bowl of mashed potatoes on the table then brushed stray wisps of dark hair out of her eyes with the back of her hand. "Bunch of government people. Apparently some space rock fell back there last night."

"A *what*?" James turned to stare at Andrea in disbelief, drops of water raining from his hands to the floor.

"A space rock…meteorite…whatever you call 'em," she said, tossing him a hand towel. "Hell if I know what the thing is. I went out there earlier, but they pretty much told me to mind my own business. I know you remember that real bright flash of lightning and that big boom that came right after it last night. That's what it was."

"You've got a smudge of dirt or something on your forehead," James said, nodding at her as he dried his hands. What he remembered was that Andrea had been in the middle of gobbling his dick when it happened and it had distracted her. He'd pushed her head back down and told her to ignore it, that it was just an early spring thunderstorm. Ever since she'd started taking 'Phyoden', the new medicine that enhanced a woman's sex drive, his wife had turned into a hot, raging slut and a thunderstorm had been the last thing on his mind. He turned back to the window. "Meteorite, huh? Ain't that some shit," he muttered with a shake of his head. "What'd they say to you exactly when you went out there?"

"I already told you. They said to mind my own business. Said I had to go on back to the trailer and stay out of their way. Now come on and sit down 'fore your dinner gets cold." Andrea set James's cup of coffee next to his plate, then went back to the counter to pour her own. What she didn't tell

James was that on her way back across the field, she stumbled and fell, landing face-first in a big puddle of something. She'd been horribly embarrassed as she pulled herself out of the sticky muck and heard laughter from the government people behind her. James didn't need to know about that. He'd be furious with her for making a spectacle out of herself. She'd come back in, stripped her clothes off and took a shower, washing the yellowish slime off and trying her best to put the humiliating incident out of her mind.

James plopped down heavily into his chair and leaned across the table. He grabbed three pieces of chicken and dropped them on his plate, then stuck his grease-slicked fingers into his mouth. Andrea put her coffee cup down, coffee sloshing over the edge to pool around the bottom rim.

"How was work?" she asked, sitting down and reaching for a piece of chicken.

"Fine enough." He glanced up at Andrea over the piece of chicken he held wedged between his fingers and frowned. "You still got that mark on your head." Andrea rubbed her forehead hard then peered at her fingertips.

"Is it gone?" She held her fingers up to show James that there was nothing on them.

James looked at her forehead again, then shook his head. "No...here, hold still. Let me get it." Andrea turned her face to James with a sigh of impatience and shut her eyes. James put his chicken down, touched his thumb to his tongue, then reached over and wiped it across Andrea's forehead. Waves of erotic stimulation suddenly roared through him and an electrical jolt zinged from his thumb, racing up his arm. He jerked his hand back with a gasp, staring with open-mouthed shock at his wife.

"What?" Andrea's eyes flew open. She reached up and rubbed her fingers hard over the spot James had just touched then looked at them again. "Did you get it? What in tarnation was it?"

James shook his head, opening his mouth and moving his lips, but no words came out.

"James!" Andrea's voice held a high-pitch of alarm at her husband's expression. "What's wrong?"

"I...I'm not...didn't you..." James stammered, at a loss. "You didn't..."

"I didn't what?"

"You didn't...*feel* that?" His voice was incredulous as he stared at her forehead.

"Feel *what*?!" Andrea demanded with frustration. "What in the world are you talking about, James?" Her dark brown eyes narrowed and she leaned close to him sniffing the air. "Just how much *have* you drank tonight? Did you stop at the bar on the way home?"

"No!" James shouted, swiftly pushing his chair back from the table...back away from her. Horror fused with fascination as he looked at the spot, unable to pull his eyes away. "No, I did *not* stop at the bar. I'm talking about THAT!" He raised his hand, pointing at the mark.

Andrea glowered at James a moment, then grabbed her spoon up from the table and held it in front of her face. Her reflection gazed back at her upside-down, elongated and distorted. She rubbed her fingers across her forehead again, then scratched lightly. She shook her head and lowered the spoon.

"I don't see one damned thing on my forehead," she said, her lips thin with annoyance. "I don't know what this game is you're playing tonight, but can we just be done with it and eat? I've got a headache and I'm really not in the mood."

James watched in stunned silence as Andrea began to spoon peas rapidly onto her plate. Questions blazed through his mind that he had no idea how to articulate. She hadn't felt it. How *was it* that she hadn't *felt* it? Hadn't even seen it? *He'd* felt it. The pad of his thumb, when he'd run it over the spot, had pushed *into* the spot. *Inside* of it. The sudden sound of voices snapped James's attention from his wife and the strange mark. His eyes fixed on the back door like he was waiting for the government officials to burst inside any moment and only when he heard their engines come to life, did he turn back to his wife. He opened his mouth to tell Andrea to go look in the mirror, then closed it and leaned closer to Andrea, frowning.

She looked up from her plate and glared at him. "Would you *please* stop staring at me? This is getting ridiculous." The blackness seemed darker now. Deeper. As if it had somehow grown *depth* in those few moments he was looking away. He stared, suddenly enthralled with the beauty of the darkness. He realized it was the deepest, blackest black he'd ever seen in his life.

James also realized that he had a raging hard-on.

What the fuck *was going on?*

The spot moved then…or rather, the blackness inside of it. James made a small choking noise in the back of his throat as he watched the darkness begin to shift and swirl inside of the hole.

The hole…

Those two words echoed through his mind as he looked into the churning blackness. It was a hole. A hole in the middle of his wife's head. *But, how did it get there?* Holes were *made*. They didn't just simply appear. And why was there no blood flowing from that wound? Just the blackness. Twisting…*pulsating*…gyrating, blackness.

James's cock throbbed against his leg. Beads of sweat glistened on his face and his breath came in ragged gasps. His hands gripped the edge of the table as he stared deep into the glorious blackness. Everything else in the room had faded from his sight but for that cavity. He couldn't make his mind think beyond that tiny abyss. He wanted to touch that darkness. Caress it. He wanted to be *inside* of it.

"JAMES!" Andrea shouted, clapping her hands in front of his eyes. "Would you stop?! You're starting to scare me!"

Andrea's words broke James's fascination and he looked at *her*…not at her forehead, but at her. He opened his mouth to say something, to try to explain to her what he was seeing, but he couldn't. His heart slammed in his chest and he shifted uncomfortably against his rigid cock. He leaned his elbows on the table and put his hands against his temples, running them over his eyes and pressing hard against his eyelids. He took a deep, shaky breath, as he looked back up at his wife. A low, shuddering moan pushed through his lips as his eyes drew instantly to the hole. A thick, gelatinous substance was bubbling out of it. His eyes dropped to Andrea's and he saw that she was staring at him, her eyes blazing furiously, expectantly, yet completely oblivious to what was happening just above them.

He didn't *want* to look again. Would have done anything he could to avoid it, but his eyes were drawn back to that sweet hole like flies to honey. The syrupy fluid coated Andrea's forehead in thick clots. It was a murky shade of dirty yellow, but transparent enough so that James could still see the mesmerizing swirl of the black beyond the jelly-like mass erupting from the hole. It pumped out faster and James brought his hand up to his mouth, biting into the side of his palm to keep from screaming. The skin beneath the gel began to crawl. It rippled like maggots under the tissue, writhing and shifting the flesh, causing it to run like soft wax. The area around the hole melted, widening a bit, then elongating, forming a vertical slit that ran from just below her hairline to down between her eyes. The edges of the slit bulged out, the flesh folding over itself, rolling together to form a thick wall that surrounded the throbbing blackness. Just above the hole, the yellow syrup flowed together, collecting itself, carrying flesh with it to form a small nub that jutted forward, quivering and trembling with its birth. The black in the hole pulsed hard, swirling fast and as James suddenly understood what the oozing solution had created, all sense of horror and disgust left his mind, leaving him feeling nothing but pure animal lust.

"That's IT!" Andrea suddenly cried, throwing down her fork. Her chair fell backwards as she jumped to her feet. "I will not sit here another second while you—"

James jumped up and grabbed Andrea by her shoulders. His eyes glowed with the frantic desire that rode in his blood. His head throbbed loudly and his cock throbbed louder as he stared at the trembling, glistening vagina in the center of his wife's forehead.

"Wh-what...what are you doing, James?" Andrea stammered. She pulled a little at her shoulders, attempting to remove herself from his grasp, but her strength left as she looked into his eyes. She saw a shifting, black movement reflected in them that sent sudden jolts of erotic desire racing through her body. *Damn those pills*, she thought fleetingly.

James leaned forward, putting his face directly in front of the foreign genitals and inhaled deeply. He closed his eyes at the shudder that tore through him from the salty, musky scent that filled his head. He uttered a deep, low moan that was filled with raw, desperate need. James opened his eyes and looked down at Andrea. He grabbed the sides of her face, steadying her, then ran his tongue from the bottom of the slit, over the throbbing black hole, to the nub at the top. A jolt ripped through both of them and suddenly they were consumed with a perverted, visceral hunger that neither could control. Andrea's fingers became talons clawing at James's pants as he pushed her backward against the table. He held her head firmly with one hand while he used his other to reach behind her and sweep everything off the table. A loud resounding crash echoed through the trailer as food, dishes, and silverware fell to the floor. Andrea spread her legs wide, her knee-length skirt riding high on her thighs as James pushed her down on top of the table. He ground his body hard against hers while his tongue explored the dark cavern of her mouth. One hand crept up the side of her face, searching. When his fingers touched the reformed flesh on her forehead, Andrea gasped hard into his mouth. She moaned loud and a violent shudder charged through her as James pressed his finger against the nub above the hole. He slid his fingers downward; reveling in the slimy wetness that coated the area and caressed the rim of the hole. Andrea dug her fingernails deep into his shoulders and pushed her head hard against his hand. He pressed one finger into the hole, then gasped loudly when he felt the thin layer of resistance. He almost came in his pants right there as the realization washed over him that this foreign pussy on his wife's head was virginal.

"Ohhhh...Jesusssss..." he whispered shakily, pulling his hand back.

"No..." Andrea moaned, her eyes still closed. "Don't...don't stop...feels sooo gooood..."

James grabbed Andrea's hand and brought it up to her forehead. He ran her fingers over the hole, coating them with the slime, pushing them hard against the nub.

"Do you feel it?" he demanded. "Can you feel it now?"

"No...It's just...I don't understand..." she said, her eyes opening to narrow slits to look at James. Her gaze was vacant but for a glazed 'come fuck me' look and she thrust her head hard against James's hand again. "Please..."

James backed off the table, ripping the shirt from his body. He fumbled with the button on his pants as he stared at the hole. The blackness churned and shuddered. Droplets of wetness stood tall on the edge of the lips, trembling. The hole shifted...*opened*...an invitation, and James snatched hard at the button, tearing it from the material, sending it scattering across the floor. His pants dropped in a puddle around his ankles, quickly followed by his boxers.

James crawled on top of Andrea and she moaned loud, clawing at his body ferociously. The hole vibrated, making the flesh quiver, almost as if it sensed what was coming. It stretched and opened wider, hungry, the blackness within pulsating in throbbing rhythm with his heartbeat that seemed to *beg* for him to fill it. He shifted his knees, moving further up on Andrea's body until he was straddling her head and his cock was positioned over her forehead. He put the tip of his dick against the hole and gasped as it suddenly sucked at him, pulling him in a little ways. Andrea's fingernails tore at his thighs as she moaned and writhed beneath him, desperately trying to pull him closer, to fill the need that was coursing through her. He pushed lightly against the thin protective layer, testing the resistance. It vibrated against the tip of his cock and suddenly James couldn't think of anything beyond the throbbing ache to shove himself inside of that blackness. With a powerful thrust and a growl of animal abandon, he buried his cock deep into his wife's forehead, breaking past the barrier in a thin spray of blood that coated Andrea's face which James never saw.

The choked sound of Andrea's screams briefly penetrated the moaning that consumed him, but it was too late. He couldn't have stopped even if he'd wanted to. The tight blackness surrounded his cock, massaged it with icy-hot strokes, sucked at it, pulling him deeper, manipulating the flesh like a hundred tiny fingers caressing him at once. He saw nothing but a hazy red lust in front of his eyes as he slammed his dick over and over into his wife's skull.

♋

James laid on the floor covered in sweat. His chest heaved as he tried to catch his breath and his body trembled uncontrollably. Tears rolled down his cheeks as he stared across the room at the dead body of his wife.

The table had broken...the two front legs collapsing just as the shuddering, violent, mind-numbing orgasm had ripped through him, spilling them both to the floor. He'd pulled out of her, his cock leaving the warm tightness with a 'squelch' and looked down at Andrea. Her eyes gazed up at him life-lessly, her forehead covered in a thick, disgusting combination of slime, blood and cum. Seeing her, realizing she was *dead* had been like a bucket of ice water in his face. That was when he'd started to scream. Backing away from Andrea, his hands covered his mouth, trying to stifle the horror that shrieked out from his soul at what he'd done to his wife, and then he'd slipped in the spilled mashed potatoes and had gone down hard, slamming his head against the side of the china hutch. Grayness washed over him, blocking out the horrors for a few blissful seconds. Far too few.

James pulled himself into a sitting position, his hand going to the aching spot on the back of his head. His eyes crawled to where Andrea lay on the floor. She stared vacantly at the ceiling, her mouth slightly open, her lips pulled down into a grimace of horror. The hole was still there, the vagina still carved into her forehead, only now it was silent. The blackness did not pulsate, did not call to him. The flesh around the hole did not quiver with invitation. It repulsed him. It looked…old. Worn out. Used. A fresh torrent of tears racked his body. He tried to clear his mind enough to think of what he needed to do now, but it seemed an impossible task. He brought the bottoms of his palms up and pressed them into his eyes, his fingers digging into his scalp, pulling his hair. *How* was he supposed to explain this?? And *who* was he supposed to—

A wet gurgling sound cut James's thoughts off instantly and his head snapped up. The gel was bubbling out of Andrea's head again, only this time it was like a volcano erupting. The yellow slime boiled up and poured out, running down her face and into her hair, then dropping to the floor in thick, spattering drops. James moaned, using his heels and hands to push himself backwards, away from Andrea and the horror she was excreting. It pumped out harder and her body started jerking up and down on the floor like she was being electrocuted.

"Oh Jesus…oh Christ…" James stammered in terror. Suddenly, Andrea's body arched and froze as the gel erupted from her head in a thick, gushing geyser, shooting straight up out of the hole, and coating the ceiling. James shrieked, the last shreds of his sanity fleeing at the sight. He knifed his body around and crawled towards the door mindless of everything except escaping. The room filled with an overpowering stench that was like dead fish and sewer water mixed together making James gag violently. A droplet of the slime hit him, falling from the ceiling onto his back. Burning heat engulfed him and he screamed, reaching his hands around to try and wipe the goo off. It seared into his flesh, sizzling as it spread out, moving down his back towards his buttocks then sliding over his sides. The pain was like being eaten alive by a million fire ants and James shrieked, jerking around in agony. Another glob fell on his leg. He turned, rubbing his leg frantically against the floor trying to get it off, but it was stuck to him, burrowing into his flesh. He tried to stand, tried to pull himself up, but the stuff on his back had eaten into him, into his spine and he had absolutely no control over his legs. With a cry, he pulled his body forward using his hands and arms. Another drop fell, catching his calf on his other leg. He gritted his teeth against the fiery pain, determined to get to the door and get out. Another fell, coating his hand and James screamed again as he watched the substance eat into his flesh. He looked up…the door was right in front of him, and an alien sense of relief and victory raced through him as he thrust his body forward. He used his shoulder as leverage against the door, leaning up to grab the knob. He turned his head as his hand began to twist it and froze with shock at the horror that met his eyes. The burning pain fled his mind momentarily as he stared into the fluid world his kitchen had become. The slime coated everything. It slid down the walls in thick rivulets and dropped from the ceiling into the ocean it had become on his floor. Only the small area around where he lay was free of the gelatinous fluid. It was at least a foot deep and it rolled thickly in waves, the body of it seeming to tremble and breathe as it lurched toward him. Almost as if it were alive and merely playing with him.

His heart hammering, the sizzling sound of his flesh being eaten away encompassing his mind, he gave the doorknob a quick twist. It opened an inch and the cool, fresh night air gusted in. He almost smiled. A large droplet of the slime shot across the room suddenly and slammed into the door, shutting it and sealing it closed. James looked up, wide-eyed with shock and horror, then across the room. The wall moved in and out, heaving, as it prepared to fire another bullet of slime. It pulsated faster, building momentum and then it shot the droplet across the room. This one nailed him in the shoulder and slammed him back against the door, holding him there as it ate into him. His hoarse, ragged screams filled the trailer as the gel fired shot after shot at him, pinioning him against the door and eating his flesh. He saw the giant one coming…as he struggled uselessly against the gel, he watched the large one form and prepare to launch, heaving in and out in humongous bursts, and for a fraction of a second after it smashed into his face, he saw through the gel. A wavering, rippling world that was filled with colors like a prism then slowly dissolved into blackness.

Mike Howard walked through the slime-covered trailer. He saw the body of the woman lying across the room, but had yet to find the man. He dug his radio from the belt of his hazardous waste suit and thumbed the switch.

"Base, this is Howard, do you copy?"

"I'm here, Howard. Did you find anything?"

"Oh, fuck yes. John, you wouldn't believe this shit. It looks like most of the stuff has dried up but there's still plenty here. The trailer is covered both inside and out with the remnants of it. I've got the body of one victim, the female…no sign of the husband yet. Do you want me to keep looking?" Mike walked over toward Andrea and stared down at her.

"Uhhhh…that's a negative, Howard. Take the samples and get the hell out of there. We're going to have a squad up there within an hour to blaze the place. Do you copy?"

"Affirmative. I'm getting the samples now, boss…you know, this is weird…I mean, beyond what this IS, but this dead woman here…I *swear* it looks like she's got a goddamned pussy on her forehead."

"Say again, Howard?"

"A pussy. A vagina. Right in the middle of her forehead."

Radio silence.

"Base…you still with me?"

"Yeah Mike…I'm trying to stop laughing. Hey, when's the last time you got laid, anyway?"

"Very funny. I'm getting the samples and getting out of here. This shit is creeping me out. I'll check in on my way back. Copy?"

Andrea Gives Good Head

"Got it," the voice answered, still chuckling. "Over and out."

Mike jammed the radio back onto his belt and bent forward, trying to get a closer look at Andrea's head. He reached one gloved hand out and touched the deformity, then jumped back with a gasp. The blackness began to shift and swirl and Mike suddenly realized that it was the most beautiful, glorious, deepest black he had ever seen in his life.

He also realized he had a raging hard-on.

N is For...

by J. M. Heluk

SMILING, MR. WISE slid the contract across the desk towards his current client, Mr. Grisby.

"Well?" Wise said, watching the man flip through its pages. "Is it to your satisfaction?"

Mr. Wise smiled as Mr. Grisby mulled over the load of paperwork. Wise knew there was still a slight chance the guy wouldn't sign it. Actually, he hoped he wouldn't. Sometimes even scumbags like Pete Grisby could surprise him, though after seeing the guy in person, he doubted it.

The entity known as Pete Grisby disturbed him. The man squirmed in that tiny metal office chair like an oversized garden slug in a salt suit. Mottled skin draped off his arms, only to spread puttylike when he finally settled them on the armrests. Grisby was way too excited. Wise hated when they got like that. The client flipped through all one hundred pages nervously, bottom lip drooping off his gum line, a meaty, red, glistening U. Mr. Wise knew the client wasn't really reading it, the man was sweating.

"You realize what this means don't you?" Mr. Wise asked, holding in the grimace that threatened to burst across his face. "This contract is good for one time…just once."

Wheezing, Pete Grisby leaned across the desk, snatched the pen from Mr. Wises' hand and signed the contact. Wise smiled, not because he was now 40,000 dollars richer, he didn't need the cash, he smiled because Grisby stood up just then. The man's erection was clearly straining against his trousers.

"I want the goods tonight," the bloated client said, gasping as he hobbled towards the door.

Mr. Wise nodded. "Seven p.m., Mr. Grisby. seven p.m. sharp."

☙

It wasn't always an easy task to get exactly what a client ordered on such brief notice but Mr. Wise had connections. His silent partner, Mr. D, always had quite a selection to choose from. Mr. Wise glanced over Pete Grisby's exact specifications then calmly dialed the phone. One ring and it was, "D? It's me, Wise."

"Hello Mr. Wise." Mr. D replied in a voice just as cool. "Did the two of you work out the details?"

The details, as Mr. D put it, were where the real challenges lay. Pete Grisby had presented quite a lot of them, more than any client he or Mr. D had to date. Apparently the fat old pervert was a bit of a perfectionist, although one look at the man would suggest otherwise.

"Yes," said Mr. Wise, "We did."

"Then go ahead. I may have a few good matches here. Been a busy weekend you know."

Mr. Wise cleared his throat. If Mr. D didn't have what he needed by tonight, then he'd have to ring up Missy X, his downtown contact. Mr. Wise began hammering out each detail to his partner on the line.

"White."

"But of course," Mr. D laughed. "Aren't they always?"

"Yes, yes. I guess they are." Mr. Wise returned the pleasantry with a chuckle then resumed. "Under twenty."

Mr. D sucked air through his teeth. Some papers fumbled on his end. "Okay, I have four of those, including one that's twelve. Does he want something that young?"

"Anything under twenty will be appropriate Mr. D, but she needs to be blonde with either green or blue eyes…and, small breasted. I suppose twelve is as small as they get!" Mr. Wise laughed. "But for god sakes, give me someone with teeth this time."

"Did he actually ask for that?"

"Yes, right here, line seventeen. Teeth. He asked for them."

"Okay…now we're down to three."

Mr. Wise heard the electric saw start up in the background on his partner's end.

"He also wants long nails, painted red."

An audible sigh came across the line. Mr. D was no beautician but they could get one easily enough. Missy X proved to be one hell of an artist when D and Wise were in a pinch.

"No exterior damage, aim for an overdose or heart failure." Mr. Wise continued, tapping his gold Waterford pen on his thigh. "No rigor mortis, but if you happen to have one that matches this, by all means, break it out manually. He wants her soft." Mr. Wise checked his watch. "It's only nine a.m., we should have until six. Grisby lives fifteen minutes away from you. Oh yeah, and I almost forgot." Mr. Wise said it slowly. "He specified freckles."

"Shit!" More papers fumbled. "Wait here one second. Carlos just wheeled a new one in. Let me go check."

With D gone from the phone, Wise could hear Carlos's stereo on in the background. He grinned. Cutting above the buzzing bone saw, Ricky Martin crooned passionately about some girl named Maria.

"Okay," Mr. D said as he picked the phone back up, "we hit pay dirt. I was left with one, the twelve year old, but then you asked for the fucking freckles. I was about to paint the damn things on her." Mr. D snorted. "Shit, I have a mortgage you know."

"I understand." said Wise.

"Okay, so here's the scoop. Carlos picked her up this morning. Police found her in a storm drain down by the old shoe factory in Linden. Overdose, nineteen years old, no breasts at all. I'd guess an A cup." A pause, then the sound of sheets sliding over dead flesh followed by, tsk-tsk.

"She has dark blonde hair, but at least it's blonde, right? Long nails too, I'll have to paint them. She croaked around 6 A. M. Should be hitting rigor shortly, but I have a few tricks up my sleeve to fend that off. Best of all, freckles Mr. Wise…she's loaded with fucking freckles!"

"Okay D, get to work. Grisby wants his date you know."

Mr. Wise hung up. Pete Grisby would be another satisfied customer and best of all; it was done in record time. Mr. D really did have the widest selection. Big, fucked up city like this, his morgue was always packed with the freshest 'dates.'

The greatest aspect of his little 'necrophilia dating service' though was that his clients were always more than satisfied. No one ever squawked and really, how could they? They certainly couldn't call the authorities, say they paid some people to have sex with a dead body, were unfulfilled and now want a refund.

It was too perfect. The bodies would just go back to the morgue no worse for wear (unless they had the shit luck to get another sicko with dismemberment on his mind) and no one would notice the absence, especially since Mr. D wasn't a Mr. at all, but a Dr. The corpse would be wheeled back into the morgue through the side entrance and tucked away lovingly in the fridge, again.

But even sick little secrets like this had ways of leaking out. Word of mouth to get them in and no words after that was their motto. Before Mr. Wise slipped Pete Grisby's contract into the handy desk side shredder, he had one more phone call to make. Mr. Smarty Pants needed to be notified of the job he'd be doing later that evening, sometime shortly after seven p.m. at Pete Grisby's mansion in Cliffdale Park.

♋

Mr. Wise grinned and slid another contract across the desk; his fifth that month. This time the client was a gentleman who wanted to be called Mr. Fister, and appropriately so.

"Look this over carefully Mr. Fister." Mr. Wise said to the gangly, white-haired man. "Make sure you've outlined everything you desire."

Mr. Fister leaned forward, Armani suit clinging to his body as he pored over the selections he made, and, Mr. Wise knew that when this man stood, he'd surely see something straining against those sleek pants of his.

"Oh, I think I've got it all here. A large man, very fat…" Mr. Fister said nervously. Noticeably capped teeth gleamed into view like tombstones. "You know, it may sound a bit sick," Mr. Fister continued, scratching his signature across the dotted line, "but I want a man with some kind of visible trauma, a head wound would be okay, but what I'd really prefer is some type of chest damage. Sounds bad, but I like…I want, very deep stab wounds."

"Oh my dear Mr. Fister! No need to feel shame." Wise said. "You see, that's why were here, to provide a much neglected service for people with your particular…tastes."

The two men smiled at each other. Wise because he was now another 40,000 dollars richer and Fister, well, he was smiling for services about to be rendered. But there was another reason for Wise's wide grin. He had the perfect match for his new client. His cleanup partner, Mr. Smarty Pants, had done a real number on that fat slob Pete Grisby the previous night.

Twenty-five-plus stab wounds to his chest if he recalled what Mr. D told him that morning. And then Mr. Fister swished in with one tall order. Chest damage like that was hard to find. Twenty-five stab wounds. Can you imagine their luck?

Mr. Wise stood and shook Mr. Fister's limp wrist.

"I have just the date for you sir. A perfect match. Shall I drop him off around, say, seven-ish?

Mr. Fister eagerly pumped Mr. Wise's hand not realizing for a moment what he had agreed to in the contract. Sick fucker never read the fine print. No one ever did. If they had they'd never sign that slip of paper.

Line 77—article 3, part 12 clearly states that the client shall be exterminated by whatever means the provider sees fit immediately after his/her necrophilia date. The client will then be brought to any one of the two area hospitals, (either to Mr. D's or to Missy X) to be recycled as dating material if another client's specifications match them.

And it was one hell of a match all right, Mr. Wise thought, watching Mr. Fister swish out of his office. When the man disappeared around the corner, Wise snatched the phone off its cradle.

One ring and it was, "Hello, Mr. Smarty Pants? It's Wise. I have another job for you tonight."

You see, no one ever talked about these dating experiences. Mr. Wise made sure of that.

The Doll, or:
What the Dead Think About at the Very End of the World

by Lance Olsen

AFTER WE WERE done doing it in a manner in which we had never done it before, she rolled onto her side and asked me:

So what's next?

I, remaining on my stomach, said:

What?

This was a frisky blue Sunday afternoon and we were in her apartment on the floor beneath the kitchen table. Several chairs were lying on their sides. The table wasn't where I had remembered it being half an hour ago.

A piquant scent of cucumber and I want to say olive oil animated the atmosphere.

Her apartment or my apartment.

I don't remember which, actually.

Her apartment, my apartment, or, for that matter, a friend's who was away for the weekend and had lent us his.

Let us call him Robert.

All the same, there was clearly a sense of upended apartmentness surrounding us.

The point not being where we were, however, but rather the gist of her question, which took me by surprise because I was at that moment busy perspiring diligently and thinking about what we had just done, and we were taking turns employing Kleenexes from a pale blue box of them with a floral design which sat on the tiled floor beside us but which not long ago had sat, I seem to recall without any real conviction about the matter, on the bathroom sink or on the desk in the foyer, where our afternoon's under-taking had originated, I want to say, although this is also an issue of some conjecture, and I was concomitantly busy, I want to say as well, wiping off various leaking fluids and/or beginning to collect vegetable refuse that had aggregated in our vicinity on the tiled floor whose squares happened, by the way, to alternate black and white, not unlike a large urban chess board.

I saw all this, for some reason, from a third-person point of view.

I saw all this, that is, as if I were standing in the doorway to the kitchen, the scene stripped of its normal saturation and hues, instead of what I must have in reality been doing, which was either wiping off those fluids or begin-ning to collect that vegetable matter.

It surprised me, her question, because we had been doing it now for I want to say three months, though undeniably it had been for no more than five, six would be a maximum, and we had done it each time, or very nearly each time, in interesting places with from my perspective interesting apparatuses while frequently utilizing unfamiliar and thus exciting postures, each posture and/or apparatus possessing a metaphoric name with great connotative resonance in certain clandestine circles.

Airplanes, of course, airplanes go without saying.

Rooftops.

A stall in the women's restroom at the Holocaust Museum in a city other than the one you're thinking of when I say the Holocaust Museum.

Double Helixes, Quantum Foam, Rabbit Mouths.

I'm not particularly proud of that, by the way. The Holocaust Museum, I mean. I'm not particularly proud of that, and I'm not particularly unproud of that, either.

Be that as it may.

It surprised me, as I say, her question, because we had been doing it now for I want to say three months, though undoubtedly it had been for no more than five, six would be a maximum.

Doing it since, that is, we met.

At an independent film at an independent-film-showing theater down-town, whose title, plot, and general theme I also forget.

We were the only ones there.

In the theater, I mean.

That part I remember.

I remember, too, how everything smelled like mildew and artificially flavored buttered popcorn.

We were the only ones there, or very nearly the only ones there, and yet we serendipitously took conterminous seats because we were both committed, I want to say, to achieving the most efficacious viewing range from the not-all-that-large-independent-film-showing-theater screen.

The Iron Man.

The film, it suddenly occurs to me, was called *The Iron Man.*

It was called *The Iron Man*, or *The Iron Man* was simply a portion of its name, and there was more to it either before *The Iron Man* or after it.

A colon, I want to say, was involved.

It was a Japanese film, subtitled in English, but you didn't need the subtitles to understand it because almost no one spoke, although many groaned or screamed, or groaned and screamed-a lot-and there was no plot, as I now recall, except for the fact that there was this man, an average Joe, who turns into a machine one day for no apparent reason, and then this woman, who is quite probably the man's lover, although this is by no means indisputable, who also turns into a machine one day for no apparent reason, unless the man was imagining the woman turning into a machine, and maybe even imagining himself turning into a machine, which always remained in my mind an acceptable possibility, or maybe there was even a third-party consciousness dreaming the immachinating couple, who knows, really, or it's not totally out of the realm of probability that I'm simply remembering the wrong movie.

The point being merely this: that I recall, I think, much jump-cutting, and, during one scene, the man doing it with the woman, or the imagined woman, with a three-foot-long steel penis that revolved like a drill and was shaped like a dunce's cap, if you can imagine such a thing, and, during another scene, both the woman or the imagined woman and the man ending up turning into parts of the same machine-a tank, I want to say, or, in any event, a tank-like mobile object-and the man speaking one of the perhaps ten lines in the film.

I've never been so happy, he said.

In Japanese, of course.

Or something like that, something with that general tenor.

It was a strange work.

And that's how we met.

She started, first, by sort of humming at the strangeness of the movie under her breath.

You know: *Hmmmmm..hmmmmmmmm..hmmm.*

Next, she began fully vocalizing about the strangeness, sometimes asking questions, perhaps to herself, perhaps to me, it was difficult to tell with any honest assurance, and sometimes she developed a running almost subvocal analysis of the film centering, mostly, on its sense of power relations and, I want to say, the hermeneutics of desire.

She had purchased, I couldn't help noticing, one of those very large tubs of artificially flavored buttered popcorn.

A vat, actually, into which you could place a small dog.

A Chihuahua, for example.

About half an hour later, I began to answer her questions, never taking my eyes off the not-large screen.

I was aware of her stealing glances at me, initially, like maybe I wasn't talking to her but to myself, just like she was talking to maybe herself and not to me, only then she plainly decided I wasn't dangerous, or I wasn't particularly dangerous, and she began to take exception with my reading, which centered mostly on the film's critique of our culture's fetish of technology, and, two hours later, we began doing it in my apartment.

Once upon a time, I was a philosophy major.

My apartment or her apartment.

I don't remember which with any convincing accuracy.

Which was, I want to say, between three and six months ago, almost surely, and without a doubt no more than let us call it eight.

Eight or nine.

So what's next? she asked, having rolled onto her side on the chess-board floor, and this, as I have already mentioned, surprised me.

Surprised and unnerved me, if I'm being completely aboveboard here, because I had been giving it up to this moment my all, and I was, not to put too fine a point on it, running out of ideas, and this question suggested to me as I wiped off various leaking fluids, some of which I had generated, some of which she had generated, some of which had been extra-corporeally generated, some more or less viscous and some more or less translucent than others, that she might be running out of ideas, too, because she had never asked it before, this question, I mean.

Over the course of the last nine or ten months, eleven was a maximum, I had it goes without saying dressed up in a miscellany of interesting apparel and discovered, among other things, how fetching I looked in a pair of red pumps and black corset, and so had she, and we had posted images of ourselves engaged in the manipulation of those myriad interesting apparatuses while utilizing myriad unfamiliar and thus exciting postures on the internet on diverse interesting amateur-submitted-images sites, and there was obviously that time we did it in an elevator halted between floors of a skyscraper, she dressed as a ponytailed school girl in All-Star hightops and I as a Nazi officer—what American didn't?—and that time we invited her friend or my friend whose apartment we were perhaps at that moment using, let us call him Robert, and his wife, his wife or girlfriend, let us call her Roberta, to join us in a seedy hotel room in a seedy section of the city with a box of matches and an alleged snuff film featuring a bound and gagged Asian teen and they did, and that time we put an ad in the paper for those little people and would have video-taped our assignation had anyone replied to said ad, which they didn't, and so forth.

Although it turned out we discovered that we were never in point of fact very keen on doing it with other couples, regardless of their stature or the subject matter of their video-tape collection, this being because we were in I think you could call it love.

Yes, I'm sure I think you could call it that.

From the day we met, that is, we pretty much never left each other's side.

Except, of course, to go to work.

Pretty much everyone has to go to work, needless to say.

Me in a Kinko's uptown, and she in a Blockbuster's downtown.

Except, then, to go to work and at several junctures during a given day to eat.

Breakfast and lunch, usually.

Work, eat, once in a long while socialize with friends or colleagues on a one-to-one basis, travel infrequently into the countryside, evacuate our respective bowels diurnally, wander the streets at night yelling at the moon, read, listen to music, bike, skate, and, upon the rarest of occasions, do it with someone else.

One could say we were inseparable, except for that.

And hence when she rolled onto her side, propped her head in her palm, and asked *So what's next?* it is I suspect no surprise how surprised I was.

How surprised, unnerved, and maybe you could even say without too much exaggeration threatened.

Her eyes were hazel, by the way.

This seems an opportune moment to mention such an important detail.

If not now, after all, then when?

Her eyes were that sort of hazel which is, if you study it carefully, and I did, multiple times, browner toward the edges of the contractile membrane and then increasingly brownish-yellow and then yellowish-brown as you move toward the fat period of the black pupil.

Her eyes were hazel and her hair shaved right down to gray skin with a razor every morning.

Unless she was wearing one of her wigs.

In which case her hair was sometimes shoulder length and sometimes longer and sometimes done in pigtails or, as I believe I have already mentioned, ponytails, and sometimes in Egyptian fashion and sometimes in a prim beehive from the early Sixties like my fifth-grade teacher, Mrs. Barnett, on whom I had a rabid crush, have a rabid crush, and always in an interesting color one tends to associate with selections of fingernail polish rather than, in fact, hair.

Her eyes were hazel and her breasts were boyish and she was thinner than what might be considered in some medical circles wholly healthy and we were, with those very few exceptions I have just adumbrated above, inseparable, and so I saw myself that frisky Sunday afternoon, as if my point-of-view were situated in the doorway of the kitchen, and not beneath the table among overturned chairs, cease wiping and say:

What?

So what's next? she repeated. You know...

Oh, I said. Oh.

I rolled from my stomach onto my back and then hoisted myself into a hunched, cross-legged sitting position.

Then she repeated her question which made the pale, thin, red-haired guy with a white-tipped pink zit on his freckled left shoulder, one on his forehead, and one at the right-hand corner of his mouth even more surprised, unnerved, and maybe you could even say without too much exaggeration threatened.

You could see him trying to think.

It wasn't a pretty sight.

Playing with the gooey tips of his fingers and trying to think, hunched in that cross-legged sitting position.

Finally, however, he cleared his throat and replied, a little evasively:

You'll see.

I'll see?

You'll see.

When?

Soon.

How soon?

Tomorrow soon.

I work tomorrow.

Tomorrow night, then. Meet me at my place after work tomorrow night.

The boy-breasted woman continued looking at the scrawny red-haired man for another few seconds, a minute at most, with her hazel eyes that seemed to lack very much I suppose you could call it emotion, then she half-smiled and rolled away from him and stood up and collected her clothes, most of which turned out, startlingly, to be scattered throughout the living room, dressed, and left without saying goodbye.

This was not an unusual mode of action on her part, exactly.

The scrawny red-haired man simply assumed it to be her way of keeping a certain sexual static sparkling through the upended apartmentness surrounding him.

He was right, he was pretty sure.

I watched him as he finished cleaning up the vegetable refuse, and righting the furniture, and so on, and then I watched him return to his apartment across town, unless this was his apartment, obviously, in which case he stayed where he was, being at home already.

All the same, her leaving proved that this place was most likely not her apartment.

This much is clear.

The following evening, I watched me pick up some things at the corner market after work, hurry back to someone's apartment, almost surely his, throw together a green salad with a light vinaigrette dressing, and sauté some onions and mushrooms in butter in a wok, some butter or some olive oil, this part always presents a number of mnemonic challenges for me-at which point the doorbell rang, or there was a knock at the door, I'm not one-hundred percent confident about which it was, actually, and in any event I watched the scrawny red-haired man trot down the foyer hall in his terrycloth bathrobe and answer the ring or knock, whichever it might have been, then accompany the boy-breasted woman in her short black dress, black high-topped combat boots, and shiny purple Betty Boop wig back into the kitchen, where they worked in harmonious tandem to set an elegant table, lit two romantic, white, vanilla-scented candles, and then the scrawny red-haired man poured the boy-breasted woman and himself a glass of brick-red wine, led her over to the counter, raised his glass in a toast, and repeated the simile he had practiced all afternoon about the evening fanning open before them like an uncomplicated space of possibility.

She reciprocated, and then he showed her the wooden cutting board on the counter by which they stood, a short time after which they ate each other's little toes (sans toenails) with a tincture of paprika mixed with the onion, mushrooms, and butter or olive oil to enliven the comestibles.

I had honestly never in our twelve or thirteen months together seen them closer than I did at that instant.

The amputation was realized, I should perhaps mention, with a meat cleaver designed and manufactured in Europe-Germany, I want to say-and was followed by an abrupt if not wholly unexpected discomfort, which was itself followed by an almost indescribable euphoria and a one could say certain intense focusing of one's perceptive abilities which maintained long after the bandages and cotton gauze had been applied to stanch the flow of what have you.

Bones comprising the little toe are, as one might imagine, fairly petite and crunchy.

Soft-shell crabs come to mind.

It was always difficult to pick a favorite philosopher.

There were always so many to choose from, of course.

I had honestly never in our twelve or thirteen months together seen them closer than I did at that instant and, afterwards, I followed us up the street of let us call them brownstones to the bus stop, we were all hobbling slightly, and watched as we kissed each other passionately beneath a halogen lamp crawling with large bugs, large bugs and small bugs, although mostly small ones.

Next day the scrawny red-haired man hobbled through Kinko's in an animated daydream.

His eyes, which by the way were an unremarkable blue, had that acute look to them of someone playing the last minute of a video game when he or she is maybe three clicks away from attaining the final level and let us say saving the princess.

He misplaced orders, employed the wrong plastic binding on two separate instances, and once produced a one-hundred-and-fifty-page double-sided copy of a literary manuscript for a local experimental writer with a mane of long blond hair, white almost, and gaps between most of his upper teeth, rather a three-hundred-page single-sided one.

But it didn't matter, not at all, as those deeply in love are wont to say.

The Doll

Habitually.

In his mind, work suddenly became little more than a means to an end.

As a point of fact, work had always been little more than a means to an end for him, a place he went to undertake the experience of not-thinking for eight hours a day, five days a week, often at odd and weirdly lit segments of the night, in order to provide himself with the primary necessities associated with living in a complex city such as this one, whichever one it was, only now the meansness of it was clearer to him than it ever had been before.

Shooting accident, he answered when his colleagues began asking.

For the sake of ease, let us call them Robert, Robert, Robert, Robert, and Roberta.

His boss's name, I should take this opportunity to mention, was Robert.

The scrawny red-haired man almost never talked to any them except to refer to immediate matters of business. He had always kept to himself. It was therefore with little effort that he continued keeping to himself now.

Shooting accident, he answered, and then, two weeks later, he answered: hatchet accident.

Shooting accident, hatchet accident, shaving accident.

Shaving accident, hedge-trimming accident, jack-o'-lantern-carving accident.

In the beginning, it all seemed more natural than one might perhaps suppose.

Then it didn't.

Then he stopped caring.

Although there is if the truth be known a very good chance he never really cared that much in the first place.

Then they began avoiding him.

Robert, Robert, Robert, Robert, Roberta, and Robert began making large arcs around him when they felt the insuperable need to pass him.

They stood in many-appendaged clusters at the front of the shop when he was busy working in the back of the shop and created meaningful gestures over their shoulders in his direction without ever turning their heads.

Then he stopped going to work.

In cases involving larger bodily emancipations, boiling water achieved both effective cauterization and a certain compounding of one's overall sense of euphoria, which the boy-breasted woman in sundry wigs began to refer to affectionately as The Angel's Kiss.

The Angel's Kiss is upon me, she would sometimes announce, trembling, trembling or shaking, folded into a fetal position on the floor, eyes rolled back in her head, or she would sometimes announce:

I have just been kissed by an angel.

Over and over.

Compared to The Angel's Kiss, drugs seemed downright drugless, other addictions little more than avocational distractions.

And so everything in our love story moved inexorably toward a happy conclusion, except that some things didn't. Several unanticipated if minor complications began to arise. One's big toes, the couple discovered much to their astonishment, for instance, provide a greater sense of balance than the layman often suspects, and, once one's feet are gone, up to the knees, the idea of gainful employment pretty much flies out the window, no matter what one's views on the subject happen to be, as does the notion, I want to add, of popping down to the corner market to pick up this item or that item or the other at eleven or twelve o'clock at night. It seems an opportune moment to mention, too, that one should never attempt to remove one's genitals, one's genitals or one's mammary glands, depending, when you are fully conscious. A series biological laws prevent such procedures from running perfectly trouble-free.

Etc., etc.

Yet what is truly remarkable is how little effort it takes one to meet one's basic dietary needs, particularly if one rounds out one's meals with a daily vitamin supplement.

Pay your rent and utilities in advance: this is a no-brainer, really. Stockpile supplies. Plan ahead.

Remember to save one's tongue until one feels one no longer has anything of specific interest to articulate.

Once upon a time, I was a philosophy major and, once upon a time, she was a film studies major, both at the University other than the one you're thinking of when I say the University.

It's a small world.

One partner should obviously also save an arm, hand, and at least two fingers, one of which should be that often-cited opposable thumb, if either partner is set on, let us say, keeping a journal of ones thoughts and feelings or composing poems or lyrics about this special introspective time in one's life, and, it nearly goes without spelling out, such appendages will further-more prove pivotal in the execution of what the boy-breasted woman and the scrawny red-haired man incrementally came to think of as The Last Waltz or, for want of a more unambiguous term, The Scalping.

Which is where they are now, where we are now, she and I, two torsos and two heads gurgling I am tempted to say happily on someone's let us guess futon.

It feels like a futon, in any event, I think.

It is dark in here, but this could be the result of the blinds having at some earlier moment been drawn, or the personal loss of what have you.

It may be a weekend.

It may not.

There is inarguably some ambient intermittent breathing taking place in addition to the aforementioned most likely content gurgling.

Things seem slightly confusing, unsurprisingly enough.

Lately, they often do.

In any case, anyhow, anyway, the saddest thing about all of this, it occurs to the scrawny red-haired man as he not very neatly jots his last impressions on this yellow legal pad on my stomach, these last impressions, mine, is how, when making love, when making love or, say, when having sex, either way, really, there is a let us call it limit case to the quantity of occasions one can in fact do it and a conceptual boundary line to the operations that comprise such an activity, this being the one secret all directors of pornographic videos never want you to understand, and beyond that is merely The Angel's Kiss, and, beyond that, every single time, nothing.

Neurosurgical
Associates
brain surgery
and a lot more...
Loose
ELL, I'LL
SHOW MOTHER
I'LL SHOW
YOU
Head Lube
COLLAGES OF MEMORY,
Erase
wake
up
and
smile
Come
Join Our
SMILES
Betray

Collages of Memory

Lesbian Whores of Broadway

by Craig Snyder

April, 2003
The Lucky 7 Motel on the outskirts of Trenton, New Jersey. It is late at night.

THERE CERTAINLY WAS a lot of licking and sucking going on, but somehow Gina's heart just wasn't in it. "I'm afraid I'm going to have to give you your money back," she said to the enormous sweating woman who had followed her home from the bar. Huffing and puffing, the woman, whose name was Sally Spears but called herself Delicious Demi, rolled off Gina and sat up. The metal frame of the motel bed protested as it absorbed the virtually unbearable pressure of her titanic rippling ass.

"Have some more wine," she suggested hopefully.

Gina sighed. "It's no use. I just can't get into it tonight."

"But whatever is the matter, dear?" asked Demi, resigning herself to a sexless night. She began settling her pendulous breasts into a pink bra with sadistically firm underwire.

Gina stood up and began to dress. The cheap motel lighting couldn't hide the incredible beauty of her long lean body.

"I don't know. Nothing. Everything. I feel like I've come to a crossroads and something's pushing me out into the traffic. I need a change."

Demi nodded. "I know exactly what you mean. This world can be hell

95

on us lesbians. Many's the time I've been just where you are now." She paused to drain her glass of wine. "But you've got to stand tall. Face to the wind and all that."

Gina shook her head impatiently. "You don't understand. I'm not a lesbian, just a lesbian whore."

"Well, now. That's a bit unusual, isn't it?" Demi was fighting a losing battle with a pair of shocking pink spandex pants.

"It's the only life I know," said Gina. "I dropped out of high school and ran away from home when I was sixteen. Couldn't stand Nebraska. Nothing but corn and dust." She pursed her lips and frowned, slipping her feet into candy apple red three-inch heels. "I got on a bus headed east. Wound up sitting next to this girl, Delia was her name. She got me into the life. Figured it was better than starving. Don't look back, she told me. And I never have."

The blue and red neon sign blinked and buzzed outside their window.

"But what about your dreams? What about the future?"

Gina's face took on a dreamy, faraway look. "I used to want to be a dancer and singer. Maybe get to Broadway. I'd stay up late and watch all those old musicals, you know; the ones where some girl out of nowhere suddenly gets to be a star, because the real star is sick or drunk or something, and there's no one else to go on in her place? I always wanted to be that girl. I can sing and dance—took all sorts of lessons. I was pretty good too; at least that's what people used to tell me..." Suddenly her face changed and it looked sort of sad and lonely. "Anyway, I can't afford those dreams anymore. They were the silly dreams of a silly little girl who didn't know what real life was all about."

Demi started blubbering. Her huge frame shook, and big crocodile tears streamed down her face, combining with her purple mascara to form garishly colored tracks on her fat cheeks. "That's the saddest thing I ever heard!" she wailed. She threw her arms around Gina and drew her head into an ample bosom fragrant with cheap perfume.

"Mmmmpphhh," said Gina.

"I can't stand the thought of you all alone, giving up on your dreams!" declared Demi.

"Mmmppphh?"

"You're going to come and live with me," the giant lesbian announced, relaxing her grip on Gina. "I know some people in the entertainment business. Maybe they can do something for you."

Gina, withdrawing from the cave formed by Demi's breasts, was drawing huge gulps of air into her grateful lungs. "I don't want to be any trouble," she protested.

"It's my pleasure and no trouble at all. Why d'ya think God spit us out onto this crazy world? He wanted us to help each other, and if we don't, we're none of us any better than the animals. Besides, I've always wanted to take a crack at being an actress. Just never had the guts to try it, I guess."

"I wouldn't know where to start," Gina said helplessly.

"Broadway dear, that's our ticket. You just stick with me. We'll do it together."

Gina had finished dressing. She looked at herself critically in the mirror, poking at her hair. "By the way," she said, "what is it that you do?"

Demi looked surprised. "Didn't I tell you? I'm a lesbian whore too! I was just giving myself a night off when I ran into you, and couldn't resist."

"It's a strange life," said Gina.

"Ain't it just?"

TWO:

45 minutes from Broadway. A dingy, spacious loft.

Two men sit smoking cigarettes and discussing a new script for a play. It is called "The United Sisters of America" and the investors are enthusiastic. The two men have been drinking, and their gestures and speech are wild, extravagant. Rehearsals are scheduled to start in a few weeks, but the cast is incomplete. They will lose financing if they don't start on time. This cannot be allowed to happen.

"We must have actual lesbians!" This from Guy Vandermeer, the director. He was a short man with oily black hair and a weedy mustache. He'd directed two successful plays and was beginning to make real money. He was a heavy drinker, but seldom got drunk.

"And if possible, they should be lesbian whores," he added. His face shone with excitement and oil.

"Realism is dead," replied Neil Blunt, the embittered and paranoid young author of a string of spectacularly unsuccessful off-Broadway productions. Blunt was in his mid-thirties, dark and tall. A handsome man, he wore a tortured expression on his face that relaxed only during sleep. "Legs are everything. What we need are sexy legs. No one will give a damn whether they're lesbians or not."

"You're wrong, Neil," Vandermeer insisted. "They must *feel* the part; they must *be* lesbian whores! This is Broadway, my friend, Broadway! The audience will know."

"Fuck it," said Blunt. "I don't give a shit. I've already been paid. But you've only got twenty-four hours to find those girls if you want to stay on schedule, and lesbian whores are scarce, even in New York."

Vandermeer lit a fresh cigarette from the stump of his old one and puffed away, waving his arms and scattering ashes everywhere. "Don't tell me about New York, Neil; I've lived here all my life. It's the home of freaks and fools, and 5 million of the most insanely hopeful would be actors and actresses in the world. Our lesbian whores are out there—and I'll find them. Then we'll make them stars!"

The irritating chime of a cell phone interrupted the conversation. Blunt went to the bar to make himself another drink. Like all writers who had any talent at all, he was an alcoholic. He'd been divorced three times. He was not a happy person. When he returned from the bar, double scotch in hand, he found the director throwing on his coat.

"We've found them," Vandermeer said happily. "We've got our lesbian whores!"

"Whoopee," said Blunt.

THREE:

The Majestic Theatre, New York City.

Craig Snyder

"I feel like an idiot!" hissed Gina. Her taut, youthful body was clothed in a silver sequined bustier, red short shorts, and black fishnet stockings. She wore black taps on her slender feet.

"Oooohh, but you look wonderful!" cooed Demi. "So sexy and fine! I only wish I looked half as good myself," she added sadly, glancing down at her own costume which consisted of a billowing dress made from a colossal American flag. The endless folds of fabric, while striking, rendered her powerful form shapeless.

"Your costume is very flamboyant," offered Gina.

They stood in the center of the stage surrounded by a restless, chattering crowd of women dressed in various costumes. Gina thought they all looked so confident and stylish, and felt awkward in her taps, which pinched her feet. On the edges of the crowd stage hands were busy adjusting lights, stringing cable, and moving sets into place. The noise in the grand, nearly empty theater was like the roar of the ocean; now swelling, now subsiding, but never silent.

Her eyes picked out Guy Vandermeer as he strolled briskly onto the stage.

"All right, girls! All eyes on me! Take your places, please!" He waited patiently until they were all assembled in a line.

"Everyone ready? Excellent. Now in this scene, you and your fellow Sisters of Justice are all marching on Washington, armed with machine guns. You are very angry. The President and Congress have been ignoring you, and this is pissing you off. You demand a separate state for lesbians, possibly somewhere in Wyoming, and higher wages for lesbian whores. Your defiance is glorious. Everyone is against you, but you stand firm confident in your solidarity, brandishing your machine guns.

"Now the President, seeing this, sends the National Guard to confront you. The situation is desperate. Suddenly you all break into song; you sing the story of your sisters' suffering and persecution at the hands of heterosexual males and anal-retentive, martini swilling housewives. You dance your way into their hearts. The National Guardsmen are moved by your story and weep; they lay down their rifles and rocket launchers and move to

99

embrace you."

"This is so exciting," whispered Demi.

"It'll close the first night," replied a stony-faced lesbian whore standing next to them. "The script reads like it was written by some dyslexic high-school kid jacking off into his word processor."

"Oh, I hope not," said Gina. "I really need the work."

"That goes for all of us, honey." The whore had great legs, delicately muscled. She was doing stretching exercises and ignoring Vandermeer as he droned on, getting more and more excited as he described the eventual over-throw of the government in the final climactic scene.

"I'm Mona, by the way," she said, introducing herself and gazing hun-grily at Gina. "You're pretty."

"Uh, thanks. I'm Gina and this is my friend Demi."

"You should try out for the lead," said Mona. "I heard you sing at try-outs and you'd be perfect for the part. Such a powerful, natural voice."

"You really think so?" The lead character was Windy Hightower, a steel heiress from an old New York family who'd formed the Sisters of Justice after her lesbian lover had been murdered by a rampaging mob of arch-con-servatives.

"Absolutely," said Mona. "You've got just the kind of fresh face they're looking for. The audience will eat you up."

Demi was bursting with pride. "Gina! How wonderful! You'll be the toast of New York Society! All your dreams are coming true!"

"Pay attention, Girls!" screeched Vandermeer. "Now remember: You're all very vulnerable and sexy, but defiant, always defiant. Now where's that prop boy with the machine guns?" He pointed his finger at a girl in the front row. "And you, honey; where are you hiding your breasts? I want them bubbling up and popping out all over! Hustle over to wardrobe—they'll fix you up. Everyone set? Ok! All together now: Step and kick and step and kick—smile now, always smiling!—and kick and kick and step and step..."

FOUR:

Washington, D.C., an anonymous federal building.

A small group of humorless, severely constipated men are huddled around a conference table in a room decorated with abstract paintings and track lighting. They are identically dressed in conservative black suits, white dress shirts, and thin black ties. Their skulls are sleek, thin lips pressed into perpetual scowls, hair beaten into submission by a liberal application of industrial-grade spray. All are wearing black sunglasses. They sit rigidly and stare at each other without speaking. In front of each is a glass of ice water, untouched, and a stack of computer printouts neatly squared. The atmosphere in the room is cold, deathlike. These men are highly-trained.

They are killers.

The door opens and a new man enters the room. His features are hard, as though chiseled from marble. He is dressed in the same fashion as the others, but he exudes an intangible aura of raw, hysterical power. This is Special Agent Tense. His authority, it is whispered, rivals that of the President himself. The silent men stand in unison. He greets them with a nod and they take their seats.

"Gentlemen. We may have a problem."

The agents at the table exchange knowing glances, grim looks, and subtle hand signals.

"Is it the Iranians, sir?" asks one of the agents.

"The North Koreans," says another, "they've been making noises."

"The Russian Mafia—we've been intercepting some signals…"

"The Pope. It's not the Pope again, is it, sir?"

"I only wish it were that simple," replied Agent Tense. His muscular shoulders quivered under the crushing weight of federal responsibility. "This briefcase," he continued, "this briefcase; the thinnest, blackest briefcase ever made, contains a top-secret report so shocking that only we of the Omega Council are qualified to judge and act on the threat revealed within its ciphered pages."

He opened the briefcase and tossed the report onto the table. "It's time we confronted the menace of the Lesbian Whores."

The lights in the chamber burned late into the night.

FIVE:

The loft again, four weeks later.

Vandermeer was mixing himself a vodka and tonic. "Opening night in three days! I think we're ready, Neil, I really do. Your script rewrites were masterful. The money people are very, very happy with what they've seen."

Blunt eyed him sourly. "It's a ridiculous piece of trash. Frankly, I'm sick to death of the thing. I wish to God I'd burned it, put it out of it's misery. The idea of my name being associated with it is giving me nightmares." He puffed furiously on a joint as thick as his index finger, filling the air with heavy, resinous smoke.

Vandermeer was astonished. "But it's going to be a smash! United Sisters of America will make your reputation!"

"Fantastic. I'll become famous for introducing the American theatrical public to Lesbian Whoredom. They'll all expect sequels: *Lesbian Whores on The Moon!*, *To Russia, with Whores!*, *Whores behind Bars!*, the list will be endless!"

A gray cat stalked across the floor and rubbed up against his leg. Blunt hurled the fat roach at it, but the cat dodged the smoking missile easily and padded away to seek sympathy elsewhere.

Vandermeer stared sadly at his colleague. "I had no idea you felt this way. Really…I think you're overreacting."

"Oh, you think so, do you? Maybe you'd like to take a look at this!" Blunt pulled an official looking envelope from his pocket and handed it to Vandermeer.

"What's this?"

"A rather stern letter from our government. They are 'concerned' about the content of the play."

"That's ridiculous!" snorted Vandermeer. "We're covered by the first amendment!"

"Yeah? Well yesterday I got a visit from someone wearing a very intense black suit. He claimed to work for some super-secret agency I've never heard of. He basically let me know that they would be watching us both— closely. I get the feeling that these people are somewhat more…dedicated, let's say, than your average civil servants."

"But they've got no right!" exploded Vandermeer. "This is art that we're creating! The revolution is a fiction! It doesn't exist!"

"*We* know that, Guy, but it looks like logic just flew out the window. They've got guns, and they've got jails. What have we got?"

"The power of art," the director said loftily.

Blunt laughed. "Well, that's very beautiful, Guy, and very deep, but right now I'd settle for a bulletproof vest and a passport."

Vandermeer looked bewildered. This wasn't something they'd taught him about at Columbia. "We've got no choice." He lit a cigarette and began to pace to room. "We go forward. We take our chances. Promise me you won't say a word to anyone about this, Neil?"

"It's cool with me. I hate the fucking government. Nothing's been the same since Reagan got elected; everyone walking around with a stick up their ass. But what about the girls, do we tell them?"

"We tell them nothing. They're getting paid."

The red, stoned eyes of Neil Blunt looked startled. "That's pretty cold, Guy."

Vandermeer finished his drink. "Sometimes art is cruel."

SIX:

The Majestic Theatre, Opening Night.

It was a perfect evening, warm, but not too warm, and the streets of New York were clogged with limousines chartered by the insanely rich. Approximately half of them had chosen to attend the opening of *The United*

Lesbian Whores of Broadway

Sisters of America at The Majestic Theatre on West 44th street. Numerous photographers, scurrying like rats on speed, overran the sidewalks, snapping pictures. Television stations had sent crews, and the metal trees of their satellite transmitters gave a festive feel to the scene. A buzz of excitement went through the crowd as the Mayor, rumored to be attending, actually showed up. Vandermeer stood out front in a flawless black tuxedo, smiling broadly and shaking hands. Adrenaline had kept him up for the past 48 hours and his face wore a slightly glazed expression.

"Mr. Mayor! So glad you could make it."

"I've heard good things about it, Vandermeer, very good things."

"We've got some lovely girls, Mr. Mayor, and a first-rate script."

"A nice turnout. Well, I'd better get inside. Break a leg!"

"Thank you, sir."

Backstage, Gina was shaking like a leaf. Having won the lead role with her spectacular body, lusty voice, and fresh-faced enthusiasm, she was, unfortunately, totally unprepared for the chaos of opening night. A dozen lesbian whores surrounded her, making minute adjustments to her costume and make-up, and sharkishly keeping the gawkers and well-wishers at a distance. "You'll do just fine, honey," said Demi, her voice unnaturally high. Her face was frozen into a zombie mask by intense stage fright.

"Listen to her, kid," said Mona. "Do it just like in rehearsals. We'll get you through okay, won't we girls?" The whores murmured agreement.

Gina took a deep breath. "It's just nerves," she said. "I'll get over it once I hit the stage."

"Sure you will, kid—this is your night." Mona turned and catching Demi's eye, drew her out of the crowd.

"Something's wrong, Demi."

"What? With Gina?"

"No," said Mona, her eyes darting back and forth, sweeping the backstage crowd. "It's Vandermeer and Blunt. There's something they're not telling us. They're always whispering together and Vandermeer looks scared, like a rat in a trap. Every time one of us gets near them they shut up and try to look casual. Something is very wrong."

"Oh my God!" wailed Demi. "What'll we do?"

"Nothing. Just keep your eyes open. We don't know what to expect. Maybe it's a bomb threat, or some crazy stalker. Stay close to Gina and protect her. There's no time to make plans."

"I think I'm going to be sick," said Demi.

"No time for that either. And don't say a word to Gina. She's got enough to think about." Mona melted quickly back into the circle of whores while Demi tried to squash a rising tide of panic. The curtain would go up in twenty minutes.

"Don't be such a coward, Demi," she muttered to herself. "Gina needs you."

♋

The Majestic was an old theater. There were many places to hide. In a forgotten tunnel under the stage, Agent Tense crouched, his body shaking violently. Streams of sweat ran down his face, a face normally impassive, but now distorted by naked fear.

"It's okay...okay...you're in control...always in control...there are no voices...no strange voices...no demons waiting to punish you...you are strong...you command respect...people fear you...you are in control... you...OH GOD MAKE THE VOICES STOP!"

A voice spoke into his ear. "Agent Tense."

"Wha...what?"

"Agent Tense, do you read?" Suddenly, the other voices faded. This one was different. It was coming from his headset.

"I...yes. I read you."

"Abort code has been received. Repeat: Abort code has been received. Do I confirm?"

Agent Tense hugged himself tightly to stop the shaking. He dug his nails into his arms until he felt the blood soak into his shirt.

"Agent Tense, do you read?"

"I read you. Negative on confirm. We go ahead as scheduled."

"Sir? Please repeat."

"That's a negative on the abort code. Do not acknowledge."

"Yes, sir. Standing by."

Agent Tense began to rock back and forth in the darkness. He sang a nursery rhyme to himself while the blood ran down his arms. After a while every voice was gone and he began to feel better. The dial of his watch glowed in the dark. It would tell him when it was time to move.

♋

Neil Blunt was drunk. He was always drunk when one of his plays opened. It was like liquid velvet—to cushion the shock. The critics hated his plays; they tore him apart in one review after another. He'd begun to think they were right. Lately he'd been dogged by a terrible dream. In the dream he took his own life as his father had years before. The twin demons of doubt and despair dragging him to the edge and pushing him over while he watched, helpless. "Hemingway," he slurred, "old boy knew when it was over, knew when he'd had enough. Izza gift, like talent—Old Papa don't need his no more—oughta lend me some, little bit, don' need a lot...ah, shit..."

Guy Vandermeer entered the room with a bottle of champagne.

"We are gold, Neil, solid gold! The audience nearly brought down the house after the first act. Didn't you hear? I just came from talking with some of the critics. They're writing glowing reviews. They love the play. They love Gina. We're gonna get optioned for a movie!"

"Fame," crooned Blunt, "I'm gonna live forever..."

Vandermeer stared at him, perplexed. "What the hell is wrong with you, Neil? You're getting what you wanted. Acceptance, respect, lots of money..."

"Tellya a secret, Guy old pal, deep dark secret. Ya listening? Good. What I really wanted was to write...what I always wanted to write...was a story that actually MEANT SOMETHING. A story that was IMPORTANT! Not a bunch of tripe about lesbians plunging their fists into dripping vaginas, or machine-gunning congressmen! Do you have any idea WHAT I'M TALK-ING ABOUT?"

Vandermeer froze in the act of pouring champagne. "Sure, Neil...I guess...I mean, yeah, I just never heard you talk this way before..."

106

"The black suits are here, Guy."

"What!?" Spilled champagne fizzed on the tabletop, forming a river that splattered on Vandermeer's black dress shoes.

Blunt nodded, suddenly sober. "I saw them sneaking around. I think there's gonna be trouble."

"Why didn't you tell me, Neil?"

"You were too busy kissing ass, Guy. You couldn't stop them anyway."

"What are we going to do? This is terrible! The opening could be ruined!"

"I'm going to drink more alcohol. You're going to get stressed out and kiss some more ass."

♋

The audience sat like fleshy jewels in the posh surroundings of the Majestic. Full of champagne and expensive hors d oeuvres, they clapped loudly, enthusiastically, completely at ease and willing to give themselves over to the evening of fantasy, singing, and lesbian whores promised them by the colorful billboards which featured Gina's half-nude body and sweet young face. They'd never seen anything like it, and the shock of the new softened the cynical edges of their corrupted hearts. Mrs. Elliot White, a wrinkled harpy, and her nephew, a bloodsucking corporate lawyer by the name of Harrison W. Caulder, sat in the front row, whispering to each other like jaded vipers and eating French chocolates.

"What is that girl doing, Harrison?" said Mrs. Elliot White.

"Having sex with her machine gun, I believe."

"Scandalous! And all of them are lesbians, are they?"

"And lesbian whores, Auntie."

She sniffed and popped another chocolate into her mouth. "Scandalous."

"Would you like me to take you home?"

"I must endure it. I feel a certain responsibility as a patron of the arts."

Harrison's lips curved into a smile. "Of course, Auntie."

"*What are they doing to that congressman*!?"

"It's called anal rape, Aunt. They are anal-raping him with their machine guns."

"Despicable women!" Her eyes were glued to the stage.

"Perhaps they'll apologize later. Offer him some analgesic cream."

"Don't make fun. Society is in ruins, and all people want to do is laugh."

"It's a new day. A new America. You must accept it."

She sniffed again. "Give me another chocolate."

Ten seconds later Mrs. Elliot White became the recipient of a brutal and unexpected shove in the back. The shove was initiated by a black-suited man wearing black sunglasses. "Watch out, you clod!" she said indignantly. But the man didn't stop. He was rushing towards the stage, and all over the theater other black-suited men were doing the same. The crowd began to stir; there was a rising buzz of voices.

"Is this part of the show?" asked a puzzled Mrs. Elliot White.

"I think not," her nephew replied.

Demi was plunging the red, white, and blue flag of the United Sisters of America through a gaping hole in the chest of the dying president when she saw the Omega agents vaulting onto the stage. In their hands they held the thinnest, blackest guns she'd ever seen.

"What will become of America now?" gasped the president, his chest dripping with fake blood.

"Shut up," said Agent Tense. He kicked the fake president in the head.

"Hey…!" said the actor, "that's not in the script!"

Ignoring him, Agent Tense turned to glare at the lesbian whores. "Whores!" he said, "your revolution, such as it is, has officially been noticed and will be terminated. Now." The Omega agents edged forward.

Gina had been in the middle of a long song about oppression, sexual freedom, and the need for strict hygiene when she noticed the strangers.

"What are you doing?" she demanded. She stepped forward to stand beside Demi.

"You are Gina Bredani, the lesbian whore?"

"I am an actress now."

"That is immaterial. You will come with us." Grinning like jackals, they converged on her, and Gina backed away. With a little thrill of disgust she noticed their teeth had been sharpened and seemed to glow under the stage lights.

"NOOOO!!!" screamed Demi as she charged. "YOU LEAVE GINA ALONE!!!" She hit the Omega Agents with astonishing force, scattering them like bowling pins.

"Stop!" yelled Guy Vandermeer, running up the center aisle, his coattails flapping. "You're ruining my play!"

Snarling, Agent Tense got to his feet, assisted by two Omega Agents.

Gina felt a wave of nausea begin to rise from the pit of her stomach. The skin on the left side of Agent Tense's face had been torn, revealing gleaming metal underneath.

Mona came running up from the other side of the stage. "What the hell!!?"

"None of this makes any sense," said Gina.

"They're fucking cyborgs!" said Mona. "Some kind of futuristic fucking cyborgs!"

"Oh, Dear," said Demi, still sprawled on the stage. "I think I've ruined this dress."

The audience, who couldn't seem to make up their minds whether to flee the theater or stay in their seats, became witnesses to the strangest scene ever to be played out on the American stage. Mona, along with a handful of lesbian whores who had taken self-defense classes and were therefore skilled in Kung Fu, specifically Monkey Kung Fu, attacked the Omega Agents, who may or may not have been cyborgs, or possibly some sort of advanced robots developed in secret by the NSA in well concealed government labs. The Omega Agents responded by firing their thin black guns at the lesbian whores, killing some of them, wounding others, before being overwhelmed and disarmed by the Kung Fu whores. A pitched battle was waged on the stage, now slippery with blood. Mona herself was pitted against the merciless Agent Tense, who appeared to have lost his mind. A steady stream of obscenities poured from his mouth, his eyes were glazed and insane looking, he growled like a dog. Mona was peppering him with Kung Fu chops and kicks, and every time she connected sparks flew from his body. His skin appeared to be melting, and his hair was on fire.

Gina and Demi were weaving in and out of the combat zone, collecting the thin black guns and distributing them to the whores who fired at the Omega Agents whenever fate handed them a clear shot. Guy Vandermeer was dancing around like an idiot in front of the stage, screeching like a banshee and wringing his hands.

"This is art!" he screeched. "Art! You're crushing its delicate soul!"

The whores began to gain the advantage. The gears and servos of the Omega Agents began to whine and smoke. Their mecha-structures were breaking down under the ceaseless assault. A well-placed kick by one of the whores snapped a metal neck, separating an Agent's head which spun around on the stage like a top spewing thick gray fluid from its neck. This was the end for the Omega Agents.

"Go for their heads!" cried Mona. "Kick their fucking heads off!" All the whores began to use Monkey Kung Fu head kicks with terrible effectiveness. Cyborg heads began flying through the air and the battle was soon won. It was during this time that the remainder of the crowd fled the theater. It had all become too Avant Garde for them. Outside, black limos scrambled onto sidewalks and gulping passengers, roared off into the night to be replaced by wailing squad cars disgorging grim-faced policemen.

Drenched in gray cyborg blood, Mona knelt and stared into the face of Agent Tense, grinning ferociously.

"You assholes sure fucked with the wrong Americans this time," she said.

Agent Tense returned her gaze with extreme hatred. His throat made a clicking noise.

"Damnable whores," moaned the head of Agent Tense.

SEVEN:

The Aftermath, one day later, The Loft.

Neil Blunt sipped his Irish coffee and looked at the picture of Gina on the front page of the New York Post.

"LESBIAN WHORES THWART GOVERNMENT CONSPIRACY!" the headline read.

Blunt didn't read the article. He couldn't take his eyes off the picture of Gina. There was something about her, he didn't know what; she had become lodged in his mind and no mental toothpick could get her out.

The buzz of the doorbell broke through his reverie.

He pushed the intercom button. "Who is it?"

"It's Gina, Mr. Blunt."

"Come on up." He smoothed his hair with a nervous motion. He hid the overflowing ashtray full of roaches and cigarette butts in a drawer and returned the bottle of whiskey to the shelf. When he opened the door she greeted him with a smile.

"Come in, Gina."

He guided her to the couch and sat opposite her in a comfortable black leather chair.

"Thanks for coming. I suppose you've heard we closed the play."

"Yes," she said. "Maybe it's for the best."

"Guy's in the Hamptons, recovering. Says there's a 'bad aura' surrounding the production, whatever the hell that means. So all the investors have pulled out."

Gina crossed her long legs. The tight fitting black jeans she wore revealed rather than concealed their tapered beauty.

"It looks like my acting career is over," she replied.

"Too soon to tell about that. I'm writing a new script; I think it'll be even better than the old one, and it'll include everything that happened at the opening. I want you to be in it. All the other girls, too, that is, if you're willing."

He was staring at her and he couldn't help it.

"Well," she said, "it sounds very exciting. Can you get the money?"

"It shouldn't be a problem. We're all celebrities now and everyone will want a piece of us. The real difficulty will be finding a good director."

She finally noticed how hard he was staring at her. A slight flush came to her cheeks.

"Is there something else…?"

"I'm afraid so," he said. "We knew about the Omega Agents, Gina. Guy and I both knew. We were just too scared and too selfish to do anything. But we didn't know that they were cyborgs, we didn't suspect they were totally insane."

"I really ought to kick you in the balls," she said. But there was no anger in her voice.

"I know. I deserve it."

"I won't do it, though, because I kind of like you, Neil. I don't know why."

Neil Blunt felt his heart beat violently.

He took a deep breath and rolled the dice. "You're so damned beautiful and I can't stop thinking about you, will you go out with me?"

"How do you know I'm not a lesbian?" she asked.

"I talked to Demi about you."

"You know I was a prostitute, a lesbian whore."

"I don't care."

"Well, okay then."

EIGHT:

The End, The Majestic Theatre, six months later.

Mrs. Elliot White sat in the front row with her nephew during the premiere performance of the new "The United Sisters of America," grumbling the whole time. It was a lush, lavish production. It would be completely sold out for the entirety of its yearlong run on Broadway.

"As far as I'm concerned, these lesbian whores, these *perverted murderers* shouldn't be allowed to perform before decent folk," she whispered.

"Then why did you come, Auntie?"

"This nation was founded on certain principles, and I for one…"

"Hush, Auntie."

Gina was about to sing.

Self Service

by Jessica Markowicz

T HE COOL CRIMSON moon bled crystalline tears as her stars glimmered like an infinite mosaic of glass shards in the indigo velvet night. The liquid shimmer of galaxies yet unborn floated overhead in the midnight abyss as Reva flicked up the lapels of her ebony leather trench against a nonexistent chill, her boots kicking up minute particles of lunar dust with each gently rolling step.

The station was just visible now above the sinking horizon, radio-active steel and glass illuminated by the intermittent pulsing glow of the violet luminescents. The sickly sweet vapor of bacchia hissed from the perimeter overhang, causing her steps to quicken then pause, drawing a long draught into her constricted chest. *Mmmmn, sweet succor nearly as comforting as mother's milk*, she thought, as the familiar ease spread through her, loosening limbs and muscles, sinking down into cramped corpuscles.

The Conglomerate had originally thought to use the pungent substance to eliminate the migrant population like so much human waste, numbing nervous systems into lethargy and submission. They hadn't counted on its psychedelic and sensually psychotropic effects. After twenty years of daily exposure, Reva was nearly immune to its effects, other than a welcome feeling of hypnotic receptivity to experience that heightened her deadened sensitivity into a state of sur-reality.

Faintly registering the shudder of muted moans and murmurs around her, Reva approached one of the semiprivate, conjoined islands lined in rows seven deep around the head enclosure where the bleary-eyed attendant monitored the master controls. Brushing aside her riotously waving electric blue hair, she placed the first pair of cool sensor discs on each temple. With several quick flicks of her wrist she unbuttoned her calf-length coat and let it pool about her boots. The balmy night air rushed against her silky flesh as the second set of sensors attached to her half-hard nipples. She shivered. The last three discs were imbedded parallel, just inside each hipbone, with the last arrowing down directly above her womb. With a languid swipe of her card, the Emjoi 3000 whirred to life.

The first aluminum tendril uncoiled, lightly tracing down the right side of her face, whispering around her ear, swirling in sinuous motions down the back of her neck, curling to hold her in a lopsided embrace as another arm snaked out, repeating the motion on her other side. She moaned at the contrast of the cool metallic fingers that warmed to her by degrees.

The center panel opened to bathe her in the mauve glow of the luminescents, where shifting patterns and designs played against the creamy backdrop of her rapidly-heating skin. Reva shifted, widening her stance, sighing. On cue, twin jointed probes curled to cup her breasts simultaneously as her nipples began to vibrate. A thin bead of sweat trickled down past the wildly beating base of her throat, slipping between the milky valley of her lightly buzzing globes, sliding across the gnawing pit of her navel before disappearing into the aching shadow between her legs. She licked wet vinyl lips, arching back into her metallic cradle, as another wave of arms released in a flurry of machine motion, slithering and undulating over each dewy inch of her bared in the lilac light, except where she wanted and needed it the most.

A slippery drip dribbled down the inside of her thigh from the slick where X marked her spot as Reva cocked her leg against the side panel. "Fill 'er up," she breathed, watching the flicker on the center console as the throaty timbre of her voice registered. A light grinding preceded the extension of the smooth, massive shaft propelled toward her core, tracing up and down the slit, teasing around her portal before smoothly sliding home to the hilt. She contracted on a groan, riding the motion of the hydraulic cock gently hammering, building the pressure in her moist depths, as all the loving tendrils surrounding her undulated to the rhythm. The fondling and fucking continued until she was nearing fever pitch when the hidden device detached from the rod and affixed itself upon her clit, sucking in time to the fucking, drawing the pulsing wave of her orgasm from her curling toes up throughout her entire body, short-circuiting each throbbing nerve ending.

The cool night air dried the sheen of sweat on her nearly naked body as she leaned limply into the comforting clasp of her mechanical lover. As the afterglow faded, her eyes traversed the confines of her fellow pleasure-seekers. Five islands down she noticed a flabby, jaundiced middle-aged man on all fours, teeth clenched around stiff leather bit, eyes glazed in ecstasy as his metal mistress paddled his concave ass rigorously. Down the aisle a bit a smooth-skinned hermaphrodite arched a golden spray from a miniature penis onto the stainless steel tub as twin aluminum palms stroked doll-like nipples in rhythm. *Cleanup on island #11.* To her right, a slender fifty-something redhead laying across the warm chrome dome gave a smiling sigh as a velvet-gloved mechanical claw gently stroked her glistening forehead while a lengthy curling tongue moved slickly and rapidly between her spread thighs.

Following her line of sight, Reva became aware of her partner on the opposite side of the island. Her gleaming eyes studied the strained visage of a muscular male, mid-30s, being caressed in the teasing torture of the Emjoi's embrace. As a lightly shuddering coil encircled his lubed cock and began to manipulate him manually, his eyes suddenly fluttered open and locked with her own. Reva felt a jolt of recognition—a sudden sinking in her stomach that made her feel both nervous and aroused. She smiled lightly as a bolt of inspiration flashed through her mind.

Detaching and extracting the sensors, then throwing on her trench coat, Reva surreptitiously sidled over to the abandoned control booth, studying the sign that read, "Be back in twenty minutes." Luckily, even after the migration, some things never changed. As a circus chorus of wailing moans groaned in her ears, she looked back towards her departed enclosure #26, noting that her mysterious stranger's eyes were curiously watching her every move. She let herself sink into the tall, raised leather chair behind the console, ensuring that the door was locked as she studied the multitude of switches and controls. It appeared that every switch had been left on "Autoerotic." With a flourish she flicked the switch on #27 to the Manual mode, noticing that an entire unlabeled panel of buttons suddenly glowed with life.

As the stranger waited expectantly for her next move, Reva was briefly puzzled over what to work first. *What the hell*, she thought and began systematically activating each switch and button, noting by #27's reaction which did what. The first lever unleashed a set of smooth ivory teeth, trailing down the tight sensitive tendon on the right side of his neck while a second compartment revealed floating peacock feathers which licked around his stiff nipples. His eyes flickered briefly in reaction. While the feather continued its loving ministrations around his chest and neck, Reva activated the second lever/knob combination. Two metal hands braced themselves upon his hips as the blower glided down, buzzing and fluttering along each bulging vein and ridge of his engorged cock, focusing on the underside where head meets shaft, alternately breathing hot and cold drafts of air across his slick flesh.

Do I have your attention now? she thought with a wicked laugh. His smirking grin had finally broken on a drawn out moan. She tweaked and switched buttons in a steadily building rhythm watching #27 twitch, shiver and shake—switch, click, moan, switch, click, groan. Reva seduced him lever by lever, pushing his buttons in rapid, patterned succession until his hips began to mimic the rhythm of the oiled coil that devoured his raging cock. In her wild button-switching fervor, she inadvertently switched the control for the entire station to "Manual, All." Now her agile lightning movements were manipulating each and every station, tapping and shifting in response to the chorus of male and female voices crying out on cue. Yet Reva only had eyes for #27. Noting the droplets of his desire seeping out from his swollen tip she initiated the finale sequence—sleek steel strokers languidly palming his tight trembling globes as the velvet vibe slipped underneath to shudder against the sweet spot. The panel began to smoke as purple lights flashed warnings. #27's eyes rolled back and he was gone. Lost in the erotic music, she became a master conductor, orchestrating the passion of the station with each rough rap of a button until the entire symphony climaxed in howling, shuddering unison as the console burst into flame, subsiding into a sparking sputter.

As a galaxy of men and women laid satisfied, soaked bodies limp and gleaming in their milky way, Reva rushed over to #27, jerking him to his feet and grabbing his pants, pulling him with her towards the exit. #27 paused outside the periphery as he pulled on his trousers, partially perplexed, questions in his eyes.

"Come on, we'll talk later," Reva promised, lightly kissing his lips.

With a dazed laugh, #27 followed Reva as they dissolved into the flickering darkness.

An X-less Story

by Perry McGee

L ISA FELT SAD.

After filming the same scene eleven times, she'd had enough. In the first place she was not gay, licking another woman's butt crack made her queasy, and in the second place, it was cold as hell in the pond.

"Can't you find one take that's good enough?" she asked Bob the director guy.

"Listen babycakes, if you want to be a big star, then you'll do it until it's perfect. Now get back in the water and give me some acting."

"Bastard," Lisa said under her breath. She waded into the cold pond, stood behind Mona, and waited for her cue.

Bob the director guy yelled, "And...action."

"Oh Monica, how I love you. Let me prove it." And again, Lisa McCallister, portraying a character named Allisa in a thinly veiled rape fantasy written by a man who couldn't get laid, knelt on her knees and stuck her tongue inside Mona's crack. "Yum," she murmured with her face cheeks squashed against butt cheeks.

"Oh Allisa, you make me cum so good. I love the feeling of your tongue in my ass. I...I...shit, I forgot my line again."

"Cut, dammit, cut," Bob the director guy shouted. "Can't you fucking girls get it right?"

"I got my part right," Lisa said in protest. "It's Mona who's messing up. I think she just wants me to lick her ass all night. That's why she keeps messing up."

Mona said, "Now listen here bitch, I'm a fucking professional. If you could rim me right instead of just tickling my ass, then I'd be okay."

Lisa wanted to argue, but she knew Mona was right. Still, sticking her tongue in another woman's ass was not her idea of movie stardom. She wanted to play nice rolls, maybe a romantic drama or an action thriller with Bruce Willis, not lapping small pieces of toilet paper from the rear end of an over-the-hill porno queen. She grabbed her robe from the coat rack and said, "I need a short break."

Bob the director guy said, "All right everyone, take five. Be back on the set in a half hour."

Lisa walked to her car. She needed two things right then, a cigarette and some mouthwash. A pack of L&Ms sat on her dashboard but there was nothing in the car to take the turd taste out of her mouth.

Lisa sat back and closed her eyes. Thoughts ran rampant in her mind; her first commercial on NBC selling tampons (*I'm fresh, are you*?), a bit part in one of the Brady Bunch movies, and finally this costarring roll in "I Really Love Your Asshole, Baby."

She was a chorus girl for the local church and a child-care specialist, and in her spare time, helped the elderly with their needs. So why in God's name did she have to lick another woman's butt? It just wasn't right.

As she drifted into an unexpected nap, her last thought was of...

Lisaaaaaaaaaa
Who's there?
Lisaaaaaaaaaa
Who are you?
I'm the ghost of lesbian past
What do you want from me?
I want to show you something. Come with me.

The apparition, who looked like Dennis Miller and spoke like Barney Rubble, took Lisa's hand and flew Peter Pan-like into the night, dragging her across the black and blue sky. As they neared a small condo, Lisa said, "That looks like the place I grew up in."

The ghost said, "It is, or rather, it was. Now watch through this window."

Inside was Lisa's mother and Aunt Matilda. They were locked in a brutal sixty-nine position, tongues flailing like earthworms on crack.

"That's my mom? I never knew she was gay."

"Now look up here," and the ghost raised her to a second story window. Inside, a much younger Lisa played with a Barbie doll. The young child wore a Pooh bear night shirt and matching pants as she made Barbie trundle around on the floor.

"I don't remember that," the floating Lisa said.

"Shut up and watch."

Lisa did as instructed.

In the pink walled bedroom, the young girl lifted Barbie to her face and said, "Barbie, why don't you go find Ken and take him for a ride in your car?"

Barbie replied "Ken is such a dolt, but Raggedy Anne can ride with me." The young Lisa could not understand why Barbie always said that, but honored the request anyway.

"I don't want to see anymore," the older Lisa said.

The apparition said, "So be it."

And flying through the sky again…
Can I go home now?
No, there's more people you need to see
Who? Who am I going to see?
The ghost of lesbian present
Oh, okay.

A man that looked very much like Don Knotts, only with more hair, said, "Lisa, watch this."

And there she was, standing in a pond licking a woman's butt and not doing a very good job. The director called for a break. The licking Lisa walked away, but the cast and crew remained.

[Camera fades in. Director stands against backdrop.]: What am I going to do with that girl? I thought she could act.

[Camera pans left to gaffer. Gaffer shakes head in disgust]

[Camera pans further left to Mona. Mona sits naked on a folding lawn chair smoking a crack pipe]: She's wasting our time. Christ, I got two other scenes with her yet. If she don't get it right soon, I'm walking.

[Camera draws in for close-up of Mona's face]: Do you understand?
[Cut to director]: Mona, we'll get it. If not I'll call Randy and have him send over another actress.

[Cut back to Mona. She exhales a large plume of smoke]: I'm just saying, you had better do something. If not, I'll personally see to it that she never works another day in this town. [Mona stands, turns, kicks the lawn chair, and storms off]

Lisa and the Knotts lookalike dude then flew upward and slightly to the left. "There's someone else you need to see."

And the skies opened in heavenly beauty. Another man, this one more like Sally Struthers with a goatee, said, "Hello Lisa, I'm the ghost of—"
I know who you are. Let's just get this over with.

Face reddening, the fat blonde ghost nodded and did the cool flying trick to a place Lisa had never seen before. "Here is your future. Watch it and learn from it."
And Lisa indeed watched. In a bed were what appeared to be herself—much older—and two old men. Several other old men stood in a line in the hallway outside the open door. She could smell the raunchiness of their breath and bodies even from her position outside the window.
The first old man in the bed said, "Take it all you bitch."

The second old man in the bed said, "Too bad you're so poor because years ago you didn't lick that woman's ass, such a shame because now you're a cheap hooker at this here YMCA and all us old men are going to fuck you every day."

The aged Lisa on the bed said, "Oh please don't shove that big hairy thing inside me all the time like that. I'm really sorry I didn't become a lesbian way back then. If I could go back in time, I'd change all that."

The Lisa outside the window said, "Well ain't that just the biggest pile of steaming horse shit I ever seen." She turned to the triple-chinned fat ghost and asked, "Who put you up to this? Was it Bob? Was it Mona? Who in the hell set this phony shit up?"

The obese ghost of lesbian future stammered, "Well...I...I..."

"I though so. Now take me back."

They went back.

Lisa awoke in her Ford's front seat. Lighting another L&M, she thought about all the trouble 'someone' had gone through to change her way of thinking about the sapho scene. Then she thought about that bit part with the Brady's and how Greg had tried to molest her. Was that what she wanted? Did she really want to get felt up by has-beens for the rest of her career? Did she really want to peddle tampons on network TV for the rest of her life?

"No," she yelled in her car.

With a new attitude, she raced back to the set. "Start rolling the film," she ordered, then knelt behind Mona. She grabbed the woman's cheeks, stared into the brown orifice, and began lapping like there was no tomorrow. Plowing her tongue repeatedly into Mona's darkest recess, letting her saliva mix with the fine butt hairs and toilet paper fragments, tasting and swallowing and sucking with vigor, Lisa felt happy.

She smiled into the other woman's butt.

An X-Less Story

Epilogue

As Lisa made passionate oral love to Mona's hindquarters, the gaffer had a sticky accident in his under-roos.

Why Don't We Do It in the Road

by John Edward Lawson

A MAN AND woman look up and notice each other while groping cuts of beef in the meat aisle of the local grocery.

The man is below average height for a male, above average intelligence, exceptionally well-hung, blond, and Australian.

The woman is average height for a female, above average intelligence, far above average whininess, above average shapeliness in all the right places, red-haired, and from a section of New York that speaks a language called Nasal.

It goes without saying that they both have incredibly annoying accents—there, I said it!

Instead of acting on their carnal instincts the pair disengage their eyes, put down said bloody hunks of muscle, and go their separate ways.

The man and woman are disillusioned with the predefined roles assigned by the fascist society encircling them.

Bored workers observe the woman and man engaging in full-fledged consumerism; these peons are too dumbfounded by monotony to even entertain sexual fantasies about the duo, despite the fact that they're attractive in the traditional, non-prefabricated way censored by the mass media.

Meaningless Muzak transgressions against the music of the 60's play heartlessly in the background, stripped of any revolutionary merit by studio musicians who are soul-raped on a daily basis.

In other words, a pleasant shopping atmosphere is provided.

Nothing carnal.

Not in the frozen foods, and certainly not at check out where burned out underachievers in varying stages of pre-suicide mechanically do their jobs (and, if they are mechanical, then surely they're rusty as all hell, slow as they move).

Nothing carnal when the money exchanges hands, when the items to be consumed are pushed out the door.

Something carnal about the shopping carts slamming into each other—man and woman banging, so to speak, loaded to the gills with enough meat products to stave off a herd of carnivores.

"What's your name?"

"Fuck me."

"All right, Fuck Me...you ever had asphalt burn?"

Forget the groceries.

Leave them for the cart collectors to ruminate over, for the seagulls to peck each other's eyes out over, for food fetishists to masturbate over.

Thunder roars somewhere in the distance.

Lightning surges through their veins, woman on top of man, a speck of roadthrill on US Interstate 30.

This isn't what anyone would call safe sex, not by a long shot, not by a cum shot.

The thunder roars closer now, an angry god protesting sinful acts.

Hips grind into hips, red and blond hairs grapple with each other, her buttocks jiggle and his get uncomfortably familiar with the ass-phalt.

The thunder isn't thunder at all.

It's a moving, living thing.

It's blasting at twelve thousand horse power, surging down the highway like a sixty minute Zulu man ripping through a diaphragm.

The woman and man don't know why they're here, doing these things, except perhaps that it seems exceedingly naughty.

Nor do they know that a "drag" race is headed their way.

Queens from San Francisco and Soho bear down on the copulating couple at 150 MPH.

It's fucking brutal, so to speak.

Screech, swerve, lose control.

Crash.

Penetration.

Total abandon.

Fenders banging, breaking, wheels spinning.

Seat belts retain only fragments of manmeat in silk evening gowns, dashboards painted red, windshields embracing male-pattern-baldness and tiaras.

Absolutely no cunt-rol.

The drag race ends in a human pile, obstructing Interstate 30 like a billy club in a colon.

And in the heart of it all, at the very center of flaming twisted-steel-and-sex-appeal, the man and woman continue to fornicate, rubber and wiring dangling around them like afterbirth, the vein-ejaculation bathing them in some madman's concept of embryonic fluid.

No longer consumers, they must feed off each other now and forever.

An ice cream truck equipped with ram plate and bulletproof armor plows through the carnage, but there are no children to be had here.

It moves on with predatory efficiency.

Sinking in a pothole the man and woman are forgotten.

Repairs are made, the carnival of death is removed; the system won't tolerate setbacks.

Now enshrouded by darkness, the man and woman continue to taste each other, while above them life speeds on by.

Abandoned and long forgotten, the abandoned food stuffs in the shopping carts jump to the pavement and—like primordial lungfish—slither back to their respective places, eagerly awaiting the next customer.

Christina Aguilera Ate My Left Testicle

by Clint Venezuela

I'M IN THE White Cockroach standing outside the door marked LADIES when I see Billy Vagina approaching.

"Hey, Dumbfuck," he says, "why are you standing outside the door marked LADIES?"

I wait a moment before I reply. Looking him directly in the eyes I say, "I'm waiting for Christina Aguilera to finish taking a dump."

"Christina Aguilera is in the White Cockroach??" he fumes.

"She is. And she's taking a dump right now."

"Hey, wait," Billy Vagina says, "just why are you waiting for her to finish taking a dump, Dumbfuck?"

Now I am in a quandary. Is it wise to explain to Billy Vagina just why I am waiting for Christina Aguilera to finish taking a dump? Am I willing to trust my neighbor with this vital secret? I gaze at his face, his thin mouth spread out wide like a horizontal vagina, gleaming with wetness.

"Do you believe in aliens?" I whisper to him.

"Well I've seen *Men In Black* two times so I guess I do."

"Okay," I say, "then I'll tell you. This is why I am standing outside the door marked LADIES waiting for Christina Aguilera to finish taking a dump…"

♋

Christina Aguilera Ate My Left Testicle

I was on my way to the library to return the book I had borrowed, which was *Impossible Encounters* by Zoran Zivkovic, when I decided to take a short cut through the woods, mainly in order to avoid Mr. Pussikeskus who had recently swallowed his bicycle and had become obsessed with discussing this.

I happened to veer away from the main pathway and in a clearing I came upon a spaceship and two funny-looking aliens. The aliens were staring at me as though my zipper was undone, and I checked to make sure I wasn't unintentionally flashing my genitals at them. I wasn't.

"Who are you?" I asked.

"We are two funny-looking aliens," they replied in unison.

"Where did you come from?"

"An unknown planet."

"Which one?"

"We don't know. The planet is unknown even to us."

"What are your names?"

"I'm Zag, and this is Zag," said the first alien.

"You have the same names? Isn't that confusing?"

"Do we appear confused?"

"Not really. How long have you been here?"

"We have no concept of your time cycles as yet."

"Is that your spaceship?"

"Well it certainly isn't a replica of the Taj Mahal."

"I see you've picked up on human sarcasm pretty quickly."

"Thank you."

"So why have you come here?"

"We crashed. We were on our way to the planet Polycarp Kusch for coffee and donuts when we ran out of fuel and ended up here."

"Tough shit."

"We have limited knowledge of human excrement but if you say so we'll take your word for that."

"Okay, so what's the plan?"

"We need fuel."

"Easy. There's a gas station a half a mile from here."

"We don't use gas as you know it. We use a different form of fuel."

"You don't say? So what is it you use?"

"On your world you refer to them as oranges."

My legs turned to blancmange and I felt an odd shiver run through my entire self.

"Oranges?" I gasped.

"Yes. Can you get some for us?"

"Wow, hey, no way. I have an unnatural fear of oranges. Those orange bastards fucked with my mind and soul and there's no way in the world I'm gonna get some for you."

The first alien then took out a ray gun and pointed it at me, an uneasy grin across his funny-looking face.

"Care to change your mind?" he said.

"Okay, okay. Where do you usually get your fuel?"

"The planet Orange."

"Sounds like a hideous place. I obviously can't go there, can I? I'll have to get some from the market. How many do you need?"

"About half a dozen will get us to Polycarp Kusch."

"Is that all?"

"Yes."

"What if I say no and tell you to fuck off and carry on to the library with my copy of *Impossible Encounters* by Zoran Zivkovic?"

The first alien didn't say anything, he just waved his ray gun around in the air menacingly.

"That might just be a toy," I said.

The alien then pointed the ray gun at a nearby squirrel and pressed the trigger. There was a silent flash and the squirrel disappeared.

"Where did it go?" I asked.

"The planet Orange," said the alien with a chuckle.

"Fucking hell. I better go get the oranges then, huh?"

"Yes. But you might just go and not come back."

"That's true," I said.

"So you require an incentive to return here."

"What kind of incentive?"

The funny-looking aliens began to babble to each other in a strange language that consisted of eerie whistles, squawks and farts. Then they both turned their attention back to me.

"Okay, we have an incentive," they told me in unison. "We know what all human males desire."

"What's that?"

"Sex."

"You could be right there."

"We are right. And for sex the human male needs a partner. Which female would you desire for a sexual encounter?"

I didn't need to ponder over that one. "Christina Aguilera," I said, "but there's no way in the world you'll get her to come here and have sex with me."

The first alien pointed his ray gun at a nearby horny toad and pressed the trigger. There was a silent flash and then to my astonishment Christina Aguilera was standing in the clearing.

"Fucking hell!" I yelled.

"Exactly," said the funny-looking aliens. "So you get the oranges and when you get back Christina Aguilera will give you a blowing job."

"You mean a blowjob," I said.

"Whatever."

"It's a deal."

I started to make my way out of the clearing when suddenly the funny-looking aliens called me back.

"What is it?" I asked.

"We require another item," they said in unison. "We require a copy of *The Kafka Effekt* by D Harlan Wilson."

"How do you know about that?"

"It's the most talked about book in the universe."

"Talked about even more than The Bible by all those holy folk?"

"Yes."

"What's in it for me?"

"We will give you a secret message."

132

"What secret message?"

"It's a secret."

"Bastards."

So once again I set off out of the clearing and found the pathway and made my way out of the woods. Obtaining the oranges was going to be a major problem for me, but the idea of Christina Aguilera giving me a blowjob was impossible to resist. With this in mind I tentatively approached the city center and the fruit market.

♋

I was standing gazing at the fruit stalls, attempting to pluck up the courage to approach one of them, when I noticed Mr. Zakarpatska walking by without his dog.

"Hi, Mr. Zakarpatska," I said with an invented joviality.

"Hello, Dumbfuck," he replied.

Mr. Zakarpatska lives in the same apartment block as me and so I know him quite well, but not his dog.

"Where are you going?" I asked.

"The abattoir."

"Why, do you work there?"

"No, I just like looking at blood and guts and dead animals."

"Cool. Will you do me a favor?"

"What is it?"

"Go and get me maybe half a dozen oranges."

"Is that all? Why don't you go?"

"I have an allergy."

"Fair enough. So what's in it for me?"

"What do you want?"

"Okay, if I get the oranges will you let me sleep with your wife?"

"Do you mean sleep as in sleep or do you mean having a sexual liaison?"

"A sexual liaison."

"My wife is available for a sexual liaison at any time."

"Yes, but I don't want to pay the twenty dollars."

"I can arrange that if you get the oranges."

"Excellent."

"However I need a second favor if I agree to this condition."

"What second favor?"

"Your copy of *The Kafka Effekt* by D Harlan Wilson."

"Awwww, man, I've only read it twelve times."

"Isn't twelve enough?"

"Certainly not."

"It's the book or no sexual liaison."

Mr. Zakarpatska slipped his hand into his jacket and produced his copy of The Kafka Effekt by D Harlan Wilson which he handed over to me. He then wandered off among the fruit stalls and I watched as he purchased maybe half a dozen oranges. I knew that I would have difficulty in taking them back to the funny-looking aliens but my mind was set on achieving the feat. Presently Mr. Zakarpatska returned carrying a small paper bag containing maybe half a dozen oranges. I shuddered as I took them from him, then nodded at him before I set off once again for the woods and the spaceship and the funny-looking aliens.

♋

When I got back the alien with the ray gun was shooting baby frogs in a nearby pond. One second they were leaping and splashing around the next they were gone, vanished to the planet Orange or some other awful place, I don't know.

"I got the oranges," I said, handing the other alien the paper bag. I then glanced around, and spotted Christina Aguilera huddled beside a prickly hedgerow. "What's wrong with her?" I asked.

"Zag told her that her latest single is rubbish," said the second alien.

I realized that these guys were pretty mean dudes and that I had to be rid of them soon.

"Okay," I said, "I got the oranges, and a copy of *The Kafka Effekt* by D Harlan Wilson." I took out the book that Mr. Zakarpatska had given to me and offered it to the alien, who took it and started to flick through the pages eagerly.

"Excellent," he said.

Then the other alien with the ray gun handed me a small note. "Don't look at this until we are gone, okay?" he warned. "It's the secret message we promised."

"Groovy. So what about the blowjob?"

The alien snapped his stubby fingers and Christina Aguilera crawled over to me. Without a word she unzipped me and grabbed my limp member. I felt an absurd tingle swim through my veins, and my penis started to come to life. The aliens disappeared into the spaceship through an open hatch which slowly closed. I heard a tinny churning sound followed by a tremendous roar that appeared to alarm Christina Aguilera terribly. She was licking my testicles and the sudden fright caused her to bite down on my scrotum and my left testicle was ripped clean off. I screamed and screamed as she looked up at me with my bloody testicle hanging from between her lips. The spaceship lifted from the ground and zoomed away into the clouds as Christina Aguilera swallowed my gonad and hurried off into the woods.

My agony slowly subsided, and as I pondered on a future with only one testicle I opened up the note that the aliens had given to me. A simple message was displayed in bold letters across the center of the sheet.

I have a message for you

I cried out in frustration as I beat the ground with my fists. And that's the story of how Christina Aguilera ate my left testicle.

ॐ

"That's weird," says Billy Vagina.

"I guess it is," I say.

"So how do you know Christina Aguilera is in there taking a dump?"

"I followed her here. She's definitely in there, I can tell you."

Billy Vagina stares at the door marked LADIES for a few seconds, as if assessing something of a paranormal nature, like Fox Mulder before his character became boring (zzzzzzzzzzzzzzzzzzz...)

"So let me get this straight," he says at last. "You plan to wait until Christina Aguilera has finished taking a dump and then sneak in there and sift through her shit and find your left testicle. Am I correct?"

"You are."

"And then you aim to take this missing testicle and somehow get it reattached. Am I correct?"

"You are. I'll see Dr. Zagduma, he'll recommend someone."

"It's a good idea," says Billy Vagina, "except for one thing."

"What's that?"

"Christina Aguilera will flush away the evidence, won't she?"

I instantly start to panic. He is right! Christina Aguilera will destroy her shit and my testicle with it, flushing it all away into the sewers where I will never find it. I'll be compelled to a life with just one gonad. Oh shit, no!

I dash beyond the door marked LADIES and quickly study the cubicles. As I do this one of the doors opens and a female appears. However it isn't Christina Aguilera, it is someone else entirely.

"Who are you?" I gasp.

"Angelina Jolie. Who are you?"

I don't reply, instead I gaze at her and realize that this surely is Angelina Jolie.

"Are you really Angelina Jolie?" I ask.

"Yes I am."

"Well to tell you the truth I have always suspected that you are really Jon Voigt in drag and that your entire existence is a sham."

"That's bollocks."

"And speaking of bollocks, have you seen Christina Aguilera?" I say.

She shakes her head, and as she does so I spot a young dark-haired man leap into the cubicle she has stepped out of. I watch as he sinks to his knees and thrusts his hands into the bowl. I hadn't noticed him before but I intend to find out exactly who he is and what he is doing beyond the door marked LADIES. I approach him, and Angelina Jolie's shit-smell hits me right in the nostrils. Then the man begins to chortle and gets up swiftly, and turns around to face me. His hands are filled with Jolie-shit, and yet among this brown stuff is what I can only describe as a left testicle. My nerves tense up immediately upon spotting this.

"Who are you?" I demand.

"John Edward Lawson. Who are you?"

"John Dumbfuck. And you have my left testicle!"

"No I don't, it's mine."

"It's mine, you bastard!"

"Wait! Did Angelina Jolie eat your left testicle too?"

"What? No, it was Christina Aguilera, she ate my left testicle."

"That's tough, man. Never trust a female celebrity."

John Edward Lawson then darts out of the room and I am left still minus my left testicle. My mind is spinning and my nerves are all over the place. Angelina Jolie is washing her hands in the sink and the world is turning, turning, turning. Everything is akin to an everlasting nightmare. Then a quiet sound interrupts my thinking. It's coming from the last sink in the corner of the room. I march over and peer into the bowl, where a horny toad gapes up at me and lets out a throaty croak.

AFTERNOTE (1)

I'm walking along the street when I see Babylonius Orgasm approaching. He spots me and gives me an enormous smile. I don't return it to him.

"Hey, Dumbfuck," he says when he reaches me. "Guess what I have inside my bag?"

I gaze at the black holdall he is carrying, deep in thought. "Kevin Donihe's ass cheeks?" I say.

"No, I don't have Kevin Donihe's ass cheeks in my bag. I have Anna Kournikova's armpits!"

He zips the bag open and there they are, Anna Kournikova's armpits, right next to the alien's head. The armpits look adorable, and I can detect a soft sweet smell, something like an exotic skin perfume especially manufactured to tackle that hideous tennis perspiration.

"That's incredible," I say.

He zips the bag closed and smirks at me.

"Wanna guess what's in my bag?" I ask.

Babylonius Orgasm is instantly enthusiastic. "Justin Timberlake's voice box?" he says.

"No."

I unzip my own bag and show him what I have.

"What is it?" he asks as he peeks inside there.

"Angelina Jolie's left testicle."

"Huh? But…Angelina Jolie is a *woman*…"

"Wanna bet?" I chuckle.

I zip up the bag, and one second later a tennis ball whizzes past us, almost hitting Babylonius Orgasm on the right temple.

"Hey, I gotta go," he murmurs, "having Anna Kournikova's armpits can be pretty dangerous. Later, dude."

He skips off down the sidewalk, and I carry on, feeling satisfied that beyond that door marked LADIES I had seized the opportunity to prove to myself and others that Angelina Jolie was really Jon Voigt in drag.

AFTERNOTE (2)

I'm sitting at the bar in the White Cockroach drinking bitter shandy after bitter shandy. There's a large bandage where my left testicle ought to be and it's still smarting like hell down there. The room is rotating and the walls are giggling at me again. I sink the remains of my glass down my throat and hand it across to the barman Szmonhfu.

"Another bitter shandy please," I say.

"Coming right up, Dumbfuck."

Szmonhfu is a large man with a bald head who looks as if he ought to be in the WWF, and I don't mean the World Wildlife Federation. Thinking again, maybe I do.

He hands me another full glass and says, "Dumbfuck, you look deeply troubled. What happened to you?"

"Don't ask."

"Too late, I just did."

"Okay."

So I tell him the whole tale about the aliens and Christina Aguilera and the missing testicle. It's a relief to get it off my chest and when I'm finished my glass is empty again and I require a further top-up. Szmonhfu starts to chuckle.

"What are you laughing at?" I ask.

"The aliens," he says. "You mean Zag and Zag, don't you?"

"Yes. Have you met them?"

"I thought everyone knew about them. They aren't aliens at all, they're students from the university in Stink City."

"*What*? But they are so funny-looking!"

"They're inbreeds from Mississippi. And they're in the Magic Circle, experts in making things disappear, like frogs and squirrels."

"*Shit*!"

"They fly around in a strange-looking helicopter-type thing, and they eat nothing but oranges."

"What a fool I've been! But wait...how could they make Christina Aguilera appear from out of nowhere?"

"Christina Aguilera? That wasn't Christina Aguilera. It was Zag and Zag's sister, Katatonia, the mistress of disguise."

"What? You mean she disguised herself as Christina Aguilera?"

"She must have done. And she's a testicle eater."

"Really?"

"Sure."

"Wait...you could be lying. This is all a pile of crap, man. Do you expect me to believe this rubbish?"

Szmonhfu seems quite aggrieved at this outburst. He lifts the hatch and comes out from behind the bar, a serious and deadly expression on his stony face. I become quite afraid when he unzips his trousers and pulls them down to his knees. Then he hauls his boxer shorts down a little and I gasp. His penis is huge, but it's the absence of a left testicle that causes me to cry out.

"She wasn't Christina Aguilera when she did this," he tells me, "she was Liv Tyler."

Christina Aguilera Ate My Left Testicle

AFTERNOTE (3)

Here I am sitting in my apartment on the sofa I don't remember us having. Mrs. Dumbfuck is in the bedroom entertaining Mr. Zakarpatska, because I'm a man of my word and don't let anyone tell you otherwise. Behind me the budgie begins to squawk, and I don't recall its name so I get up and walk into the bathroom. It's still there, sitting in the bath tub; the horny toad.

"Come on, Horny," I plead, using the nickname I've supplied.

The horny toad just gapes at me, its large eyes unblinking. I go back into the lounge and pick up the phone. I stab a few numbers and listen to the ring tone at the other end. Someone picks it up and I recognize the voice that belongs to Anus Ignatowski.

"Hello?" he says.

"It's Dumbfuck."

"Hello, Dumbfuck. How's the testicle?"

"Still missing."

"Not very cool."

"No."

"What can I do for you?"

"What do you know about horny toads?"

"A little. Be more specific."

"Like how long before they take a dump?" I ask.

The Hotel Detective

by Alec S. Scott

TIJUANA, SATURDAY NIGHT

I am sitting on the hotel room floor with a freshly rolled joint.

I have pulled the mattress off the bed and stood it on its side, creating a barrier between myself and the rest of the world, as there are no curtains in the front window, and outside, in the red and blue blinking neon of the courtyard (*does that make purple?*), several aging drag queens are laughing and stumbling drunkenly about.

My best friend Terry is out getting us food. I try to wait for him, hold out, remain loyal, but that blunt is staring at me, smiling even, and soon I have no choice but to give in...

I am about to light up and take a toke when the hotel detective, glowing and beautiful, floats over the sidewalk outside the room, past the picture window, oblivious to the crowds upon crowds of drag queens (*have they multiplied?*) who have begun fucking and sucking each other in the most amazing ways, and knocks on my door.

I crouch down and peek past the barricade—even though, from my perspective, the mattress is now transparent, the color and consistency of honey or amber or stale lemon Gummy Bears.

Unsure what to do, I toss the joint into my mouth and swallow it. (Not to worry, though, for I have a chute, or tube, made of all the bubble gum I swallowed but shouldn't have swallowed when I was a kid, that leads, somehow, from the side of my stomach to the tight right pocket of my short-

141

shorts, gay issue, where I will soon find the spliff waiting in a pink sticky mess—*ahhhh…*)

The hotel detective knocks again, and I decide that my best course of action is to play dead.

I lay face down on the floor and let a line of drool crawl from my mouth and dangle, just so, above the carpet. ("Of *course* he's really dead; just *look* at that saliva!")

Out of the corner of my eye, crouched behind squinting lids as I was behind the mattress, I watch him reach into his pocket and produce a cluster of keys. He brings them, one at a time, to his luminous ear and listens, hearing who knows what before he finally finds one that is identical, by the way, to a slot car I once had as a child (*is my slot that big*?) and unlocks the door with it.

When he steps inside he is no longer glowing or beautiful, just short and pudgy and pale with glasses on.

He sees me lying there and is immediately suspicious.

He walks over, toes me, no response. He squats, runs his middle finger up and down, up and down the crack of my ass, almost to the hole, and— switching my act from dead to asleep—I pretend to wake up. "Huh? Uh? Wha?…what are *you* doing here?"

"We've received complaints that someone is smoking."

"Smoking?! That makes no sense, I specifically requested a *non-smoking* room!"

"I know, but you can never be too sure. Just a routine inspection."

He starts snooping, poking, nosing around, peeking in closets, sniffing trash cans and beer bottles, picking up pieces of shiny colored paper from the floor (which is really quite filthy, I didn't want to get into it earlier, but since *he* brought it up, let me tell you: always damp, and it smells like a vagina with a yeast infection—*yecch*!), and when he has collected enough of these he tapes them together to form a photograph (*did I tear that up*?) of a man's dick (*my dick*?) which is actually a big huge blunt that a beautiful blonde (not like the carpet; it's a redhead) is sucking off with little or no enthusiasm whatsoever. Bitch.

142

Seeing this, I instinctively grab my crotch. My dick is still there, but it does feel like someone rolled it too tight. I've gotta get this dick (the detective, that is) out of here so I can loosen up.

Not sure what to make of what he hath wrought, the detective tosses the photograph aside—it flutters end over end to the floor, where it suddenly bursts into blue flame—and advances into the bathroom, peering inside the empty medicine cabinet, the filthy shower-stall, the coke-filled toilet tank (that's another story), then unzips his pants and begins to pee.

"Aaaahhhh," he moans, a spastic stream of urine finding its way, more or less, from his short fat junior detective into the toilet bowl.

At the same time Terry appears outside the room. His arms are full of groceries, so he Wills the door open. (By this I mean he kicks a dwarf named Will into the door and knocks it open; the dwarf tumbles into the room, climbs to his feet, farts at Terry, farts at me, farts at the world and then leaves. [*Four foot three-inch stilts give the illusion he's as tall as the rest of us, but he's fooling no one...*])

Terry steps inside and models for me; while he was out, he not only got us food but he also got a lame-ass haircut, the kind that looks like a lopsided animal has died or shit or both on your head, the kind that skaters in my old neighborhood used to get to make them better skaters but it never worked, because all they ever could be were uninspired, untalented, retarded reproductions of their fathers, and their fathers' fathers, and their father's fathers before *them*, and *their* fathers' fathers before *them*...(Do you understand?)

I put the mattress back on the bed and Terry dumps the groceries out. Hundreds of stale taco shells, a few dozen cans of refried beans and no can-opener. Great.

"Hey, man," says Terry suddenly, casting a worried glance at the bathroom and the stout figure pissing within; "Who the fuck's in the—"

I put a finger to my lips. "There's a dick in there," I tell him. "There've been complaints."

"Oh," he nods, and the pissing peters off; then, as the dick zips up and returns to the room, Terry shoves his hands deep inside his pockets and turns away, ever the innocent bystander.

"Nothing in there but a leaky valve," says the detective, attempting levity.

I bend over the bed and ignore him, pretending to scan a can of refried beans. (The joint has reappeared in my pocket, and I'm afraid if I stand that it will be seen by its shape, or worse, that it will fall out—*how embarrassing*.) The dick spies my ass again, comes over and runs his middle finger under my shorts, down the crack, and tickles my bald (*bald*?!) testicles before standing, turning, and going back into the bathroom.

"I forgot to do something," he says, and closes and locks the door behind him.

Terry turns around and gives me a smug, idiotic grin. I look him right in the eye and say: "You know, I think you're one of the best actors I've ever seen. I mean, no matter what you do you're always believable. You have instant credibility."

I know this hurts him; he suddenly frowns, turns away and goes to a corner to pout. I don't care, though, 'cause I'm pissed—I'm not going to take this kind of abuse. (Other kinds of abuse, maybe, but not this kind.) I stand up, even though the joint is now bulging in my shorts pocket (*has it grown or was it always this big? and if it was always this big then how did I swallow it in the first place?*) and pass through the peeling wall into the bathroom, where the hotel dick is sitting on the stained, encrusted toilet, frantically jerking off.

With some effort, I pull the gargantuan doobie from my pocket, slip it between my lips, and light it with my forefinger. "You know what?" I say in my best (though actually pretty bad) hard-boiled voice. "I'm tired of your shit. I don't care if you know things or not. Know this. I think you suck. Fuck you."

"Oh yeah," he moans, stroking his cock even faster, "bring it on!"

"Fuck off."

"More, more…"

"Eat shit and die, motherfucker."

"More, more, please, oh yes please more…"

"I hope you get warts on your cock and polyps in your rectum."

"Uh-huh…"

"I hope fifteen escaped convicts rape your mother and father and grandmother, then force t hem to rape each other."

"Uh-huh, uh-huh..."

"I hope every time you think of me you know I never thought of you."

"Oh God yeah..."

"I hope that your pain is like a bell on a bike, being rung repeatedly by a slowwitted choir boy on his way to church."

"OhGodyeah, oh*God*yeah..."

"I hope...I hope..." I finally give up. "Ah, to hell with you," I say, waving him off.

And that, apparently, does it.

The detective's eyes bulge out, his breathing accelerates, he starts to make choking, sobbing sounds and his hand becomes a rhythmic blur. (Within this blur I can make out, flickering and faint like an early silent film, a voluptuous 1920's nude, dancing and frolicking with a candor and innocence I think has been lost from pornography today—I really do.) "Oh yes!" he cries. "Oh yes, *that's* it! That's it, yes! *Yes!*"

He comes all over the place—on the tub, in the tub, on the sink, faucet, mirror, walls, soap-dispenser, folded and unfolded towels; even, somehow, on the enclosed ceiling-fan above us—but none of it gets on me, thank God, and I return to the room...

Terry is still pouting in the corner, arms folded. He glances briefly, ruefully in my direction, revealing a drop or two of semen on his flat nose and chipmunk cheeks.

"Want a hit?" I offer him the joint, which is now a tiny tube of lipstick ("Cherries in the Snow," circa 1949, by Charles Revlon).

Terry walks over, opens the lipstick and paints his mouth. He closes it, hands it back and returns to his corner.

Meanwhile, the hotel dick has showered, shaved (so *that's* why they itch!) and changed his clothes. (The hotel management, such as it is, keeps a clean new suit in a special compartment under the intestine-twisted pipes of every bathroom sink for such "unforeseen circumstances [*wink*]".) Drying his hair with a small pink towel, he comes back into the room and smiles at me.

"What's your name?" he asks.

"Guy."

"Guy?"

"Yeah, but it's pronounced Ghee."

"Gee," he snorts, "a guy named Ghee. Whatta you fuckin' know about that?"

Dig made, he saunters, hands on hips, to the bedroom door and opens it. (Outside, the drag queens are now smoking, talking, taking a break.) He drops the towel—which has become a big pink wad of bubblegum—to the floor. He aims his ass like a gun at me and Terry and farts, but somehow it sounds all wrong, like mushrooms in boiling water.

Then he steps outside and closes the door.

He goes back the way he came, and though he is still short and fat and pale, two small white wings have sprouted from his back and are flapping, flapping slowly as he floats, a fairy among queens, through the red and blue and purple haze of the courtyard, then circles up into the night sky and out of sight...

I open the tube of lipstick and fix my mouth. "He was some kind of man," I say.

Terry just glares at me and spits.

Eat Me, Drink Me

by Alyssa Sturgil

I AWOKE TO find Myrtle lying beside me, fishing hookworms out of her bellybutton with a kind of morbid fascination. She looked as if she were about to say something stupid, like what a nice day it was, or wouldn't the hookworms make a gorgeous pair of earrings. She rolled over to face me, the waterbed mattress lovingly conforming to her contours.

The bones of most of my now-former girlfriends could be found inside the mattress. I looked up at the ceiling. I couldn't bear to watch it swallow her up, no matter how inane she was. I had watched it devour Elenka, Margaret, Anastasia, and Louise. It allowed me to have sex with them first— it liked the feel of it. It would begin to ripple softly, then pull them down, thrashing and screaming, into the putrid seas below.

Elenka was the first, and I had to sleep on her innards after that. I awoke to the smell of her each morning, along with the innumerable others whose entrails squished about inside the hungry mattress. None of the women I brought home ever seemed to notice the horrible stench.

Once I was sure that Myrtle was gone, I tried to go back to sleep, but Margaret would have none of that. Her amorous brain wrapped itself around the back of my head, with nothing but a thin layer of vinyl and a sheet separating us. Leave me alone, Margaret, I muttered, and rolled over onto my stomach. The brain worked its way down to my cock and there was a slapping wet sound as it tried to attach itself. Margaret was a whore before she died. I often wondered what my furniture saw in the women I brought home.

Eat Me, Drink Me

Stop it! I snapped at the pulsing, sucking brain. It shunted off into the murky abyss within the mattress, hurt by my rebuke. Anastasia's intestines went to comfort her. She had always been secretly in love with Margaret, even while they were alive. I eventually gave up on getting back to sleep.

I stood, put on my skin, and went outside to pick up the paper. The paper read Doomsday where the date should had been. All the other pages were blank. I went back inside and into the living room.

The wall clock was watching a porno film and was too distracted to tell the correct time, so I had no idea how long I'd been sleeping. The couch grinned as I went past, bones spilling out of the cushions. The poster of Jean-Claude Van Damme frowned. He was above all this. He was slaughtering a small white rabbit he planned on cooking for supper that evening. I was very hungry that night, so I was all the more displeased when Sully got to the rabbit first and ate it all before I got there. Sully was the goblin I kept in my kitchen, and he usually got to the dinner table before I did.

We argued for several minutes before I made my decision. I decided once and for all to stand up to him, and to get my dinner back. I pried open his snarling, gaping mouth, and leapt.

I was first met with utter darkness. Sully's stomach pulsed in the oily blackness. I tore through its outer skin. It smelled like meatloaf and raw sewage. It was delicious. I climbed through the rip and found myself at the edge of a vast pit lined with the bodies of dead movie stars. Clark Gable, Fred Astaire, and Clara Bow gaped stupidly at me.

But Marilyn Monroe smiled. "Eat me," she said, licking her lips. Marilyn was as sweet in death as she was in life, and fucking her eviscerated corpse invigorated me. Feeling energized and refreshed, I then set off into the yawning pit.

Well, set off may not be the most appropriate phrase. To be more precise, I stepped out of my skin and used it to parachute into the pit. Upon landing, I stepped back into my skin.

The topiary was amazing.

What made it so amazing was that in lieu of plants that had been sculpted into people and animals, the topiary was instead populated by the bodies of people and animals that had been sculpted into plants. A large Lipizzaner stallion had been carved in the image of a delicate, if somewhat muscular, white orchid. To the left of it stood a woman in the shape of a cactus, her frozen hair standing up to resemble the delicate spines. She had blonde hair, and was wearing a blue dress and white pinafore. And at her feet quivered a small white rabbit.

I pounced on it with stunning ferocity, crushing its bones with my body. I slammed into the feet of the cactus woman, shattering her on impact. She screamed as she came down, showering me in razor-sharp crystals of ice. I looked down at the rabbit that lay beneath me, still quivering, one of my ribs stuck through its chest. It raised its head slightly. I tilted my head to listen. "I…I am your father," it said. Then it died.

I ate it anyway. An instant later, I found myself lying on my living room floor, my father in my stomach, a book in my hand. The couch was gleefully snacking on Marilyn, smacking its blue plastic lips. Her small blonde head bobbed up and down between the cushions as the flesh was pulled from her bones. The words "DRINK ME" were carved into the flesh of her back.

I looked at the book in my hand. The picture on the cover was moving. The White Rabbit, now humanoid and muscular, had Alice bent over the hood of a rusted Chevy that stood up on cinder blocks, and was fucking her mercilessly in the ass. I opened the book to the title page. There was an inscription there. It read: *To me—Have a Great Summer, Yours Truly, Lewis Carroll.*

Whisper

by Michael Amorel

SHHHHH...

She wasn't sure if the wind of the cool October evening had made the sound as it picked up dry, dead leaves and careened them down the sidewalk. She froze for a moment at the sound, not enough to really be called a stop but maybe a stutter or perhaps an uncertainty. Yes, she definitely oozed uncertainty, not so noticeable from sight alone but it could be smelt, tasted more like, a crisp electrical tang, slightly too liquid or smooth, and filled with the dull presence of mold. It was this scent, mingled with the touch of growing cold from inside, which drove her forward, her furtive glances revealing no one in the darkening park.

Shhhhh...

Again she was stopped by the sound, a dry rustling taking on the tamber of snow drenched and rotting foliage uncovered by the spring. It wrapped around her, enfolding her with the sound, now but a recent memory, and mixed with the scent to hold her still. She tried to turn around, hoping to catch sight of the origin of the peculiar shushing but found it had become tangible enough to restrain her. The touch of cold progressed at this point to engulf not only her center, where it had originated, but her bowels and lungs with a fiery intensity, making her want to puke or curl up and hug the warmth of her knees to her breasts or both. Instead, she became paralyzed by a conflict of thoughts, emotions and senses, withdrawing her consciousness into the dark behind her eyes in an effort to retreat from the over stimulation.

Whisper

"Shhhhh…keep them closed," interrupted a voice, tugging her to the surface of the cold, black fluidity. The sound's caress warmed lightly, dragging its decomposing heat through the depth of her skin, fighting at the cold pool until the climate changed in the exact way she had felt her lover's lust explosively burn her fingers with molten quicksilver, encompassing, slight tension against every point of contact. Here, she was safe for the first time, wanted and wanting, every inch of her body electrified with subtle touches, tongues of flame awash over her, pricking, soothing, stroking.

She felt a gentle motion as something entered into her, exactly where was beyond conception to the melting vinyl that had been her skin as she floated in blackness. The warmth grew ever more intense with the almost timid penetration, filling the spaces with rouge smears like the aftertase of whiskey. The gentle blush in the dark became heated to a crimson as it filled her further, her center rocked with the violence of thundering horses but the joy of winter swaddling. The light began to strobe in yellow flashes across a plane of goose bumps, infinite hairs vibrating in the summer breeze recently so far away, while a tingle raced behind her, its cold needles drawing the ends of her nerves into a symphony of strings, all connected to the burning scent of sound entering her again and again. The tingle was joined by more and her lost flesh yearned for the stretch of muscle in release, a cat's arch in the morning, a lover's arch in the night.

With the release of her prismatic voice from the pool of protoplasmic jungle she had become, her eyes opened. She was herself again, in a park on an October evening surrounded by shadowy voices, surprised at the puddle of liquids beneath her legs and the hot, moist scent of sex in the air. Her skin aflame with pleasure, her mind left for voyages among the inner stars, her eyes still staring vacantly at the twisted lump of boiling, bubbling, gibbering flesh before her, spurting gore and ichors that withered the vegetation where it landed, tentacles swirling with miasmal gasses, its huge member, a pulsating, writhing appendage whose terminus was between her legs, pounding into her again and again.

Shadows

by Vincent W. Sakowski

I STOOD ALONE in the park in the shadow of a giant maple for about fifteen minutes, just to be certain everything was going according to plan. So far, so good. No one else had come around.

I was nervous but exhilarated. I also had a bit of a headache and my stomach was cramped up. I had been feeling this way for the last day or two, but I chalked it up to anxiety in preparing for this night. Earlier, I had gone to the bathroom—but I still had the cramps—worked-out, showered, eaten, and I wore fresh, clean clothes: all black.

I didn't have to wait very long before she came by—Rhonda, from the 7-Eleven two blocks from the park. We didn't make plans together for this night or anything. Truth be known, she didn't know I was here...and...she never really even knew me in the first place. I had "met" her at the 7-Eleven a few months ago, and she was very nice, very sweet. She was young—I discovered soon afterwards that she was only twenty—polite, courteous, and once she got to know a customer, she would joke around with her or him like an old friend. Rhonda was just one of those few people who was friendly to everyone she met. She had a great personality and anything it might have been lacking, her body and her face more than made up for it: five feet tall, with a very full, hour-glass figure. A natural blond with large, clear gray eyes. They were so limpid and luminescent—just so alive! I could've looked into them for hours. Her whole face was very pretty and elven-like, and that's how she carried herself—so gracefully, like a little elven beauty.

Shadows

I was very attracted to her, but I kept it to myself. I didn't tell any of my friends. I didn't think she would go for someone like me, for more reasons than one. I wasn't seeing anyone at the time, but I couldn't get up the courage to ask her out. Way too shy. Temperamental too, I guess, but it kind of comes and goes, depending on the time and the circumstances.

So...Rhonda passed me by and didn't notice me hiding. I came out of the shadows, quietly fell into step behind her, and cut the distance between us. When I was close enough, I reached out with both my hands and wrapped them around her throat. Startled, she threw up her hands to free herself, but I was too strong and tightened my grip. She started to thrash around, making little sounds—calling for help, or for me to stop, or gasping for life—I don't know. Rhonda put up a good fight, so I slammed my knee as hard as I could into the small of her back—drove her down, and knocked out what bit of air she had left.

I'm sure she had no idea who was killing her, or why she was the victim. But, I didn't want her to know it was me. I felt much stronger remaining anonymous, being a shadow, and having complete control over her. Even after I was sure she was dead, I kept on throttling her, just out of the pure enjoyment of the power racing through me.

I noted the time, then picked up Rhonda's body and threw it over my shoulder in a fireman's carry. It wasn't easy to do, but I managed. I looked around on the ground to make sure I hadn't missed anything, then went as quickly as I could through the shadows to my car parked close by. No one was around, so I carefully placed her in the trunk and covered her without any troubles. I got in and drove off to my house, which I was renting on my own.

There were no problems getting home, and I pulled into the garage with a feeling of great relief. The neighbors nearby knew I kept odd hours, so there'd never been any trouble coming in late at night. With the garage door closed behind me, I got out and opened the trunk. She was there. Still. Dead. Truth be known, I was almost disappointed by that—I would've enjoyed fighting her again. She died almost too easily. Rhonda was good, but after I had some time to reflect on it, I realized I could've handled an even greater challenge. I took her up in both of my arms—she seemed even heavier than before—and strained my back again. Then I carried her into the house. My head pounded furiously, and my whole mid-section seemed to be rebelling against the rest of my body. But I had much more important things on my mind.

Keeping the lights off, I made my way with her through the house and upstairs to my bedroom, where I laid her on my king-sized bed. I double-checked the curtains to be certain they were completely closed, before I turned on the lamp on the nightstand beside my bed. I loved the way the dim light cast subtle shadows across her face, softened her features, and made her even more beautiful.

I caressed her cheek and I found it cool to my touch. So, I wasted no time, but got a small pail of hot, soapy water, a washcloth and a towel, and then I undressed her. First, I removed all of her jewelry: an inexpensive watch, a simple gold chain with a crucifix, and a pair of scrimshaw earrings. The earrings were very interesting: a serpentine dragon was carved into each nickel-sized piece of antler. I placed everything on the nightstand so I could inspect them later. Next, I removed her runners and socks. Her feet were tiny and very dainty, although the bottoms of them were worn and callused. But, her toenails were clipped and clean, which I really appreciated. I moved up alongside her and took off her jacket, then her long sleeved shirt. Her skin was delightfully pale and it was very smooth and soft. Rhonda wore an off-white cotton bra, which was relatively modest in its design, and I gazed long-ingly at her full bosom and admired it in its confines. She had very large nipples and they were poking through the material without any shame. I didn't take her bra off yet. First, I undid her pants, pulled them off, then checked out her panties. They too were made of cotton, but were low-cut on her hips. Short sand-colored pubic hairs poked out on the sides.

My heart pounded in my chest, and I decided it was only fair to even things up before I went any further. I pulled off everything—my jacket, sweatshirt, shoes, socks and pants. (I didn't have any kind of underwear, as I normally don't wear any.) I felt chilled, covered in goose-flesh, but warmed again as I took in the elven beauty lying so still on my bed.

Her body was absolutely magnificent: all very pale—which I just adored—with a number of scents. There was the musky odor of sweat; a powdery deodorant; and a light flowery perfume—like dried roses—which I couldn't recognize; and her hair smelled like fresh apples. I admired her form awhile longer before I sniffed her groin, which had a heavier, "eau de saumon" smell. I inhaled deeply, like it was an addictive drug.

Her skin was relatively unblemished—mostly free of scars, pimples and other assorted skin ailments, and it was also particularly soft. (I break out periodically, and I was undergoing my latest attack at the time.) Both her armpits and her legs had been recently shaved, and with great care—there were no nicks or scars to be found anywhere. Her flesh was very meaty; that is, there were no bones poking through and she had very little fat on her.

I couldn't wait any longer. So, I put my hands behind her back and rather clumsily undid her bra—I've never been good at undoing those hooks—then pulled it away from her. I threw it with the rest of her clothes on the floor, then turned back to feast in her glorious breasts. Her nipples were a warm pink, and they were roughly the size and hardness of a pair of thimbles. I closed my eyes and lightly tongued one of them—it was absolutely exquisite! They were so cool and erect! I caressed her amazingly firm breasts with both of my hands. Especially for their size—they were the firmest breasts I have ever had my hands on, but their texture was like silk! I was in absolute awe of her bosom. I nibbled and sucked and fondled her breasts quite greedily for several minutes before I got a hold of myself and decided to stop.

I shuffled down along my bed and slowly removed her panties. I ran my fingers through her pubic mound and loosened the light, fine hairs that had been compressed by her tight panties. Then I ran a single finger across her labia and sighed, but I only dwelled there briefly.

Before I went any further, I planned to wipe her down and freshen her up a bit. I'm not a clean freak, but I thought since we were going to be intimate for awhile she should be fresh. I dipped the washcloth in the water and wiped her down, beginning with her face. As I cleansed each part of her anatomy, I studied her form and grew melancholic.

I knew this was one of the setbacks of my plan—with her dead, our time together was very limited, and I wouldn't be able to enjoy her for very long. At the time I rationalized it by thinking that if she were alive we never would've been together anyway. Although, there're times when I wonder, "maybe if I'd only had the courage to ask her out, then things would be different now." I couldn't have handled the rejection though if she had said "no." I'm uncertain if I—no, *wait*...I made the right decision...Or...maybe I...whatever...I have to live with it now, so it doesn't matter.

Anyway, after she was cleaned and dried off, I got into bed beside her and pulled the covers over us. Her body gradually grew colder and I wanted a little extra warmth. I kept the lamp on to admire her for as long as I could. I held her close to me for several minutes then I allowed my hands to wander over her body again. As I continued to explore her with my hands, I lightly nibbled on her ear lobes and planted soft kisses on her face and shoulders. As I grew more excited by her cold silky flesh, I became bolder and worked my way down to her breasts. There, I spent an extensive period before I moved down lower until I had my head between her thighs, where I also dwelt for a considerable length of time. Finally, I worked my way back up along her stomach until I maneuvered into a scissors position—which has always been my favorite—and then I dug in. It was awkward, and I kept my movements very slow at first. But then, as I felt my orgasm building, I ground myself harder and harder against her until I exploded. It was so intense and exquisite! So unique! At that moment I realized I had made the right decision.

I had to stop for awhile to catch my breath. Then I pulled up the covers around us again. Basking in that wonderful post-orgasmic afterglow, I snuggled in close and reminisced about making love to her...all I could hear was myself—*my* breathing, *my* body rubbing against hers, but nothing else from her. Her eyes were closed and it was like she was asleep, and not really dead. Her body was cold, yet it was solid and soft in all the right places. When I had explored the inside of her vagina, it was also delightfully frigid and rough—it was all so extraordinary!

More than content, I desired to remain snuggled in beside her and fall asleep for awhile. But first I had to fit her with an adult diaper, as it wouldn't be long before she let go of her bodily functions one final time. Mentioning it takes a bit away from the romance of the scene I suppose, but it was a necessity: better to keep everything contained.

Enough said about that.

Soon afterwards, I fell asleep. My dreams were pleasant, if not mundane at times, and I took them as a good sign. Rhonda appeared in two of them—neither of those was mundane, of course. One was taken from a memory of meeting her for the first time at the 7-Eleven. I remember her sweetness, my shyness, and desiring to be with her even then. The other dream was an alternate vision of our time together in bed. In it, she was very much alive—but not in a nightmarish sense, and she was a *very* willing—if not an aggressive—partner in our lovemaking. As the dream developed, she ravaged me instead. In the end, we lay beside each other gazing up at the ceiling, and I asked her *why*? She seemed puzzled for a moment, then repeated my question several times. I think she was asking me the same thing, but before either of us answered, I awoke feeling somewhat uneasy but also extremely aroused.

Several hours had passed but I was still draped across her. She was mine! It wasn't just a dream, a fantasy, something beyond my reach. It was *all* real and that made me very happy. Yes. Yes! YES! Oh, I was in a state of absolute bliss—for the first time in a long time I felt in control of myself and of my destiny. I was feeling so utterly fantastic that I had sex with her again: it was "giggle-sex" this time though, as opposed to the slow, passionate sex we had earlier. Or the lazy-assed sex I usually have by myself in front of the television, with one of my dozens of porn tapes in the VCR. I was too giddy to take it slow, and "make love" or anything. But I had to clean her up again first, which was not a pretty sight—or smell for that matter—I won't get into the details though. Anyway, it was as wonderful as it had been only hours before—still awkward, but very satisfying. *Very fun*. Afterward, I lay beside her, softly caressing her, then drifted back to sleep, quite content with myself. My personal pains were temporarily forgotten, and I looked forward to our next day together.

I woke in the morning feeling very refreshed and I examined her briefly. Rhonda was as motionless and quiet as ever, lying flat on her back with her eyes closed. She seemed so tranquil, so much at peace; except of course, for the dark bruises around her neck. I never really paid much attention to them the night before. I guess I didn't want to be reminded at the time that I was her executioner, so I had ignored them. Now, I couldn't turn away, but stared at them until I couldn't help but cry for awhile. After that release I felt so much better and continued on with my original plan.

So, during the following day and a half, I spent most of my time with Rhonda. I ate sitting on the bed. I read, sometimes out loud, but not really *to her*. I watched a bit of television, and I explored her body some more; and not just sexually, but to see what was happening to her. She was slowly rotting, of course, but I still had some time before she started to stink or anything. I continued to give her dry baths, and I even brushed her teeth a few times, which is more difficult than it sounds. (Trying to rinse her mouth out was a real bitch.) For the most part, I kept her face up, and I didn't like to look under her—the blood in her body had stopped flowing, of course, and it was settling into the lowest parts of her body: her back, her buttocks, the back of her thighs, and so on.

As for myself, I was still cramped and nauseous, and the headache would come and go. But I felt so full in so many ways, and I didn't want my time with her to end. I found myself rather emotional about the whole idea of losing her. Occasionally, I cried for long periods when I thought of how it would be to go on without her. Yet somehow, whenever I got close to her, my sadness dissipated, and I felt very warm and loved. Then I had to laugh—at least a little, anyway—for what I had gotten away with, and I would never be suspected. As long as I continued to be smart of course.

In any case, my feelings for Rhonda had grown tremendously in that brief time, and soon I found it very difficult to be away from her for more than a few minutes. Our time together was drawing to a close, and I kept trying to come up with ideas on how to keep her longer. Unfortunately, I didn't have the time, money, skill, or connections to make something like that possible.

Late that night, it was time to go. I carried Rhonda and her things down to the garage. She'd begun to smell a little, and it felt very weird, holding her around her back and under her thighs, which were thick and black with her blood. Down in the garage, I tied her knees against her chest, then tucked her legs in and tied those to her as well, and finally I wrapped her arms around her legs and tied those down. So, in the end she was a tight little ball. Rigor mortis had settled in long ago, but it had been gone now for a short time, which made me quite glad. For some time earlier, every time I had to bend one of her joints, there was a long and loud crunching and crackling sound, which I found very unsettling: "KrrrrrRRRAACKKK!" It sounded so unnatural and painful, and I didn't enjoy doing it. Tying her up was so anti-climactic and depressing that I couldn't help but cry through the whole ordeal.

Also, seeing her tied up that way made me so depressed, because it seemed to go too much against what we had shared together. So, I closed my eyes and gave her one last kiss on her forehead and said good-bye. I pulled several large green garbage bags around her, and put her things in a separate canvas bag, which I also filled with several large rocks.

Initially, I had wanted to have something of hers as a keepsake, but I was well aware that that would've been a mistake. I would've loved to have kept her earrings, or possibly her bra and panties, but I kept nothing. This also made me extremely sad, because I knew very shortly all I would have left was my memory of her.

Getting her body in the trunk was much more difficult than the last time, and I ended up hurting my back again, but this time it was much worse. It was almost as if the magic was gone, and the last two days had simply been a beautiful, warm dream. This last little bit of our time together felt unwholesome, and I wished I hadn't had to go through with it. I didn't like how it was changing my feelings back to rage and frustration, and how it was tainting my view of Rhonda and of our time together. I just wanted the whole episode over, so I quickly threw her stuff in the trunk beside her. Then, I covered everything with several blankets, containers, and other odd pieces of junk.

Finished, I was on my way out of the city. To the north there was a large river, and that's where I planned to dump everything.

On the drive to the bridge, I reflected on our time together—trying to exclude tying her up in the garage—and it made me melancholic. It didn't take me long before I was balling my eyes out again, because it felt as though I was losing a part of myself forever—the *better part* at that. Perhaps, surprisingly, I still didn't feel bad about wrapping my hands around her throat and choking the life out of her. It was so enjoyable...almost purifying, and it was *necessary*.

It was after one in the morning when I reached the bridge and I worked very quickly. I hurt my back—for the third time—lifting her body out of the car and throwing her in the river. Rhonda made an enormous "BUHHH-WOOOOOOSHHH!" of a splash, and I saw her slowly sink down into the black water as the current carried her away.

I wished I could've stayed and seen her float down the river, but that wouldn't have been wise. I only said a simple last good-bye and threw the canvas bag in the river after her. Its splash was much smaller and rather anti-climactic.

I started to cry again though, and those tears didn't feel good at all. They were hot and burned my face, but I didn't bother to wipe them away. I turned around and I was on my way home without a second glance. Again, I felt that need to look behind myself, and I almost did—I expected to see Rhonda there in the rear-view mirror, either in the back seat or standing on the high-way. Maybe to exact some sort of revenge on me, or maybe, as I've often dreamt since that night, she wanted to come back and stay with me, and live "happily ever after." I never looked back though, and if she *was* there, I'll never know.

I made my way home without any incidents, then I took a shower and went straight to bed. I felt lonely and extremely sad—I really missed having Rhonda beside me. The bed seemed so large and empty without her, but it still had her scent—a soft mixture of flowers and a deeper, darker redolence.

I fell asleep thinking about how much I missed her, and I woke the next morning with a little visitor—my period had started, and my sheets had got stained a bit. It sometimes happened to me during the night like that before, but not in a very long time. I guess I was so pre-occupied with Rhonda, that I wasn't paying attention to my own body. It was no big deal though, and the blood reminded me of how much I missed Rhonda, and what we had shared together.

Speaking about Rhonda—her body was never found. She became anoth-er headline then another statistic. I will always remember her though, and how special she was to me.

As for myself, I returned to my regular everyday life—for awhile. However, I was still having problems. I was frustrated and lonely again, and now I had some other new desires I wished to fulfil. So, it wasn't long before I was in the shadows again. And I was through with crying. Time to get some fun and laughter back into my life again, with no looking back. The next one I chose though was a man—I didn't wish to discriminate against women, and besides, I heard that newly dead men can get fantastic erections.

Is Your God Good
Enough for Religion?

Is Your God Good Enough for Religion?

Heresy

God's Will

'Slaughtered Souls'

Sam Thompson in Love:
A Case From the Annals of the
Lavender Investigative Agency

by J. Scott Malby

LIVING AS WE do in a culture of erotically charged hedonism we can't help measuring ourselves according to the length of our performance. In our lusty and hopelessly male souls we secretly dream of unbridled bitches daring us to wank them for hours, knowing inside ourselves the reality of such a fantasy is one of muscle cramps, skin abrasions and the torture of combined body parts twisting into all sorts of uncomfortable, agonizing and seemingly impossible positions. Just one critical word about our performance and we deflate into a flabby mass of resentment and self recrimination.

As the mind is such a terrible thing to waste I maintain that we should waste it on something good like fantasies that aren't pricked by commercialism or cut by the unforgiving, stainless steel, boil-lancing edge of reality. Was there never a male on the make who didn't prefer to be lied to rather then told he's a big disappointment in bed?

It's not that our obsessions suck. Reality does. When everything fails for us we fall back on the comforting proof of our basic animal superiority represented by our ability to pee standing up. We're plunderers, you and I. We yank at things. We're dribblers and droolers grabbing at whatever's in reach. Plunging into the middle of things. Forgetting to wash our hands. Ours is a world of red meat, potatoes and booze. A man's made for one thing. We're sex machines. Exhibitionists, walking around in a constant state of semi-arousal. On the prowl for broads twenty-four hours a day, diving without thinking into the honey pot of life. Looking for a quick score regarding our insatiable appetites.

My name is Sam. It's my birthday. I'm twenty-five but look younger. I scam for a living and am committed to the proposition that we should pro-long adolescence as long as possible. Boys don't turn into men. Men secrete a protective cocoon around the little boy inside themselves. Pleasure, greed and the primal urge for conquest are always with us no matter how we try to deny or hide it. The truth is that when you strip away the politically correct, civilizing veneer of the basic male and get to the animal essence of any guy, you will find that his fingernails are dirty, his hair is messed up, his pants are stained and he's either got an erection or is just losing one. It's not that we don't give a damn about anything but our own gratification. It's that our testosterone levels short-circuit our thinking process.

Why am I telling you this? I'm hunkered down in Lost Bay, Oregon. Shivering beneath the overhang of a coffee shop that's been closed for hours. I'm so bored I'm periodically rubbing myself. It's pouring rain. Behind me is a wall scrawled with graffiti. I've read it over a hundred times tonight. It's a quote from a song made popular by the infamous new age punk rock band called "Kenneth Rexroth."

"Life is just a mess," the lyrics go, "full of tall children, grown stupider, less alert and resilient, and nobody knows what makes it go, as a whole or any part of it. But nobody ever tells."

I'm drenched while on a stakeout for the Lavender Investigation Agency. Across the street are a series of storefronts. Above them are apartments. I've been observing the lighted window of one of them. The apartment in question was rented 2 months ago by a Disney Chase. Chase is an excommunicated Jesuit priest. A man of unimaginable perversions. He uses the apartment to meet with his pickups. Tonight he's with a delectable piece of goth cheesecake going by the name of Bambi. Her real name is Cherry. She's Mayor Hymen's nineteen-year-old daughter.

When not involved in his perverted sexual escapades, Chase is the head of The Millennial Church of Rapture. His critics call him the voice of religious rupture behind his back. My research leads me to believe he's a fundamentalist whacko who stumbled on a million dollar racket and is now intent on turning it into a dangerous sexual cult.

Penny Lavender roped me into this gig. I work for her because I have to. Without her intervention I would now be doing jail time. I owe her. She never lets me forget it.

Bambi is naked. So is Chase with the exception of a red cardinal's hat he has on his head. He's playing some kind of instrument. I think he's playing his bongos. Bambi is dancing. I'm watching Disney making it with Bambi. Wait a minute. The shape of a moving shadow in the room is just barely visible. It looks like some kind of argument has started. Abruptly, the apartment plunges into darkness accompanied by shouts.

Running to the corner of the block, I place a hurried phone call to the police. They want to know who I am. Instead of answering I hang up. I've no idea what exactly happened. It's dangerous for an unconnected nobody like me to directly confront a man as politically powerful as Disney Chase. Others have tried. They're singing the blues from their jail cells located six feet under the ground. Besides, if I'm found to be even remotely involved with a perv party the fuzz will have me booked and before I know it I'll find myself on the bony knee of some hairy prison ape called Waldo. It would take a week before Lavender could bail me out.

Climbing into my white Ford Tauras station wagon I speed off down the road. I drive this bucket of crap for a reason. It keeps me from getting pulled over by the police. As nobody even remotely considered cool would be caught dead driving such a vehicle, the police haven't bothered to profile it. It's a dud. Not on their *socioeconomic to be ticketed* or *criminal vehicle of choice radar*. I pull into the Mill Casino parking lot. Turn off my motor. Two police cars race by. Sirens blare. Lights flash.

Besides the elite 36-hole golf course, the casino is the Mecca that draws the big honchos into town. I know I'll find Lavender here. Penny Lavender is a gambler. She approaches life that way. I don't make moral judgments.

After all, Penny gambled on me and I won. At least for the present that is. She's at a special poker table. In front of her is a pile of chips that represent thousands of dollars. More money than I see in a year of hustling. The table is roped off. A crowd is milling around it. You can cut the tension with a knife. This is a high stakes game. It appears Lavender is winning. A casino employee approaches me and asks to see some identification. I oblige, handing her my drivers license.

Her black leather slacks hug her body suggestively, revealing attractive, enticing hips. Her silk shirt is left unbuttoned just enough to reveal the velvet texture of her soft, heaving breasts. The outline of her nipples presses against the silk. She teasingly brushes against my chest with her boobs and smiles as she hands me back my license. It's more than a smile. There's something about it suggesting an invitation.

"My name is Angel. I'll be off work in a few minutes. Why don't you hang around."

Smiling back, I make a mental note to follow up with her when and if time permits. As Angel turns to go her hand lightly cups my crotch. My face turns a bright shade of red. God, this is no lady but a dame chaffing at the bit. A tease. Ripe and ready for a romp on the hobby horse of my uncontrollably induced passion. I gulp and look around. No one seems to notice her flagrant and slightly demeaning gesture. Except me of course. I revel in it but find that the pistol I pack down below is growing into a loaded cannon with a dangerously short fuse.

Replacing my wallet in my jacket, draping my jacket over one arm to hide my excitement, I look around for some way to gain Lavender's attention. Mingling with the crowd I finally notice Miss Blandish standing alone in a corner. She's Lavender's personal assistant. Lavender has a penchant for attracting beautiful people into her orbit. Miss Blandish is no exception. Blandish is a brunette bombshell who compliments Lavender's raven hair and exotic good looks. They make an arresting pair when seen together which they are most of the time.

My curse in life has always been my height. At five-foot-four I'm often overlooked despite my muscular body and relatively good looks. It may be that in trying to compensate for my lack of height I get into more trouble than most. My insecurities and shortcomings seem to be most pronounced when approaching beautiful women. Both Miss Blandish and Lavender are real knockouts. They dress unbelievably well and look like models out of some exclusive woman's magazine. They're tall. Both are just this side of six feet. As I approach Blandish she lowers her head so that I can whisper into her ear. I can actually taste the expensive perfume enveloping me from between her ample cleavage. I'm aroused and dizzy at the same time. It's hard to concentrate.

Hearing me out, Miss Blandish nods. Pursing her lips together as if in a coy pout, she thinks a minute and then enters the restricted enclosure of the poker game. She walks casually, swinging her hips as if she owns the joint. I see her bending over Penny Lavender. Penny listens while playing her cards close to her chest without a trace of emotion. She strokes her chips with sensual, teasing fingers.

When Miss Blandish returns, she smiles and runs her fingers through my hair playfully brushing it back into place. "Penny said you need to go home and get some rest. You look like a damp gerbil. Meet us at the office tomorrow morning. Bring the newspaper with you."

If anyone else dared to use the term "gerbil" in referring to me I'd smack their face. If I could reach it that is. What I lack in height I make up for in attitude. One of the few good things about my relationship with Lavender is that I seem to be mellowing out, exerting a little more control over my tendency to take offense regarding personal comments. Nevertheless, the description rankles me. There will be no orchids for Miss Blandish tonight. Not that I've ever given her any, though I've fantasized about making love to her on a bed of them. They're her favorite flower.

Before I can say anything, an audible gasp rises from the crowd observing the game. Miss Blandish tenses and looks over at the players. It appears that Lavender has won another big pot. Miss Blandish begins to jot some notes down in a little pad she'd withdrawn from her purse. I take advantage of the disruption to slip away. The events of the evening and my interaction with Blandish generate a strange sort of appetite in me. I'm ready for some action.

Sam Thompson in Love

It's time to follow up regarding that angel that bumped into me earlier.

I finally locate her sitting at a table in the bar. She is surreptitiously holding hands with someone. That someone's face is familiar. I can't believe my eyes. It's Bambi! Both girls are in deep conversation. Angel raises her free hand and gently wipes away tears from Bambi's eyes. In the dim light Bambi looks like a fragile, frightened doe. I watch as Bambi rises, kisses Angel lightly on the cheek and quickly leaves the bar. I take a step backward attempting to leave. Angel sees me. She waves in my direction. There's nothing for it but to approach her table. She's drinking a beer. There's a half finished brandy opposite her with Bambi's black lipstick mark on it. I drink from it as I sit down.

Angel grimaces quickly and then grins. Her blond hair is cut fashionably short. Her smile reveals dazzling white teeth outlined by full, well shaped, fleshy lips. She has the youthful, poised body of a gymnast but is also entirely feminine as well. A number of the other men in the bar are stealing appraising looks at her when they think no one is watching. It appears that Angel can't help but turn guys on. She stares directly into my eyes. I find myself getting lost in them. I'm unable to turn away.

"You took your time finding me. Sam, isn't it? That's what it said on your license. What do you do for a living, Sam?"

I immediately knew I wanted to go to bed with her. There was something in her voice that was forthright and disarming at the same time. I wanted to be honest with this woman. I didn't want to lie despite my misgivings and better judgment. Besides, I could tell that this was a person you hid things from at your own peril. A direct, frontal approach would be best in order to gain what I wanted. There were enough people in this town that knew me. My cover was already blown or very shortly would be.

"Right now, I'm in private dick training."

Angel paused and blinked. "You're what?"

"I work part time for the Lavender Investigative Agency. Who was that girl you were sitting with?"

"That was Bambi. She's the mayor's daughter if you want to know. She's in some kind of trouble. Had a bad shock earlier tonight. I think she

170

could use a detective right now. Even if it is one in training."

Angel had provided me with the opening I needed without my even having to ask. "Why? What happened?" I tried to sound concerned and surprised at the same time.

Angel drank from her bottle. "Long story. This town has gone to pot since the big money moved in. Marijuana money I mean. Näive girls are seduced by it into providing sexual favors to big shots. That Chase fellow for instance. He has a thing for lesbians. He thinks he can set them straight by introducing them to his sexual wand of enlightenment. He got Bambi high tonight and tried to rape her."

"Are you a lesbian?" I asked.

Her eyes narrowed. "I'm bi if you want to know. Got a problem with that?"

"No. Not at all. If it feels good do it."

Angel's taught body involuntary shuddered. It seemed to be calling out for me to caress it. Clearly, Angel appeared to be relieved by my nonjudgmental attitude. The chip on her shoulder fell away as she began to relax. Her words came out in a flood. "I work for the woman's crises center in my spare time. We've been getting some real horror stories regarding Chase but the police won't do anything about it. He's got the whole political structure in his back pocket. The lesbian community is becoming radicalized. They're threatening to deal with the problem themselves. I don't blame them. It's getting ugly. Someone accosted Chase tonight. They tried to castrate him. Bambi was there. The police arrived. Bambi said Chase called it an attempted burglary. They'll keep it all hush hush of course. Poor Bambi. Chase is fixated on her. He won't leave her alone till he has her and makes her straight. That's an impossibility. If you want to know the truth Chase is a pervert whose out to pervatize the world."

I was glad to know that Bambi was safe. The question had been bothering me. The gay community on the rampage would be a terrible thing to behold. In my mind I imagined a mob of butch lesbians with lighted faggots in their hands, besieging Chase's church at night. Screaming for him to come out. And if he dared to, having their lustful way with him. If it happened it wouldn't be a pretty sight. Chase was wrong all right. The only person I knew who stood a chance of introducing Bambi to an unforgettably successful hetero experience was me. The opportunity might arise. Good things happen on my birthday. I couldn't help thinking of Angel, Bambi and myself getting it on. I considered it for a moment before returning my attention back to Angel. This was a mistake. Angel was looking at me intently. She had been asking me something.

"Well? Did you hear me? she repeated.

"I'm sorry. I'm a little tired tonight. What did you say?"

"You were daydreaming. Fantasizing about something. Right?"

Angel was smart. She was catching on to me pretty fast. I had to cover my tracks, "I'm just amazed that I'm the fortunate one sitting next to you and not someone else. What was it you said?"

"I asked you if you wanted to meet Bambi. She could use your help. I think I trust you. I like you. Who knows? Something interesting might develop between us later."

"When do we leave?" I answered back.

The idea of breaking this case by myself clouded my judgment. Besides, Lavender wasn't the only one capable of handling an investigation. When it came to the Lavender Investigative Agency I was low man on the totem pole. Showing a little initiative now might just provide the break I needed. I lusted after both Lavender and Miss Blandish and wanted to impress them. They failed to realize how capable I really was.

Angel's eyes brightened, "Bambi's at Shore Acres Park. I told her I would meet her there. We can go in your car."

The trip to Shore Acres was not a long one. I could feel the body heat of Angel sitting beside me. She put her hand on my knee. My mind was steaming due to the intoxicating proximity of her fingers to the most active and unpredictable organ I possessed. I tried to focus on what I knew about the area we were approaching. Concentration was almost impossible. Angel kept kneading the flesh of my thigh.

Shore Acres was the hangout of choice for the gay community. The park was dangerous at night due to the cliffs. The police seldom ventured there and never without extensive backup late at night. It extended over several miles. The wooded trails were winding. They passed by numerous little alcoves protected by bushes and the overhanging branches of trees. It was in these secluded spaces that countless late night sexual trysts were arranged for and consummated. It represented an underworld theme park for sexual perversions and fantasy enactments.

I was ready to call the whole thing off just as Angel pointed to a space off to the side of the road. "You can park here" she said.

I pulled the car over. It was dark. The sound of ocean surf could be heard in the distance. There were no other cars nearby. "Do you have a flashlight?" Angel inquired.

Reaching into the glove box I handed her one. She opened the car door and stepped out. Walking around to her I was accosted by the sound of frogs and chirping insects. The ground was damp. My feet made crunching sounds as they stepped into a bed of decaying pine needles. Angel seemed to sense my misgivings regarding this escapade. She placed her free hand on my back and began making circular motions with it slowly massaging me as her palm traveled down my spine toward my hips. My back tingled. It straightened then curved into a pleasurable arch.

"Don't lose me Sam," she volunteered, "this place is scary at night."

Whem my arm slid around her she shivered, then moved out of reach, heading toward a break in the bushes where a trail started. Angel had the flashlight on in front of her pointing down at the trail. I stayed right behind her as we walked. Angel's pace was determined. She knew the terrain. Within the first ten minutes of our trek the twists and turns we made had thoroughly confused me. I was hopelessly lost. Finally she stopped. We were in a clearing of grass surrounded by trees. In the middle of the clearing was a particularly old tree with peeling bark. Its sloping branches were denuded of leaves. In the moonlight it looked like an eerie arm jutting up from the ground and ending with a series of gnarly, arthritic fingers. Someone had carved a pentagram into its base. Beside it was a fallen trunk where Angel now sat. I sat beside her. It was growing cold. From her back pocket she withdrew a flask. She opened it and handed it to me. It smelled of whisky. I took a long swig and handed it back to her. She screwed the cap on and sat the flask between us.

"Aren't you having any?" I asked suspiciously.

"In a minute. I don't want it on my breath right now." With that she raised one leg and rested it on my lap as she turned toward me, pressing her flesh against my body. Placing her arms around my neck, her lips met mine as her tongue moved into my mouth beginning to gently explore my teeth and throat. She smelled of leaves and mint. I could feel the growing excitement of my own body responding to her caresses. My tongue circled hers even as hers retreated and I entered her hungry mouth. She made me dizzy. I wanted her so much but suddenly felt sick. Turning away from her I barfed, feeling embarrassed but unable to help myself. I tried to rise but couldn't. All the while sexual flames of excitement continued to increase in intensity and duration in ever expanding waves threatening to drown me.

Angel stood up. She moved away from me. "Don't try to stand," she said, "it will only make things worse."

"Why?" I asked. "What have you done to me?" I bent over and barfed again. My hands were now cradling my face.

"When you wake up the nausea will have passed. You won't be out for long. Consider yourself fortunate. I included an ancient Egyptian aphrodisiac with the whisky I gave you. You're my birthday boy. It will last for hours. Your penis will grow up to three inches. Your erections will be rock hard. Your sex drive will be supercharged. Your orgasms will be more intense." Angel turned to face the sounds caused by someone else now entering the clearing. It was Bambi. In the process of losing consciousness I swore to myself as I watched Bambi and Angel begin removing each others clothes.

I woke in pain. My wrists were tied together. I was hanging by my arms from a branch of the dead tree. My feet were almost touching the ground. With difficulty I could just stand using my toes. I teetered for a moment trying to understand what was going on. There was a small fire not far from me. Bambi and Angel were standing by it. They were naked. Fondling each other. Kissing passionately.

I groaned. My body was hot. My flesh felt smothered by my clothes. My skin had never been so sensitive and electrically charged. I was sweating. The pain seemed to merge with a sexual longing for release that was unbearable. Both girls turned to face me. Angel had a leather harness on. Attached to it was the wicked shape of an obscene, curved protuberance over 15 inches long, jutting out from between her thighs. Bambi stroked it absent mindedly while looking at me. The remarkable bodies of both girls glowed. Despite my predicament I began to feel an erotic excitement. In my imagination both girls appeared to be wild, uninhibited denizens of the wilderness.

Angel bent down and picked up a knife that had been heating near the fire. She approached me with it. Bambi moved in my direction as well. Angel raised the knife to my face. I could feel its heat. "I wouldn't move if I were you," she said as she pulled my shirt out of my pants using the knife to cut the buttons away. The shirt singed and melted where the blade touched it. Bambi helped her with one hand and caressing my inner thighs with the other.

"Why are you doing this?" I whispered. "This isn't necessary. I want you both. I must have you!"

Angel sneered. All the while cutting my clothes to smoking shreds. "We know you do. Haven't you figured anything out you male pig. I killed Disney Chase. Bambi saw you from the window. You're the only one who can connect us with the murder. Oh, you have no idea what it woke in us. It freed us. It opened our bodies and souls to pleasures you can only guess at. I hope you don't suffer from premature ejaculation. When you come we're going to kill you. Just like we did Chase."

Bambi whispered in a low seductive growl, "I had no idea men could excite me so."

My shirt was now totally destroyed. The little fragments that remained hung from my exposed shoulders. Bambi moved closer to me. Her tongue lightly licked the area around one of my nipples. Angel put her hand around Bambi's chin bringing their moist lips together. Bambi's hands began to explore my armpit. Teasing the hair that grew there. I moaned in unbearable ecstasy. I wanted to touch them back. I ached to take their quivering breasts into my hands. Moving back from me they began to fondle each other in the most intimate places while staring into my eyes as if feeding off my hunger, pain, yearning and the rising surprise of my unbearable excitement.

Angel suddenly looked shocked. "Oh Sam, they made your pants too long!"

Bambi laughed. She hurriedly unbuttoned my belt and pulled it free. Angel took her knife and began slicing into my pants until they fell away. She caressed my groin before yanking my shoes off my feet. My socks went next. Nothing was left me but my shorts which both girls started tearing at with their teeth.

The girls rubbed themselves in gyrating motions up and down the length of my frame. Angel began to tickle my feet while Bambi held me still by wrapping me in my own belt. Bambi then grasped my pulsating shaft while Angel spanked me. I found myself on a plateau of indescribable sensual passion that I never dreamed existed. I was dumbfounded. Continually brought to the cliff of total sexual release I found instead another plateau and yet another and another.

The girls now began to explore themselves while watching me watch them. It was the ultimate tease. From Bambi's pack they each removed a bottle of olive oil. Angel moved in back of me. Bambi moved in front. Pouring olive oil on my hair they began to massage it thoroughly into my skin, working it slowly down the length of my body. Their hands going everywhere as my whole frame fell hostage to a series of unforgiving spasms. I was unable to escape from the innumerable explosions wracking me from the inside out. My flesh quivered and pulsated when Angel began to kiss and nip at my skin.

Removing her wicked tongue from my ear Bambi whispered, "Men know so little about women. You just dive right in. That's not what a woman wants. The real treasure is closer than you think. Stimulation takes time. The whole body needs to be involved. I can tell you're beginning to have multiple orgasms. Too bad you won't be able to benefit from this experience. Hold off as long as you can because when you come for us it will be the last load you'll ever shoot."

Angel laughed, "The gate to a man's soul is through his body. Your soul is what we're after. You'll beg us to take it. They all do. It's a pity that you know Bambi was with Chase tonight. I could spend weeks feeding off your prolonged passion."

Angel approached me from behind and put her arms around me. She began to dance suggestively. The terrible dildo she wore slipped between my legs. I knew she was playing with me. The true function of that rubber monstrosity was reserved for Bambi alone. Bambi's eyes grew bigger as she watched us. She turned away from me to put a log on the fire. The outline of her body glistening with olive oil increased my sexual arousal. Feeling my renewal of interest, Angel joined Bambi by the fire. They began to wrestle with each other. My chest heaved as I watched. My hips began to jerk back and forth to the rhythm of their movement.

Angel was a serial killer. I could see that now. She was using me to teach Bambi. These two gave the mysteriously wonderful world of Lesbianism a bad name. They were a curse to their sexual persuasion. Theirs was a world of male entrapment. Their evil minds thrived like Venus Flytraps on predatory pleasures and passions. I was their fly. If I ever managed to break free I swore to myself I would treat the women I knew with more compassion and caring.

I thought of Lavender and Miss Blandish. I thought about how good they were to me and how I repaid their kindness and concern with pettiness. I knew I was going to die tonight but it was becoming impossible not to surrender totally to the perverse sexual ecstasy the aphrodisiac was causing. The dildo was a turnoff. Thinking about that helped. Though I couldn't tell for sure how I'd feel when Angel started to use it for real on Bambi.

Both Bambi and Angel were turning into horny sluts. Screaming and moaning in pleasure. I moaned with them. I begged them to cut me loose that I might join them. The damned have no interest in or time for pity. Passion has an uncontrollable heat when loosed. Angel was right. I was losing all perspective. The sexual energy inside me was a tornado increasing in severity beyond my wildest imagination. Every pore tingled, crying out for satisfaction and release. I closed my eyes knowing that if Angel or Bambi merely blew in my direction I would burst apart. The dam would break. They would kill me. My mind began to drift off.

Suddenly, all my senses jumped to attention. My eyes opened like saucers. I was convulsing from shock. Angel was standing before me. She was holding an empty bucket. The evil witch had thrown ice cold water on me. My ardor cooled. It was not a reprieve but a temporary respite. Steam was literally rising from my body. "The devil made me do it. You looked too hot to handle," she mischievously intoned, mocking my vulnerability. "You were having too good of a time. You needed a break."

"Well, he's had one," Bambi angrily interjected, "Let the real pleasuring start. I want to feast on his unfulfilled longing. I want to watch it grow and expand. I want to dominate him just as he's dominated so many of our sisters." She kneeled seductively before me and began cooing in admiration. Then without warning she thrust her hand and then her arm between my thighs, moving her fingers back down between the crevice of my cheeks until she reached my scrotum which she cradled firmly in the basket of her hand. Her other hand grasped my growing rod. Her wet tongue moved back and forth over her lips. Slowly she brought her mouth toward me. Her tongue teasingly moving everywhere at once. I let out a gasp in response to the thrill she was causing. She held me so securely down below that I was helpless to move. Her control and mastery were now complete. I was putty in her hands. "Very soon you will sing for us." She intoned, "You will sing like you have never sung before."

Playing the part of a cruel dominatrix, Bambi withdrew her ministrations just as I was about to come. I cursed her and her more experienced partner. I could tell Angel was hot and impatient from watching her protégé at work. Her face and body were flushed. Pink nipples pointed up and out from her pert breasts. She fondled them as she watched Bambi's nubile, naked figure kneeling before my elongating member. Angel was pleased with herself. She was right. Looking down I was amazed to find that I had grown over three inches in length. The fact was not lost on Angel. Her eyes wandered over me appraisingly.

While stroking Bambi's radiant hair Angel spoke in my direction, "I picked you out when I noticed it was your birthday on your license. This ritual works only on such as you. You can't imagine my joy when Bambi told me that you were the one she saw below that apartment window. Everything comes to the she-wolf who waits. The drug I gave you is not for you alone.

The longer your arousal, the more potent it becomes. When we collect your blood, just a drop of it will convey to another the peak of arousal you experience tonight. It will prolong life and restore youthfulness. Thanks to you, Bambi and I will rule the world. No man will be able to deny us anything. Know that I have lived for centuries by having my way with men like you for I am Sinifre. A Princess of Isis."

Bambi began to sing and dance before the fire. Angel joined in. Their voices were beautiful. The words were in an ancient tongue that caused a renewal of longing and desire in me. My body felt weightless. The flickering light off of their backs and rounded buttocks made my heart pound faster. A warmth swam through my blood. It seemed to respond to their song. Angel placed her hands on Bambi's glistening thighs. Both girls danced closer to me. They faced each other as Angel brought her lips to Bambi's welcoming mouth. Bambi's tongue extended out as Angel's own tongue met it while Bambi's fingers played over Angel's breasts and nipples. It felt as if a river moved through me extending out to become part of them. The urge within me was too great. "Release me!" I screamed. "Oh god, I'm so ready! Let our desires mix that we all might be fulfilled!" Bambi danced closer to the fire and picked up the pail that had once held icy water. Angel took up the knife she had used earlier and danced toward me with it. Holding it up as if to bathe the blade in the milky moonlight.

"Sing!" she called out to me. "Sing with us."

From somewhere within me a voice rose that I did not recognize. It was the primordial voice of seduction and fulfillment. A voice at once deep and mellifluous. The words coming from me were not recognizable. It was my blood singing as if from a grove or shaded temple beside the Nile. The moment merged into an infinity of moments extending through time calling out with urgency for me to become part of it. I was the pharaoh whose monumentality was carved in stone. My erect penis an unashamed symbol of strength and manly fertility extending out and over the world. The earth blessed and made new again because of the power hidden inside its massive shape. Mine was the humongous rod that generated the magical fluid, that essence making all things new again. I was everywhere and at once a god.

The sun itself exploding out and up separating the earth and sky. Yes, I sang as I realized that that music in me made me immortal.

And yet, from the corner of my consciousness the little that remained of me picked up a series of shapes and lights charging into the clearing. I could see Angel with her upraised knife turning to confront another figure. A gun went off. I saw the outline of Angel fall to the ground. Bambi now held the sacrificial knife meant for me. I threw my hips outward that I might meet it's sharp, glistening point. But Bambi's arm failed as she too fell mortally wounded and dying. Someone cut the rope above me. A blanket was draped over my shoulders. Vaguely, I recognized the voice of Penny Lavender and Miss Blandish as if talking to me from a great distance. Opening my eyes I found myself in a bed. Light from a window. The smell of gardenia perfume.

Penny Lavender was sitting in a chair beside me. A racing form was in her hands. I tried to sit up but couldn't quite manage it. Miss Blandish helped me. She placed a martini glass in my hand. Penny filled it while talking to me. "Sorry to put you through all that but the doctor said you'd be none the worse for wear except for a strange enlargement in a place we won't, out of delicacy, mention."

I looked under the sheet covering me and blushed to find myself still intact and better then ever.

Miss Blandish began to scold Penny. "I told you we should have filled him in."

Penny shook her head. "No, Beebo Brinker would have been on to him. We had to do it my way."

"What are you talking about?" I asked impatiently.

Penny smiled, looking as glamorous as ever. "You were our bait Sam. We had you tailing that Bambi girl in order to bring Brinker out of hiding."

I was confused. "Who in the hell is Beebo Brinker?"

Miss Blandish answered, "Brinker was Angel. She went by many names, and was wanted out of state for a number of murders."

Lavender continued, "Her m.o. was strange. Each of her murdered victims were men in their twenties. Their private parts were cut off with a knife and they bled to death. We heard that Brinker was in the area but didn't know what she looked like. When we got the rumor that she teamed up with Bambi, a.k.a. Cherry Hymen, we saw our opportunity."

Blandish continued, "By having you tail Bambi we hoped that Angel or Brinker would connect with you."

Lavender interrupted, "It worked. We followed you both to Shore Acres but lost you."

"It was a close call," Miss Blandish volunteered. "We had the police with us but you seemed to have disappeared off the face of the planet. Than we heard you singing. I never realized you had such a beautiful voice. We got to you just in time. A few seconds later and your voice would have changed for good."

Penny Lavender sipped from her glass. An amusing but faint smirk passed over her face. "Sorry about the deception Sam but you will be pleased to learn that because of your fine work I'm going to promote you. You played a key role in helping us solve a very difficult case. We're all proud of you."

I frowned. Took one more look under the sheet covering me and smiled. I felt different, as if there was something in my blood softly singing. Perhaps it was worth it after all.

Revenge of the Living Masturbation Rag

by Kevin L. Donihe

THE MASTURBATION RAG hated living in the dark beneath the bed. It hated Roger, hated him with every fiber of its being. The man had taken the rag from its home in a duck-shaped wicker towel holder and turned it into a crusty monstrosity. The rag especially hated sharing space with the briefs that housed Roger's short, stubby lizard. Roger had a habit of keeping them under the bed, unwashed for several months.

The rag recalled its first rub against the penis Roger called *Laser Roboto*. It initially assumed the hairy growth was some deformity or disease. Then it realized Roger took pride in the thing. The guy stared at it in the mirror, measured it, even spoke to it. Roger couldn't keep his hands off the lizard. Sometimes he whacked it six to eight times a day and, each time, the rag experienced revulsion, then agony. Roger's explosions shot through the rag, leaving it feeling raped, eviscerated. The worse aspect was the drying-surfaces becoming hard and crusty like a dead sponge. After a year, once pliable fabric had grown so stiff and brittle that an edge broke off when Roger used it last.

The wound still throbbed.

If the masturbation rag were ever to develop a sex organ—which was very likely—it would not whack it into oblivion. There was no question about that. The rag was borne of man, yet it considered itself superior to

183

man. Especially Roger. Whatever he did, the rag did not wish to do. But it wished to whack Roger into oblivion. It wanted to use *him* as the ultimate masturbation rag. That would shut the lizard's spurting mouth-give it a taste of hell.

Such things were destined to happen. The masturbation rag felt it.

Self-awareness was a yearlong process. The rag spent the first six months of life as pure consciousness. It sensed stickiness and darkness in ever-increasing intensities without knowing what stickiness and darkness were. With the passages of time-and the constant infusion of seed-the rag had developed individual eyes within each tiny gap in the fabric weave. Most were rendered useless, however-either gummed up by Roger's lizard or shot out entirely. Though the rag now bristled with microscopic, sound-sensing feelers, not much had happened in the last two weeks. No further development. No heightened senses.

But today was a special day; time for a new mutation. Locomotion would take some getting used to-perhaps years of being carried around had spoiled the masturbation rag. Undaunted, it extended crusty pseudo-pods and slithered out from beneath the bed, leaving a fetid slime-trail in its wake.

Halfway up, the rag heard all-too-familiar sounds: heavy breathing, squelching skin, bedsprings in motion. It didn't want to see the act. Seeing hurt too much and brought on flashbacks-but the masturbation rag steeled itself. Snail-like, it slid up the comforter.

On top of the bed, the rag turned one of its functioning, non-gummed eyes toward the sound. Roger was indeed going at it. He rested on his stomach, his ass hiked to allow the free access of his hand. Roger didn't notice the mastur-bation rag-not at first. His neck was turned; he faced the opposing wall.

The masturbation rag's mouth-slit opened to reveal whirling yellow teeth.

"Daddy", it said.

Heaven

by Christian Westerlund

A SAD AUTUMN landscape.

Dead leaves fluttering in the darkness and empty moments passing in the cold. I came walking along the sidewalk, watching the familiar city.

There were only a few other people out there, in the smell of greasy machinery and electricity. You could see the pale autumn lights in their eyes.

October fluttered in their minds.

Then I raised my arm and one of the sloshing cabs stopped. I got inside and the interior of the car smelled like musk and stale hospital air.

The driver looked at me in the rear-view-mirror. A filthy Hispanic man with bloodshot puffy eyes. He clenched a wrinkled cigarette butt between his long teeth and there were food-stains all over his cheap cloths.

"Where to?" he asked with a heavy accent.

I gave him the address. The smell of musk and rot around him was sickening. He was unshaved and there were strange stains all over his crotch.

There were photos back there, nailed to the seats before me. Most of them were old and yellowed. Others had been taken more recently.

Shots of empty hospital beds, rusted factories, long corridors, vomit in the gutter...

Then I watched the world outside.

An empty wastescape of frail buildings, growling like cancer out of the concrete. Dead shells of warehouses, skeletal and rusted in the darkness.

Heaven

I rolled down the window and the cold air numbed my fingers. It was probably going to snow soon. It would be December in a few days.

The driver let me off somewhere among the dead buildings and I felt lost. I stood there under the broken streetlights, staring at the decay.

There was another photo on the ground: a close-up on a wrecked anus, filled with insects.

A gentle snowflake touched my cheek.

And then I knew where I was…

♋

The hospital had been abandoned years ago, due to a bacterial infection. It stood like a shell in the darkness now, old and forgotten.

The stale hospital air filled me as I looked out of the window. I could see more of the city from up here. Skeletal factories and empty warehouses. Dead slums stretching out into forever.

There were hospital beds lined up along the walls. Most of them were rusted and probably hadn't been used for several years.

I'd been here before.

There were broken cardio monitors on the floor, wrapped in rotten cabling, flickering in the darkness. A dark gas mask lay abandoned on the floor.

Then I was down in one of the lower wards, wandering endlessly among the heaps of broken cardio monitors and oxygen masks.

Everything reeked of formaldehyde.

The girl was there, waiting for me. She looked up with rust-colored eyes.

"Please do not let them do this to me," she whispered.

She was lying on the floor, with her legs stretched out in unknown spilling. She was naked and they had forced a greasy tube up into her anus.

The tubing was connected to a oily machine and differently colored fluids were being pumped out into her twisted little body.

She might have been lying there forever.

More tubes slithered up into her mouth and nostrils. She looked at me and I saw recognition in her eyes.

I left her there—alone with the sound of the strange machines that kept

186

her alive. And I knew that she would never again be alone.

☞

Then I found the man.

In one of the lower wards, sealed-off due to the bacterial infections, where everything still smelled like almond and musk.

"I am becoming part of something bigger," he said. He stood in his own spilling—a stocky black man with hair like rotten satin. He had pulled his pants down and he was just taking off his underwear.

His thick penis hung semi-erect between his legs. Several tubes slithered up into the sockets in his skull. His eyelids fluttered rapidly.

"I am closer to god," he whispered.

He reeked of vomit and semen. More greasy tubes slithered up into his anus.

Then he started to ejaculate. He moaned and grabbed a rusted tin cup and held it to his penis. The slow, thick sperm flooded the cup.

"They are keeping it. They are saving it all for later."

There were five TV-screens in the darkness, flickering endlessly. They were linked together, connected with dirty cables.

And on the dark screen—a single phrase.

YOU ARE ALL ALONE.

A white hot flash in the dark, appearing simultaneously on all five screens. The smell of static and burnt metal filled my head.

There would be more phrases like that. The low electrical humming grew louder as the images fluttered inside of me.

The stocky black man stood there—still with sperm dripping from his soft penis—trying to understand.

"I am closer to god," he whispered.

And I knew he was right.

☞

It was still cold when I left the hospital.

A nighttime scene of dead leaves and flickering neon. The buildings around here were all abandoned, boarded up with planking.

I found a rotten little pink-plastic doll in the gutter, staring at me, all dull-eyed and limp. It had vomit all over it and it stank of burnt plastic.

I picked it up and it reminded me of something.

And then, in the end, there was only one picture left, glued to a brick wall. A close-up of me, taken years back:

The interior of a dim hotel room where I am sitting on a decaying mattress, with steel-tubes disappearing up into the rusted sockets where my eyes should have been.

Then I walked away because I did not want to remember. It started to snow and I did not even know where I was going.

Sometimes I will just sit down on bench somewhere and watch all the people—all the forgotten moments that flutter in their eyes.

And I know that they will never be alone.

Surgery

by Simon Logan

Pre-op

T HEY LINE UP outside the rear entrance to the labs like Auschwitz prisoners being ushered into gas chambers and they do this willingly, handing themselves over for what, twenty, maybe thirty notes? It depends on what they volunteer for. It depends on how desperate they are and what wonders we've dreamed up to put them through.

I've handed out lists to them of what's on offer, let them figure it out amongst themselves who'll be taking the risks—and the money—today. The ones that aren't desperate quickly shuffle off when they realize that what we do here is more than just drawing blood or getting them to drop a pill, leaving only the regulars and of course she is amongst them.

I call her Mine.

Threads of red hair, threads of blue, blank bleached chunks in between. A bomber jacket to try and stave off some of the chill she must be feeling in such a short skirt and what look like army surplus boots with no laces. I've watched her each week since I started at the labs, trapped her in my head like one of my favorite schematics. She's noticed me watching, too. Lately she's been watching me back.

She interests me for no particular reason. There is nothing special about her, nothing at all. She is not beautiful, nor strange, nor intriguing. I watch her because she is mundane.

Surgery

"Females only," Ulrich had told me three days ago but his only elaboration was a deep smile that excavated his scraggy, veined face like an explosion in a Soviet mine shaft.

Everything that went on here was illegal but Ulrich was always the one pushing things to the limit, even amongst the rest of the researchers. People who wouldn't think twice about slipping a drunk fifteen notes for allowing us to inject him with viral chicken cells just to see what would happen felt uncomfortable around Ulrich.

I can feel his breath on my neck as he watches the line progress. "I want her," he tells me, nodding down the line towards Mine. "But don't offer her any more than thirty, she's not worth that much."

"She's no good," I tell him. "She's a troublemaker."

"She'll know better than to cause me any trouble. We're fucking paying her for this."

"She's no good," I repeat and feel the sting of a scalpel blade being pressed into the webbing of my left hand.

"Don't forget your place, you little fuck. You're just here to organize them all, nothing more. I *want* her, do you understand me?"

I nodded, then went back to the line, giving them their instructions one by one until I came to the girl.

"How much for this one?" she asked, pointing to Ulrich's experiment on the sheet of paper she held. I could see her teeth were starting to rot from drug use and her eyes glittered with what I imagined to be the myriad of chemicals coursing through her wiry veins.

"Ten," I told her, and glanced back at Ulrich, standing cross-armed in the doorway.

"You're fucking joking. Forty."

"Twenty."

"Thirty."

Another glance at Ulrich, sweating in the midday heat, lab coat smeared with dried agar. "I'll give you forty to go now. Forty."

"To what? Go where? I want this one here."

"Just go. Get out of here." I try to urge her with my eyes but she's too wasted to notice. "Sixty. I'll give you sixty to not do it. Don't do it."

"What? Why not? Is this some sort of…?"

I have the money in my hands. Ulrich is coming towards us, he knows something is up.

"*Sixty*. Please. Just go now."

"What for? I don't…"

"This is my experiment," I lie and Ulrich is almost with us. "*Run*. Just go. Come back later and I'll tell you what I need from you.

"Not unless you tell me what I have to do."

"I'll tell you later for seventy," I snap.

And she bites because I'm talking the language of hits, of addiction.

Money means nothing. Money is not paper, it's liquid or little rocks or small mountains of powder.

She takes the notes and she runs.

The first incision, onwards

I didn't know what to do with her at first.

She presents herself to me as a walking, talking piece of clay ready for me to sculpt from and I have no inspiration from which to draw. Her expectation gnaws at me as we linger by an incinerator at the back of the hospital, away from the labs and the legitimate workers, the mournful noise of its chemical churnings loud in my ears. She stands before me, arms and skinny legs crossed. Waiting.

"Well?"

I'd given her seventy…for what?

"You want to fuck?"

"No," I tell her.

"Jesus." She stares at her feet impatiently. "Then what?"

Then what. Then what. Then what.

"I want you to get inside that incinerator. For one minute." I say this because it comes from nowhere, because it comes from a place inside me that is a secret chamber or bomb shelter. I say this. "I'll turn it off. I know

191

how. The machinery won't harm you but there will be toxic fumes."

She seems reluctant at first despite everything she's been willing to put herself through at the labs but I've been around her type for months now. I know how they work.

I offer her another ten, enough for a couple of low-grade rocks.

"How do I know you won't turn it back on once I'm inside?"

I let the ten touch her palm but don't hand it over. I want to see what she does. "Another ten once you're out," I tell her.

Money means nothing. Money is control, that's what it is.

I wonder how long it's been since she's dosed as she climbs inside. Her hands are shaking, this I notice. The machine is deafeningly silent. She has to cover her nose and close her eyes because of the fumes and tries to back out but then sees the ten in my hand. I close the hatch and start counting.

I don't hear her whimpers but I imagine them and they are like fresh tears or pure, clean blood.

Ten.

Twenty.

Thirty, forty. Fifty.

I reach sixty and open the hatch and she bursts out past me, gasping for breath, clawing at the fume-laden air, collapses to the dusty ground. I watch her lurch around there for a few moments before I help her up and she's spitting blood.

Her eyes are streaming, sweat covers her ragged features like fragments from a nail bomb. I check that she is okay and offer to take her to the ER to get some treatment, I tell her I know some people who will help her, no questions asked. I tell her this.

"The ten," is all she says, and holds out a hand with chemical burns up one side.

But I hesitate before giving her what she wants. "I don't want you to go back to the labs again."

"Don't tell me what to do," she says, and, "you don't own me."

I give her the ten and when she takes it we both realize that I *do* own her, if only for a few moments in time. For that minute I owned her and I want more.

"Tomorrow. I'll give you twice what they would give you at the labs."

Money means nothing. Money hires souls temporarily.

The Healing Process

The money flows.

At first I run out of time to keep up my other interests—my studies into mathematical theories, the concepts of structural engineering—but then later I willingly give them up one by one, replacing each with more time spent with her.

I give her sixty and she cuts herself open. A single, clean line from wrist to elbow that is deep enough to require stitches and I give her thirty and she lets me kiss her blood.

I give her eighty and I hold her head in the dirty canal water until she passes out and I fuck her as I do so but the sex isn't important, it just happens. I remain inside her as I pull her back from the water and we collapse to the ground like weeds sprayed with pesticide.

We fuck each time after that but it still doesn't matter. We just do it, we don't have to. We just do it.

She takes me in her mouth after I've smeared myself with an hallucinogenic paste that burns me and makes her think my hands are clawed as I wrap them around her neck and decorate her body with more incisions. I give her twenty.

I give her thirty to tell me everything she can think of that has happened in her life from the moment she was born until the present. I scribble notes and diagrams and timelines on scrap paper as she talks and I force her to keep going even when she insists there is nothing more to tell. I want to claim all her experiences because they make her what she is.

I sell all my pieces of art from an underground graffiti artist whom nobody else has ever heard of, pieces I have studied for hours on end to know and feel every inch of the canvas.

Money means nothing. Money grants you freedom to destroy yourself and those around you.

I give her only ten to inject herself with a potent mix of drugs I made myself because I figure she is getting what she is wanting in the process. Her throat bleeds for several days afterwards but it takes her that long to become lucid again anyway.

I quit the labs because I don't need them any more and Ulrich knows I am up to something but he no longer has control over me for he no longer pays me. He cannot stop me, this he knows. This I know.

I'm running out of money but I'm filling myself full of her.

I tell her to come to my apartment and it is near-empty when she arrives because I've sold the furniture.

Money means nothing. Money is fun, is games.

I give her one hundred this time, more than I have ever given her before and she knows that this means something.

"I want you to go cold turkey. For one week."

"I can do that."

I feel like smiling but I don't. "When was the last time you went a week without a hit?"

"I can do it," she repeated. "For one hundred and fifty. In advance."

"Fine. But I want to know you've done this. I want to see it. I don't trust you."

I show her the bathroom, with the extra locks on the outside that I have fitted, the boarded up windows, the small mattress on the porcelain floor.

"In there for one week. No drugs. One-fifty."

I can sense her hesitation and it thrills me for this is the first time I've felt real resistance from her since that first night and this is a great thing, this is what I have been searching for. I challenge her submission but she accepts everything I put before her. I want to make her do something she really doesn't want to do -and she wants it just as much. I know this.

"Two hundred. Up front."

"One hundred," I tell her.

"What?! You said one-fifty!"

"Now I say one hundred. Take it or leave it."

Money means nothing. It means desperation. It means suffering.

And one hundred still means enough to keep her high for days. I hand her the money because her stupid fucking junky brain doesn't realize that it makes no difference whether she gets it upfront or not because she won't be able to do a damn thing with it.

Later I think of the notes as she screams and lashes out at the door, threatening me, hating me, pleading with me. I open the door only when she goes quiet and she is asleep on the mattress with goose pimples the size of golf balls. I strip her and fuck her and her eyes are still closed when I lock the door again.

The week passes in fluctuating rhythms of time.

Money means nothing. It means days, minutes, hours, seconds.

She has all the water she needs. I feed her occasionally but it usually only stays there for a matter of moments before she pukes it into the toilet or onto the floor. She tires on day three, murmuring constantly and I think perhaps hallucinating. She begs me to bring her some rocks when I go in late one afternoon and ends up unzipping me, slipping me into her wet mouth as if her lizard-brain had somehow become ingrained with these prostitutional survival functions. A new evolutionary mechanism for this new age.

I watch her almost constantly through the window and by day six her skin seems to hang from her and she moves like a lazy insect. She slides around in ice cold bath water and sings to herself then attacks the door with all the fury her withered body can manage. Later that night she is peaceful and warm when I go to her and I open her legs slowly, gently. I treat her like a lover and notice the awkward chemical shine has gone from her eyes as I lean into her. I lay with her that night into the next morning and we talk whilst saying nothing.

She seems reluctant to get up from the floor she has become used to sitting on when I tell her it's over. She is uncertain how to deal with sobriety, with this defeat, this I know.

I help her up and out of the room, towards the light pouring in through a large window on one wall. She shivers and I embrace her and at the same time slide the hundred notes into her hand. It takes her a few moments to comprehend what this means, this gesture.

Money means nothing, it has lost all meaning. Just paper.

Her skin seems to be absorbing the daylight, gaining color with each moment that passes.

"I need to go." She says this. "Where are my clothes?"

"Go where? What for?" I ask as I hand them to her.

"I need to go."

"How do you feel?" I ask as she clips her skirt and pulls on her boots.

"None of your business," she says.

"Twenty," I offer her but she ignores me.

Then she is gone, along with my hundred.

Remission

Four days pass without her and I find her in the accident and emergency one night because I've asked the duty nurse to call me if any overdoses of young women come in.

Her bed and chin are bloodstained, her eyes hollow once again. An IV drip pumps itself into her bloodstream. I carry her away before the attending doctor can return and take her back to my apartment, lay her on the same mattress she spent the previous week on.

She is barely conscious when I ask her to undo the stitches that still crisscross her forearm.

"How much?" She asks me this.

"Money means nothing," I tell her, and hand her a surgical pick.

She can't focus on me. Morphine overdose, the medical notes had read. This report is now pinned to my wall along with x-rays and blood charts that had been in her file. I place the pick in her hand and lay its metal tooth under one of the stitches.

She pulls weakly and at first all she manages to do is stretch her skin and draw blood but then the thread snaps. Piece by piece she undoes the binding, grimacing as she pulls the thread through her puckered skin. She presents me with the wound when she is done and I kiss her blood afresh.

"No more drugs," I tell her.

"I don't need them anyway."

"Don't come back here."

"I don't need you either."

"Of course you do."

We fuck slowly just as we had that final day of her incarceration and the blood from her reopened wound blesses us, smears us.

She is still an addict but she is my addict. I have become her addiction and she has become mine.

This I know.

Money has no meaning. It has no place. It is redundant.

Addiction shall never be so.

"Anything?" I ask her.

"Anything," she says, and squeezes her vaginal muscles. We are in the lotus position, her nestled in my lap.

"Knowledge means possession," I say.

"To know is to own," she recites from one of our first nights together.

"I want to know you completely."

She squeezes again. "Anything."

I am a rock. I am a line of powder. I am a syringe.

Surgery

It takes a few days to organize but I want to do this right.

We arrive at the hospital at 3 a.m. and I take her to the old surgeries on the eighth floor. They haven't been used in years, at least not officially—this I tell her.

Kubrick is medium height, bristling with stubble, 8% body fat. He holds a clipboard with nothing on it to give this all some air of normality. He leads us into an OR with tiling on the walls that has been cracked and displaced by subsidence and everything is ready.

We lay her down on a gurney.

There will be photos I say, and video footage. I want to capture everything. I want the x-rays and the sample jars. I want to see her bottled and scanned and magnified. I want to know her and I want her to see herself like this when she awakens afterwards.

As Kubrick washes up I lean into her ear and whisper, "I want to fuck you from the inside out." A faint sigh escapes her cracked lips as the anesthetic begins to flow.

I give the surgeon his money and he scrubs her bare belly with iodine before he makes the first incision.

Post-op

I remember staring at the rocks I bought one night. It was the night he fucked me with my head in the canal's poisoned waters and I held those little gems in my hand several hours later, trying to divine their meaning. My hand shook because it had been days since my last hit, enough to make the bruising on my bare legs blossom like blood clots that had burst. My stomach was a raging, tormented fire.

I cooked up to kill the pain as always but this time I thought of him as I did it. I fell back onto the cold concrete floor of the fire damaged building I had been squatting in and his face appeared above me in the chemical haze.

I was his toy, his own experiment. I'd watched him being browbeaten by the scientists and I could see that intense desperation in his eyes from time to time, enough to make me wonder if he was a secret junky too. When I had climbed into the incinerator I had been prepared to die. I had been prepared for a long time. When I came out I knew I would never need go back to the labs again.

I let him think I was a worthless piece of scum, that I was nothing but just another desperate morphine-hound, because this is how I saw myself.

It was the greatest pain I had ever known to be locked inside that dirty tiled bathroom of his, a pain that had no boundaries between drug withdrawal and the ugliness inside my stomach. I fell into the agony, it embraced me just as he did, and I thought of the time before the drugs when I had tried to confront it by myself. By day five the worst of the withdrawal was over leaving me with the cluster bombs of my intestines exploding inside me. My head cleared to let me fully appreciate the pain and I hated him when he came into feed or clean or fuck me but I didn't have the strength to do anything about it.

He gave me one hundred and I already knew by that point how I would use it. I knew the pattern of my life. I gave it to a nurse at the hospital and told her to fake an overdose for me then to let him know where I was. It felt like a cleansing wash to be bathed in his hatred of my weakness. He told me to give up the drugs and I let him believe that I hadn't already.

I took out my stitches that night and let the sharp spikes of pain replace the menacing ache that he been haunting me deep within. I wondered how far the growths had reached when he told me about the surgery. The growths, the tumors. The source of my addiction, the cancers that made me into an addict.

I had never told him but now I wanted him to know. I wanted him to see for himself the true ugliness in me, the dark shapes that had been growing inside me for over a year, that would take my life any time now.

I wanted him to witness this in the stark surgical light and really see what I was because I felt like he was already so close to it.

I was pretty certain I wouldn't survive the operation but that was unimportant. As long as he stared down into my abdominal cavity, as long as I meant something to him…at least then, finally, I meant something.

Black Wings

by Jeffrey Thomas

THE PALACE WAS called Urian, though amongst themselves the Demons liked to joke that it was Castle Urine. It was a great square block worked from a single stone, its luridly red-orange surface pocked and pitted as pumice, with no towers, no carven decorations, just far-spaced slits for windows and only a single door. This red cube rested at the heart of a desert of red sand, and on the rare occasion that it rained, the scarlet powder would reveal itself to be dehydrated blood, and would liquefy, become a sludgy mud flat of gore. From the desert sprouted a dense forest of bare, treelike growths as white as coral. The surfaces of these coral trees were so rough that to rub against them was to draw blood, like the rasping skin of a shark. Their leafless, lifeless arms wove jagged thickets of bone that had never worn flesh.

There was a path through the coral reef, however, that ran to the door of the castle. From one of the narrow windows, the Demon named Xaphan peeked out at the approach of the carriage that was delivering Urian's latest guests. The carriage itself was a featureless, black iron globe between two huge wheels, pulled by a harnessed team of two dozen naked Damned children, so Xaphan could not as yet spy the guests themselves.

He started as another figure slipped beside him; he had been so intent he hadn't heard Vjeshitza's approach. She pressed her face into the crook of his neck, and bit him hard there without breaking his dark skin. While doing so, she held onto his folded wings, which like her own were feathered and black as a crow's, though the wings did not permit their species of Demon to fly.

Black Wings

Xaphan and Vjeshitza both possessed skin of a deep chestnut hue and luster, both of them hairless, even without eyebrows. And both wore no garments. Their only embellishments were black onyx rings pierced through their nipples—and on their upper chests, raised keloids like the healed wounds of a tiger's slash, four of these tracks above each breast, where they had marked themselves with their retractable talons upon having completed their warrior's training in the city of Tartarus, where all the Demons in this region of Hell were mass produced before marching to their assigned cities, forts and outposts.

Vjeshitza lifted her face, smiling, and traced her tongue—more tender now—along the rim of Xaphan's ear. "They're newly dead," she purred, "and this is their first visit to Hades."

"Their first vacation?" Xaphan snorted. "Are they bored with their celestial pleasures so soon?"

"The man wants to hunt. His wife will be entertained here. Come away now, before you're seen loitering about. We must all be prepared to serve them."

"I hate when their kind come," he said.

"Shh," hissed Xaphan's lover, looking over her shoulder in case one of the Baphomets might be near. "You mustn't appear sullen."

"Should I appear giddy, then? I'm a Demon."

"You should appear dignified, but servile. We must assemble now. They're almost here." As she withdrew from him, she lightly raked the tips of her mostly-retracted claws across his hard belly, as if to mark him with scars again.

♋

The Demon population of Castle Urian gathered in the high-ceilinged entry hall, the ranked warriors with their wings folded, but a few superiors, at attention near the door, with their wings opened in a majestic display. Looming over these Demon officers were the three creatures that presided over Urian, nicknamed Baphomets by the Damned laborers who manufactured them in Tartarus. The Baphomets concealed their pillar-straight forms in black robes, their bodies surmounted with the charred heads of goats, though the white flames that enveloped their skulls radiated cold rather than heat. They never spoke, but the winged Demons could read their meaning in the lapping of their flames.

A heavy, hollow rapping of the outer knocker, and a Demon lunged forward to creak open the black iron door. Into the hall walked a small procession of four white-robed Angels. The Angels were not homunculi like the Demons, but had once been mortal, had died and been resurrected in Heaven. One of them wore a white, starched head covering pointed into a cone, the other three simply with cowls that they slipped off their heads as they entered. Xaphan could see that one of these latter Angels was a woman.

They had met the one with the cone-like headdress before; his name was McDonald, a used car salesman who had died in the 1960s and found employment for himself over the past few decades as a guide leading other Angels on vacation tours through certain areas of Hades. The other three were his current tour group, who one of the Demon officers introduced to the assembly. "These are the brothers Anthony and James Colombo, and James' wife, Teresa. They will be staying with us for an indeterminate time. During that time, we are all to be at their service."

As one, the assembled Demons gave a deep bow.

The party had strolled further into the hall, slowly, as if to inspect each of the Demons in their rows. They were close enough to Xaphan now that he could hear the Angel named James Colombo snort and comment, "Haven't they heard of clothes around here? I feel like I walked into *National Geographic*." Over his shoulder, he said, "Check out their color, Tony. Big surprise, huh?"

Their guide, McDonald, put in, "Well, guys, these aren't the only sort of Demons. Some look like whites, some like orientals…"

"How politically correct."

"I think they're beautiful," said Teresa Colombo, who unlike her husband had a British accent, dark and smoky. "In a scary way."

"They're okay," Anthony opined, flicking the nipple ring of one of the female Demons. Xaphan saw her jaw twitch slightly.

The woman's husband stopped, turned to her with a cocked eyebrow and said, "You do, huh? Well…they're not as bad as those things." He gestured openly at one of the towering, immobile Baphomets. Xaphan could tell by the fluctuations in its caul of cold flame that it was displeased by the comment, but he knew it wouldn't have given voice to its disapproval even if it had had a voice.

"Right," said his wife smartly, spinning to address McDonald, Mick as he insisted on being called. "Mick, can those poor children be unharnessed now from that awful contraption we rode here in, and given some food and water and maybe some rest? I never should have stepped into that thing when I saw what was pulling it."

"Uh, this is Hell, sweetheart," said James. "There's a good reason for those kids to be here, I'm sure."

"It's their parents' fault if they weren't baptized…"

Uncomfortably, McDonald chuckled and put a hand on her arm. "Don't worry, Terry—we'll take care of them. And when you leave, I promise we'll have a carriage pulled by animals."

"What kind of animals? A team of a hundred kittens with their fur on fire?"

Her brother-in-law laughed. "Whoa, that I'd like to see. Terry, you should be one of the torture designers down here."

The guests were shown off to their opulently-appointed rooms, and the ranks of Demons broke up. Xaphan found Vjeshitza and muttered, "I could devise or administer no greater torture than the smile in an Angel's voice."

While Xaphan and Vjeshitza made love, a sandstorm howled outside. Xaphan hoped the two brothers and Mick were on a hunting excursion at this very moment, and had been caught out in the storm. He pictured them hunkered down in the inadequate shelter of the forest of antler-like bone, covering their faces against the stinging sands of dried blood.

That was the main reason the brothers had come to Hades—to hunt the Damned for sport. Though they had brought their own rifles, custom-made for them in Heaven, Castle Urian opened the doors of its armory to guests, and Xaphan had heard that earlier today the brothers had gone down into the tunnels below the palace to fire crossbows into targets. He didn't know if the targets were Damned prisoners from the palace's cells, but he didn't doubt it. These prisoners were released as hunting stock when the free-ranging Damned outside grew scanty in this area.

They were in Xaphan's room, which was tiny—but he counted himself as lucky, since Demons in other outposts and cities often had only communal barracks to rest in. A red silken tapestry covered one entire wall, the symbol for Castle Urian embroidered on it in metallic purple thread. The sheets of the small cot-like bed were of the same red material. Xaphan was raised over Vjeshitza on the strong columns of his arms, the muscles and cords in his neck pulled taut, his tight chest looking carved from polished ebony. Her powerful legs wrapped around his lower back, Vjeshitza had one finger hooked through both the rings pierced through his nipples, pulling on them just enough that the pleasure didn't stray too far into pain. Her feathered wings formed a black pool under her that looked like it might swallow them. His, half open, were a canopy that seemed to be casting that intimate pool of shadow.

"I helped prepare a perfumed bath for the woman today," Vjeshitza cooed, staring into her lover's eyes, which were both intensely focused but oddly detached, as if he stared at some small object that was the only detail he could recall from a dream.

"Yes?" he grunted absent-mindedly, rocking her hips with his own, their pelvises locked like the antlers of fighting stags. "I imagine she was imperious. Insulting…"

"No. She was polite. She's bored, though. She's only here because of her husband, I'm sure. But I saw her body when she disrobed. She's a horrible thing. Fat, like a white leech gorged on blood. Like fruit that should have fallen from a branch long ago."

"She wasn't born a warrior, like us. And how old is she?"

"She was forty-two when she died, I heard. Young…for one of them." Both Xaphan and Vjeshitza were only eleven years old. They had left the city of Tartarus, where they had been made, as adults. Had, in fact, been born as adults.

"She doesn't strike me as being terrible. For one of her kind," he said.

"Don't let her mislead you. They can't be trusted. They are all of one evil heart…such as we Demons can only aspire to." Suddenly she darted her head like a snake and nipped him on the neck. His eyes clicked onto hers at last, and she grinned bright teeth in her lovely dark face. "Look at me." Then, more seriously, her smile becoming more subtle, she whispered, "Look at me…" She smoothed her hands over the black globe of his skull, as if to read the future in its surface.

♋

Earlier in the day, Xaphan had passed Mrs. Colombo in a hallway. He had lowered his eyes and nodded his head respectfully, but when he glanced up he saw that she had given him a smile. Changed out of her Angel's customary garments, she was wearing a black long-sleeved pullover and black slacks with flared legs. Her clothing was very tight, emphasizing her over-ripe figure.

Xaphan felt that his lover had been uncharitable in calling her fat, a leech. Though her body was more voluptuous, more indulged than those of Urian's devils—which might be taken as a sign of grossness, decadence— he found her shape an artistic abstraction of the features associated with the feminine: her breasts plump, her hips wide (had she birthed children in life?). Also, whereas he, Vjeshitza, and the others had no hair, Teresa Colombo's flowed down past her breasts, was thick and parted in the center, as black as his own wings. It waved about her face when she moved, and she was always brushing a curtain of it aside to clear her face (with its dark eyes, heavy brows, strong nose, pink lips pressed into that little smile she gave him). Again, compared to one of his kind, her long, heavy hair might seem a sign of lush overindulgence. But the contrast was eye-catching…just as was the brightness of her skin compared to his own.

Later in that same day, as he was turning into a corridor, he heard her voice behind him (its British accent distinct), and turned to see that she was moving briskly to catch up with him. "Excuse me?" she called, gesturing. She smiled more broadly this time, showing large white teeth. He went to her.

"Madam?"

"Can you help me move something?"

"Of course, madam."

He went to her, and she led him back around the corner, down a hallway and to a door of one of the opulent guests suites. He realized it must be her own.

She opened the door, led him inside, and she closed the door after him.

"The desk under the window," she said, pointing. "Can you move that to the corner, and replace it with that arm chair? I like to sit and read, but I prefer natural light."

"Certainly, madam." He did as she had instructed. As he lifted her desk, he noticed there were a few books strewn upon it. They were some of those written by the Damned themselves, and published by them as well in the larger cities like Oblivion. These crude booklets had found their way to Castle Urian in the possession of this and that Angel over the years, and Xaphan himself had read several of them in his idle hours (though Vjeshitza had scolded him for it, and had hissed that she didn't think it was wise for Demons to allow the Damned to express their thoughts in this way, let alone disseminate them to other Damned). He saw that she had a bookmark in one slim volume titled *Letters From Hades*, the author calling himself Dan Alighieri.

Seeing his eyes on it, Teresa lifted the book and riffled the pages. "There isn't much to do here while my husband's out hunting."

A little while ago, Xaphan had heard distant gunshots. "There is a subterranean garden, and a pool, down in the labyrinths," he offered.

"I've been to them. Yes, the pool is nice and hot, and the garden is pretty, if you like mushrooms and moss. A bit dungeon-like down there for my tastes, though." She set down the book and unexpectedly moved closer to him, reached out a finger that almost but not quite touched one of the perfect, unbroken onyx rings that passed through his black nipples. Her almost-touch made him flinch harder than an actual touch would have. "How do they get these things in you? I don't see a break in them."

"They put them in my species of Demon while we are still forming."

"Huh; I see. How strange. And these?" She indicated the slashed scars on both his breasts. He explained to her that he had inflicted the wounds upon himself, in a ritual marking the end of his training as a demonic warrior.

"Rrr," Teresa said, pretending to slash her own fingernails down the raised scars on his chest. Then she chuckled smokily. "Sorry." He didn't know whether to smile or to feel mocked, so he remained stoic.

She moved around behind him now, and though they weren't as sensitive as his skin, he could tell she was fingering the glossy black feathers along the edge of one of his folded wings. "Pretty," she said behind him.

"Thank you, madam," Xaphan muttered.

"Do you really fly?"

"No, madam."

"Hm. They're rather pointless, then, aren't they?"

He found their reflection in a mirror over a dressing table. She was obscured behind him in the silvered glass, but he felt her hand alight softly on his lower back. Slide into its hollow. Then around his side, along his hip. Now he could see her white hand on his dark skin in the mirror. He saw it glide over his hard belly, and then lower. Until it cupped his prick and his balls, and held them firmly. Her thumb stroked his demonhood, coaxing blood into its tubes.

"I'm bored," she whispered against one wing, as she slid her cheek back and forth across its silken sleekness.

"Yes, madam," he managed. She was pumping him languorously now. He grew hard quickly. Her hand barely fit around his black-veined dusky shaft. Its glans gleamed like the head of an obsidian scepter.

"My God," she husked, and she ran her tongue along the skin of his hard-muscled shoulder as if to taste its salt. Then she moved around in front of him, and sank to her knees. It made Xaphan uncomfortable that an Angel should kneel in supplication before a Demon. But when she took as much of him into her mouth as she could accommodate, he let out a small groan, and a moment later could not restrain himself from putting both hands to her head.

He had never touched a human woman's head before, except in the course of tortures he was obligated to perform. Her hair was a mass that shifted under his palms. That tangled between his fingers. His listened to the slick sounds of her mouth as her head worked forward and back. He felt her nails against the balls they cupped. Sharp, but not painful like the teasing claws of Vjeshitza.

Before he could find release inside her human head, Teresa rose before him, her dark eyes shining with something like a madness. "Undress me," she whispered.

And he did. He pulled off the formfitting black pullover, the tight-fitting slacks, as if unpeeling a fruit. Her breasts hung heavy in her bra, and he held them in his hands, his thumbs spiraling across her nipples until they pressed at the restraining material. Then he lowered one of his hands, slipped it under the elastic waistband of her briefs, and fingered open the moist slit hidden in the coils of her secret hair. He had never touched this hair before, either, Vjeshitza as denuded there as a newborn mortal. A dark musk arose, and liquid sounds like her mouth had made at his cock.

"Fuck me," she murmured against his chest. With her tongue, she flicked the ring through one nipple, and then pulled slightly at the ring with her teeth. Then, again: "Fuck me."

He fumbled at her bra; she helped him. He skinned her panties down her legs. Seeing her entirely nude, he nearly ejaculated into the air itself. That vista of white flesh, its whiteness only heightened by the black growth below her rounded belly, and pouring down across her rounded shoulders. There were no hard ribs, points of hip bones, sharply defined arm muscles. She was like the offer of a soft bed to a monk who had been sleeping on a stone floor.

He took her body up in his arms, carried her to the bed she shared with her husband, and lay her on it. And without hesitation, he was on and in her and already plunging, pumping, making the bed dip like a boat on a storm-tossed sea, and her breasts jounced and she threw back her head and moaned deeply.

His wings opened full above them like a black canopy.

Distantly, Xaphan heard the crack of a rifle shot echo across the desert flatness. Somewhere, a Damned had probably just died. But he or she would resurrect. Being already dead, a Damned or an Angel could not be killed a second time. In this way, the Demons were more like the mortals had once been than the mortals were themselves. Though their powers of regeneration were great, a Demon could be killed. And so the gunshot made Xaphan tense up a little. What if the husband should return and find them this way? Would he allow his wife this entertainment, see it as nothing more than a dip in the spring-fed pool? No more than his own entertainment hunting the Damned? Or…

But his mind drifted from the gunshot, as Teresa took his head in her hands and pulled it down to her breasts. He lost himself in their white soft-ness, as if they filled all creation…all life and afterlife. Xaphan had never seen the Creator—not even Angels had seen Him—so he could blasphe-mously imagine that He was a She. An embodiment of fertility, like this woman. He imagined all life pouring forth from the hole he was now stirring (like an alchemist's pestle in a mortar), and all life feeding at the orbs he himself suckled at avidly.

Yes, she was a goddess…and he worshipped…

The bathing pool below Castle Urian, fed by hot springs that made steam curl from its surface, was enclosed by a circular wall carved out of solid rock as red as muscle. Into this curving wall, small curtained nooks had been incised so that visitors could change in and out of their clothes. The pool itself was currently empty—no Demon would dare use it while Angel visi-tors were staying here—but one of these small changing niches was cur-rently occupied by the Demon Xaphan and Teresa Colombo.

She had bent over a stone bench carved into the wall, her palms spread on it, while Xaphan gripped her waist and took her from behind. When they were finished, she sank down onto her knees, her breasts and elbows resting against this rock ledge—Xaphan sinking with her, still embracing her, gen-tly wilting inside her. On impulse, he pushed aside some of the thick black hair that was stuck to the expanse of her back with sweat, and he kissed her on her damp shoulder.

"Sweet," she whispered, in almost a little laugh, reaching up to cup his cheek for a moment. She lay her head down on one arm and sighed heavily. "Well—that was rather nice, wasn't it, my Demondingo?"

"Demondingo?"

"It's a joke. Mandingo? Demondingo? Never mind. *Mmm*…keep doing that."

Xaphan was running his hand across her back, spreading the spilled ink of her hair, feeling the bony plates of her shoulders like unsprouted wings beneath her taut skin. "I hated you when I first saw you," he muttered, more to himself than to her.

She lifted her cheek off her forearm a little, seeming amused by his confession. "You did? Why?"

"I'm sorry…"

"No, tell me. Why?"

"Because you are valued by the Creator. And we are nothing more to Him than inanimate things. And sometimes, we don't see the difference between us. We can't understand what it is He values in you."

"Well, perhaps if you could understand that, then you would be the same as us." After a moment, Teresa twisted around to look up at him, no longer smiling. "Sorry, X. No…I don't suppose there is much difference, is there? I was going to point out the horrible things your kind do to the Damned. But right now, my hubby is out in the desert hunting some teenage boys that he saw and liked in your bloody kennels down here." She snorted, lowered her head again. "I don't want to know why they aroused his interest, in particular. Aroused perhaps being the key word."

Still rubbing her skin, as if contemplating it, as if expecting to at last discern something about it that would distinguish its illusory substance from her mortal skin, wherever that lay moldering right now, he asked, "How did you and your husband die?"

"In a plane crash. Private plane. We were going skiing, in Colorado. We met on a skiing trip in Aspen, actually. I'd moved to the States a few years earlier, and…"

"Did you have children?" Xaphan interrupted.

"Two. Ten and seven. They're still alive." A few empty beats. "I don't want to talk about them, X."

He changed the subject, his voice retaining the quality of a sleepwalker. "Your flesh is so different from Vjeshitza's," he murmured.

"Whose?" A look up at him again.

Tensing up a little, Xaphan let his hand go motionless upon her.

"A mate?"

"A lover," he admitted solemnly. "We don't need to mate."

"But you fuck." A carnal smile. Was there a hint of jealousy in her dark eyes, or was it merely flirtation that pretended jealousy? He hoped she was jealous. It would cause him pain if she wasn't, he realized.

He was jealous of her husband, he realized…

"Yes," he whispered.

"I'm different from her, am I? I won't ask who you like to fuck more. It's apples and oranges, isn't it? A bright morning sky is lovely. And so is the black night sky with stars."

Xaphan grunted derisively. "Your theologian Swedenborg said, 'corporeal loves appear gross, dusky, black and misshapen, while those that are heavenly loves appear fresh, bright, fair, and beautiful.'"

"That must bother you, to have troubled to memorize it."

"It bothers me," Xaphan admitted.

She took the hand that didn't lay upon her skin, brought it to her lips and kissed it. "Don't worry—you're a beautiful midnight sky, aren't you, my love?"

"Don't say that."

"Say what?"

"Love. I'm not your love. You don't love me."

"Why are you…" she began to chuckle.

"Don't mock me!" he hissed.

"I'm not mocking you, X! It's an expression, isn't it? I didn't realize love was such a touchy subject for Demons. I didn't even know whether you can feel it." A moment. "Well…can you?"

"I'm not sure I understand it," he grumbled evasively.

"Well I guess we're not so different after all. I don't understand it either. I mean, I know I loved my mother, and my children…there's no ambiguity there." She veered the conversation, again, away from the children who had survived her. "I used to have a neighbor, who told me that he and his wife had once taken in a stray cat. They had it for about ten years, I suppose. My neighbor was an older man, very gruff, an old war vet. And he told me his cat was hit by a car in front of their house one day. He said to me, in his very gruff way, 'I don't know why we ever got that damn cat.'" Teresa smiled. "That was the greatest avowal of love I've ever heard…"

"Terry?" a voice called out, echoing in the circular, domed cavern beyond.

"Shit," Teresa whispered, getting to her feet as Xaphan let go of her. She grabbed up her balled robe from the stone bench, and began slipping into it. In so doing, her elbow struck the deep red velvet of the cubicle's curtain, causing it to sway.

"Terry?" The voice had turned in their direction. "You there?"

Pushing Xaphan back against the wall with one hand, Teresa parted the curtain with the other and slid out into the humid air of the bathhouse. "I was just going to take a dip, darling," she said. "Want to join me?"

Xaphan peeked out through the slit in the soft curtain. He saw James Colombo's loathsome face. Could he not smell the sex on his wife's sweat-moist body? The film of slickness spread across her inner thighs? With his superior sense of smell, Xaphan himself could clearly detect the musk of his own lifeless sperm, nestled inside her in a miniature version of this secret closet he lurked in.

"Mm." Colombo reached his hands around and cupped Teresa's full bottom, pulling her against him, kissing her on the mouth. Open mouth. Xaphan felt an animal growl rumble in his guts, fought to keep it contained. Breaking free of their embrace, Colombo groaned, "I'm beat…maybe after supper."

"How was your horrible little fox hunt?"

"I got one kid. The other got away. But the one I hit, I got with a clean shot right through the eye." He jutted a finger toward his own eye, and sniggered.

"I suppose I didn't really want the particulars," Teresa said, turning and walking back toward the row of cubbyholes. But, she was moving toward the one directly to the left of the one Xaphan was hiding in.

"They don't die, you know!" Colombo reminded her. "They regenerate…"

"Whatever. I'll join you for dinner. I still want to have my dip."

"You should," Colombo teased, turning away, "you smell sweaty."

"Thanks, James. Ever the romantic."

"Hey, you love me for my honesty," called his diminishing voice.

"Do I?" she called back. "And do you love me for my honesty?"

"That and your tasty ass," his voice echoed.

A moment later, Teresa ducked back into the closet with Xaphan. She curled her fingers into his nipple rings, drew him into her arms. "Mm," she moaned, as her husband had done while embracing her, running her hands around his shoulders and across the sleek feathers of his folded wings. "Thank God he's gone. I don't know why I married him, X, I really don't understand it…"

Xaphan was not moved by her statement, whether it was an honest sentiment or meant only to reassure him. He said nothing, looked over the top of her head at the dark red curtain. Its featureless smoothness soothed him a little, as her skin had done a minute or so earlier. Now that skin, bending with oppressive pleasure against his own, only confused him. What a curse, the skin. There was no escaping it, even in Hell.

♋

As had been the case over the past several days, Vjeshitza was one of the Demons who accompanied the visiting Angels on their hunt. Because of this, Xaphan relented when Teresa insisted he take her to his own tiny room, with its red tapestry bearing the symbol for Castle Urian and the matching red sheets on its narrow bed.

Teresa sat astride him, his hands gripping her breasts, claws extended just far enough to indent their soft flesh. Rolling her ample hips in a slow, circular rhythm, Teresa husked, "I think we're leaving tomorrow." She said it without lead-in, without segue. Its unexpectedness shocked Xaphan, although the information itself should not have shocked him.

"Your husband bores so soon?"

"I suppose so."

"And you?"

"Me? I'm not bored, X. But what am I to do?"

"What are you to *do*?" Xaphan repeated hotly. He calmed his tone, but stammered with a raw discomfort that made him bitter, "Will you return, then? Or am I never to see you again?"

"Ohh…darling," Teresa purred, cupping the side of his face. "I will come back to see you again, I promise. We're both immortal, aren't we? We have all of eternity to see each other again..."

"You're immortal. I'm not."

"You won't age. And you won't die, unless you're killed. So don't get killed, all right?" She smiled down at him. "What is it with me? I've always been drawn to either bullies or brooders."

She slid off him, left his cock suspended naked and vulnerable in the air. She rolled onto her belly and raised her rump a bit. "Here," she whispered. He got up over her, lay atop her, began to ease into her again. But she took his shaft in hand, and nuzzled its tip a little higher up. "No—here."

Lubricated with her juices and with the inner mucus of this orifice, he pressed gradually inside her. She winced, gripped the sheet in her fists, tensed up hard beneath him. A little alarmed, Xaphan said, "Do you want me to stop?"

"No," she breathed. "All the way."

"It's hurting you."

"I'm immortal, aren't I? And since when is a Demon afraid of hurting someone?"

He did as she asked, until he was in her to his hilt and rocking forward and back atop her. Teresa's eyes were clenched shut and tearing at the corners, but she gasped, "You love me, then, don't you?"

"Please don't make me say it."

"Say it. You're torturing me. Let me torture you."

"Yes," Xaphan said through gritted teeth, increasing his rhythm now with each thrust until he was slapping against her, until the bed rocked and she began to cry out a little with each stab, "I love you...I love you..."

♋

There was a commotion in Castle Urian, which Xaphan with his heightened senses detected, raising his head alertly. Teresa only became aware of it when he halted his thrusts, and she rolled over, her hair in her face, as he slipped out of her. "What is it?"

"The hunting party is back early," he hissed. "You'd better get out of the Demon quarters..."

Teresa got up, pulled her robe on. "Bloody hell. James must be more bored than I thought. Or he wants his lunch early, poor dear." On her way to the door, she gave Xaphan a quick kiss on the cheek. "I hope that wasn't our last time, love," she cooed, but he didn't think she sounded mournful, wistful. Or would no measure of emotion satisfy him, any longer?

After cracking his door and peeking out, she darted through it, and closed it after her without a look back at him. Xaphan watched the door nonetheless, as if she might reappear.

♋

James and Anthony had indeed wanted their lunch early, particularly since James was in a foul mood. He had wounded a teen age boy by blowing off one leg at the knee, and when he got up close to the boy to finish him off (or to play with him, Xaphan thought, hearing the story at the banquet-like dinner table), the boy had thrown a rock at James and hit him over the eye, splitting the skin and drawing blood. There was no longer any evidence of this wound, but James was still livid.

"I want that kid tortured for the rest of eternity, Mick," he snarled to their guide.

"I've already had him taken to the tunnels, Jim," the Angel assured him. "They'll straighten him out for ya."

"Better straighten him out on a rack," Colombo grumbled, picking through a plate of edible mushrooms grown in the subterranean garden. Vjeshitza had just placed it down in front of him. Xaphan saw the Angel look up at her small, hard breasts as she straightened to remove another cart from her wheeled serving wagon.

Xaphan was one of several Demons merely standing in attendance like living statues. He had offered to take the men's guns to their rooms, since their weapons merely leaned against the wall behind their chairs, but Anthony Colombo had waved the Demon away. "Don't touch our gear, boy," he warned him absent-mindedly, while looking at freckles of drying blood that he had just noticed on the white sleeve of his robe.

Xaphan watched Vjeshitza place a glass of wine in front of Teresa Colombo, whose hair had been quickly bunched back in a ponytail to hide its disarray. She did not look up at Vjeshitza. Did she suspect that this was

216

her lover's lover? Or didn't she even care? She had not made eye contact with Xaphan once.

But now Xaphan returned his attention to Vjeshitza, muscular and brown, candlelight fluttering on her polished skull. She had placed the glass down already, yet still hovered over Teresa's shoulder, slightly bent, as if expecting another order.

Oh Creator, Xaphan thought, realizing what was happening. When he widened his nostrils, he could smell it over the aromas of the food, too…even from across the long table he could smell it. The musk of sex on the Angel woman.

The Demon sperm, inside her. And with her superior senses, Vjeshitza would even recognize which Demon it had issued from.

From deep inside Vjeshitza's guts, from some microcosm of Hades within her, arose a growl that erupted as a bellow when it escaped her wide jaws. Even as Xaphan's wings spread open (uselessly, as if he might fly over the table), Vjeshitza seized hold of Teresa's ponytail in one fist, jerking her head back. Her other hand rose, and panther-like claws slid out of her fingertips. In a flash, she swept that hand down, and ripped open the front of the human woman's arced throat. Blood leaped like an freed animal, landing in the wine glass, toppling it, and rocking an empty soup bowl which quickly filled to its brim.

"Mother of God!" James Colombo shouted, bolting upright. Both he and his brother scrambled to grab up their guns.

"No!" Xaphan roared, leaping up onto the table.

Vjeshitza turned her feral eyes on her lover. "Traitor!" she hurled at him.

Then one gun roared like the voice of yet another Demon. Followed by several more deafening shots.

Xaphan alighted beside Vjeshitza and caught her just as she fell. Her eyes were still on his, though in those last seconds he knew she might not even be seeing him. As practiced as the hunters were, all three bullets had hit her in the chest. One of these projectiles had struck her in the nipple, punching it in, a leaving a hole streaming blood like a profusion of poisoned milk. Below her, on the stone floor, Xaphan could see a fragment of the once unbroken onyx ring that had pierced her nipple, like his own.

He lowered her slack body to the floor, then reared and spun around, wings still open wide, talons fully extended. He saw Anthony Colombo's gun swing in his direction.

One of the goat-headed Baphomets, also in attendance like a statue, drifted forward a foot or two so smoothly that it seemed to float. Apparently having seen this, the guide McDonald raised his arms and shouted, "Whoa, whoa, whoa! Let's not go crazy here, people, please! Please!"

Anthony lowered his gun warily. His brother James helped support his wife, who despite the fact that the front of her robes were soaked in gore was able to stay on her feet. Because she was an Angel, she could heal faster than one of the Damned that her husband hunted. She was in agony, Xaphan knew, but unlike a Demon, she couldn't be slain. She had an immortal soul, where the Demons had been fashioned without them, like a tin man without a heart.

"We're out of here!" James Colombo cried, incensed. "This is outrageous! Fucking outrageous!" And he began half-dragging his wife toward the doorway, with Anthony covering their retreat and McDonald still blubbering for them to calm down.

Another Demon had come forward to rest a staying hand on Xaphan's shoulder, claws extended to bite into his skin. Xaphan shook him off, and before he knelt down beside his lover's corpse, he met Teresa's eyes for a final time as she was swept backwards out of the dining chamber.

Her eyes were wide with pain. But was it merely physical anguish? The Demon had no way of telling if there was loss…regret…guilt…or only severed nerve endings that would soon weave together again, leaving no scars behind.

Though as a Demon, Xaphan was expected to be a master of pain, he realized its nuances were as mysterious to him as the emotion of love.

He took his eyes off the retreating Angel, and crouched down over Vjeshitza, picked up the halved fragment of her onyx ring. Clenched it in his fist until it bit into him. Clenched his eyes shut like fists, and wished he could take her in his arms and spread his wings and fly both of them directly up, up into the very eye of their Creator.

    Not so that He might heal her.

    So that they might blind Him. If He wasn't blind, already.

God on Television

by Carlton Mellick III

CHANNEL ONE

"LAST NIGHT I had sex with my goldfish. Well, I didn't do it in on purpose. I really didn't want to fornicate with the little slimy creature, but she gave me no choice. In fact, the goldfish didn't even ask for consent, jumping up on top of me and screwing me right against the tile floor. I guess it was a rape or molestation. I didn't know what to do. I just lied there with a squishy look on my face, the cold slimy creature holding me down, slipping her breasts all over me. I didn't know how it could breathe out of the water, gills gasping and fish lips opening for air, as it wiggled on top of me. It was so cold inside, but nice and smooth…I guess it wasn't an unpleasurable experience, but ever since then I just can't seem to get reality straight. I can't even look my goldfish in the eyes anymore."

My mind twitters and I forget what I'm talking about. I don't remember where I am. What's going on?

"Mr. Edson?" asks a voice in my ear, making me jump from my seat.

Oh yeah, I must be talking on the phone to somebody.

"Who is this?" I ask the voice.

"It's Saul, from the Porchlight Project," says the voice.

My face continues confused.

"The person you've been speaking to for the past twenty minutes. You keep changing the subject, but I think you were beginning to tell me that you

221

had some food and clothes to donate to our cause."

A clicking noise in my head, "Oh yes, I remember now!"

Long pause.

"Well?" asks the voice.

"Well what?" I ask the voice.

"Do you have anything to donate?"

"Oh yes, I have a ton of that stuff. It's ridiculous. I was just going to throw a bunch of it out before you called."

"Great, just leave the items in a box outside and I'll send someone to pick it up tomorrow morning."

"Oh, never mind," I tell the voice on the phone.

"Never mind?"

"Well, I don't want some strange person coming to my door."

"Strange?"

"I thought you were going to come," I tell the phone. "I don't trust that other guy with the rusty pickup truck."

"It's a woman in a mini van, not a guy in a pickup truck."

"Even worse. I don't trust those women things."

"Well, you're on my way home. Maybe I can come by after work. Is 5:00 okay?"

An image of my goldfish flashes across my mind. "I can't believe she slicked her fin into my butthole!"

"Okay, make sure the food is in a box outside and ready to go," says the voice in the phone.

I continue, "And it even cried out when I came inside of it. I think we climaxed at the same time…"

CHANNEL TWO

There is a knocking sound annoying my ear.

It happens in short bursts twice a minute for five minutes.

It's so annoying.

"Annoying, annoying!" I scream at the knocking sound in the air.

"Mr. Edson," says a voice from behind the front door.

The door opens all by itself and then appears a short young balding man.

"Fucking, who are you?" I shriek at the man.

"Saul," he says. "We spoke on the phone just a couple hours ago. I came to get your donation."

"I didn't donate anything," I tell the short man.

"Per our conversation earlier today it seemed clear to me..."

He is cut off by a crackling sound. It comes from the kitchen.

"Oh no, not again," I say to the kitchen.

"What is it?" the man asks.

Saul doesn't look like the most intelligent creature in the world, scratching his head like a not-very-smart thing.

From the kitchen comes my hermit crab, hammering towards us. It is now as large as a person for some reason, squatting by the sliced-sausage table.

"What is that?" Saul asks.

"My pet hermit crab," I say. "I call him Hammerskins."

"It's gigantic," Saul says, stepping back to the door.

The hermit crab shuffles twisty black and red legs slowly across the carpeting. Its eyes curling, glaring at the young man.

The man screeches, turns away to run as the crab scurries its eyes up and down his body.

"Don't run," I tell him. "Hermit crabs don't like you when you run."

But Saul is already running out of my front door and before I can tell him to stop the hermit crab shuffles after him with violent pinchers.

CHANNEL THREE

Hammerskins returns, dragging the bloody corpse of the donation man as if a bone was retrieved.

The crab gnaws on the man's leg, ripping open the meat like a mutant dog.

"You are not a doggy," I tell Hammerskins, and the crab becomes sad.

The hermit crab claws strips of meat from the man's back and stuffs them underneath its shell. Not eating the flesh, just hiding it up inside of its house.

Gripping the young man between its claws and spidery legs, the crab slowly disassembles the man's head. Crumbles of bone and blood ruin the nice sea-green carpeting. An eyeball pops out into the foyer and Hammerskins jerks a limb at it, snatching it up into its shell. The skull splits open and Hammerskins removes the brain.

It places the thinking organ onto its face as if to eat it, but the nerves dangling from the brain start squirming. Like wiry fingers. They hook into the crab's head, digging inside, molding onto it until the brain is a working organ on the pet hermit crab.

CHANNEL FOUR

"I am terrified of God," says the hermit crab in a shaky tone, the donation man's voice.

I cock my head at the hermit crab.

"I don't want to die," says the hermit crab/donation man. "I'm far too scared to see God."

"Are you an evil person?" I ask.

"No, I am too scared of what will happen to me if I do anything wrong."

I sit myself on the couch in front of the television.

"I help unfortunate people the best I can," says the hermit crab. "For years, all I wanted to do was help people. If I finish college, I plan to join the Peace Corps. But for now I work with churches and nonprofit organizations. It is important not to be self-centered."

The hermit crab spiders up onto the couch, claws in its lap, sinking into its shell.

"What are you doing?" I ask Hammerskins.

"I want to watch television."

"That television isn't for watching," I tell the hermit crab. "Go watch your own television."

"I'm a hermit crab now," says the hermit crab.

CHANNEL FIVE

I am asleep.

No, I'm awake now.

The goldfish is on top of me again, rubbing my penis with her slime-skin, trying to make me hard.

She is more woman-shaped this time, with arms and legs. They are still fins, but now much more limblike. And the head is more like a woman's head, slender neck. She is still cold and wet, gummy scales, fish eyes, fish lips. But now she has a long white tongue gooing out of her mouth and creeping up my face.

Gills pulsing slowly on her neck as her wet kisses wrinkle my chest skin.

We make love three times.

Lying there, glaring into me with her big fish eyes, slicking back her scales.

"Love you," I tell the goldfish for some reason.

And she kisses me all over with her fishy lips.

CHANNEL SIX

She doesn't go back in her bowl this time.

We are sitting on the couch, watching television with the giant hermit crab who has not left his seat since last night.

"Television is not good," says the hermit crab/donation man.

"I hate television," I tell them. "I never watch it. I don't know why I have it at all."

The fish girl swallows at the air.

"I usually love television," says the hermit crab, "but today TV is very boring. God is on every channel."

I look to the television to see a portly southern-styled man with brown-dyed hair and a white beard.

"Who is that?" I ask.

"God," says the hermit crab. "I already told you."

"What's he doing on TV?" I ask. "What's he saying?"

"I don't know, I put Him on mute."

"TV is even worse on mute," I say. "It captures your attention but you don't know what's going on."

"Well, I don't want to unmute it. I can't handle hearing God's voice."

We continue to stare at the screen. The slimy fish woman rests her head on my shoulder. Clicky fluids flowing inside of her.

Wondering if I can read lips, "What do you think God is saying?"

"He's probably fed up with our disobedience," says the hermit crab. "He probably wants to create hell on Earth."

"Why would he do that?" I ask.

"I think He's ashamed of our imperfections," he replies.

CHANNEL SEVEN

There's nobody outside anymore. Not sure what happened. All the buildings disappeared. My home is still here though. Or perhaps my house has been transported to nature?

"I don't like this," says the hermit crab. "God has more power in nature than in the city. Everything natural comes from God, everything unnatural comes from the devil."

"Is God more dangerous than the devil?" I ask the hermit crab.

He says, "God doesn't like us because we build too much. We make unnatural things and live in unnatural environments. God wanted us to stay like the apes."

The landscape is a forest painting. Sandy purple emotions from behind the deep green trees.

Twilight loneliness.

CHANNEL EIGHT

This morning I am growing grass instead of a beard. It is that itchy kind. The pubic hair of grass.

I glide a razor across my face. It smells like a freshly cut lawn now. The hair on my head is still real hair. And my eyebrows are normal. But all the new stuff is vegetation.

I wonder if God has a beard of grass...

I wonder if he has tiny fairylike angels that mow it for him when it gets shaggy.

The fish girl is lying in the tub next to me. Fish face bug-eyed at me. Her lower body is now that of a human's, with a slight pattern of scales that look more like tattoos. But the texture of her skin is a woman's.

CHANNEL NINE

Later today, outside:

I can't go to the supermarket to buy food because supermarkets no longer exist.

"We're back in nature," says the hermit crab. "We are hunters and gatherers again."

"Who is the hunter and who is the gatherer?"

"I am a bit of a hunter."

"Crabs are scavengers."

"Fine then, I'll be a gatherer."

"I'm too tired to go hunt or gather food," I say. "There's got to be some kind of civilization. We can order a pizza maybe."

"Let's go inside. Nature makes me nervous."

CHANNEL TEN

There is something in the walls, worms and soil and water, as we enter my home. God is still preaching on television, my goldfish examining her privates as God points at her from the television screen.

I kiss her big fishy lips for some reason and see her eyes are turning more human, turning blue. But they are still big. Cartoon eyes.

"Maybe we can eat your fish?" the crab asks. "She reminds me of something tasty."

"Or maybe we can eat crab?" I ask the hermit crab.

"Let's not eat seafood then."

We decide to open up the walls in the dining room and eat all the worms inside. There are many worms, but we also find a beetle, a bottle of dirty water, and a couple severed fingers.

After a few weeks, we decide to conform to God's world.

"It's hard being an animal," the crab says. "But an animal is much safer in nature than a human."

We sit and watch God speaking and eventually take him off mute.

"This is bad," I tell the fish and crab.

"Yes, but there is nothing to do in nature. It is so boring after living in society for so long. As bad as it sounds God is the most entertaining thing there is."

We listen to God for the afternoon. I do not understand a word that comes out of his mouth.

"His accent is messed up," I say. "Is that the accent of Heaven?"

"No, it's just a southern accent."

"What's he saying?"

"He says that we are free of the devil now, free of social organization, free of corporations, free of technology, free of education, free of the system that has corrupted our world."

"What is wrong with all those things?"

"They are unnatural, I guess. He wants us to be animals."

"Well, at least animals are free to do whatever they want."

"No, he says we aren't allowed to do what we want. We have to watch God on television for an hour a day every day and all day Sunday. And the rest of our time we spend finding food, making shelter, and raising children. The world will continue this way for the rest of eternity."

"Well, at least we can mate," I say, wrapping my arm around the fish woman.

"Actually, you can't. He says you have to get married to have children. And you must only marry within your race. And impregnation can't be done through sexual intercourse. It must be through artificial insemination."

"But that's not natural!"

"God says what is natural and what isn't."

"God has made everything far less natural than it used to be. Talking crabs and sexy fish women are the most unnatural things I've ever seen."

"Perhaps God is going through a mid-life crisis," says the crab.

"I hate TV," I say.

CHANNEL ELEVEN

The coffee table thinks it is a buffalo now, grazing on the green shag carpeting.

"That's very unnatural," I tell the crab. "It was a table and is alive now."

"Does it have meat inside of it or can an animal be made of wood?"

The table steps closer to my feet to eat some coffee-stained carpet, balancing on the wobbly leg that is missing two screws. I grab the loose leg, a cracking sound and it breaks off. The table rolls over squeak-screaming, blood gushing from the missing limb.

I examine the leg hole. It is wood on the outside, but meat on the inside.

"We'll have steak tonight," I tell the crab and fish.

CHANNEL TWELVE

"There's something wrong about nature that makes me feel small." Sitting with the crab man on the roof at twilight. Eating barbecued table meat. Looking into distances. "I mean sometimes it's overpowering."

"God made it that way on purpose," says the crab. "He wants us to feel small in His world. It's how He proves his power over us. Like a tyrant."

"And now we have to watch him on TV."

CHANNEL THIRTEEN

Back in front of the muted television.

God on Televsion

People like to watch television. It is what we are supposed to do. Just like how we are supposed to want to live with God when we die.

I think I'm being punished for not liking television. Whenever I used to go outside and somebody would try to talk to me about something they saw on some sitcom or kooky news show and I told them I don't have a TV, they would drop their mouths like I told them my child just died. And they ask if I'm going to get one but I just shrug and then they become suspicious of me. Like there is something very wrong with me and they should get away very quickly. Tell the authorities on me.

CHANNEL FOURTEEN

Weeks pass and I become a small lawn on the living room floor. The fish woman has mutated into a normal woman, but she can't grow any hair and still has a goldfish smell to her. She doesn't talk and doesn't think to put on any clothes.

The crab man has disappeared. I heard some screaming coming from the other room and I think the fish woman killed and ate him. Or he might have run away.

She spends must of her time on the couch watching television. Her bare feet scrunching against my back. I can sense she is smiling. Smiling at God. Like there is something about him that makes her happy. I have no idea what it is, but I'm sure he's got her brainwashed. She has forgotten all about me. Doesn't remember her lover who has mutated into grass. I know we can't have sex, but she can at least kiss my blades from time to time.

All that she ever does is watch that evil television.

God, I hate television.

The Unauthorized Woman

by Efrem Emerson

NONE OF US has ever seen Wally Wooten's "mother," except for Wally of course. We all wonder what she looks like and what, exactly, her problem is. She's been locked away in the bedroom for over a month now. As senior resident, Wally has bedroom privileges. We're beginning to get a bit nervous though, because it's against the law to have more than five people living in one apartment. Wally's "mother" makes six. We said nothing at first, thinking perhaps that it was a temporary thing. It's certainly permitted to have one's mother for brief visits, but to keep her locked away in the bedroom *is* rather odd. Wally probably has her pee and shit in some kind of container or something, because she never leaves the room. He must be sharing his food pellets with her too. He confessed to sneaking her in during the middle of the night when we were all asleep. He told us that she had nowhere else to go, and we should be grateful for not being in her shoes. He told us that it wouldn't be for long.

"Who *is* this cunt?" asks the Pretty Face, our sole female roommate. "What's her trip? We could get in trouble for this, you know. Why in fuck won't she come out and party with us?" She smoothes down her green flower-print dress and flips her long red braids back over her shoulder. The Pretty Face feels it's her duty to question Wally as much as possible.

"Why, she's my dear old mother, of course," says Wally, pulling nervously on his thin moustache. "A helpless woman in need of my...our...assistance, and let's not call her a 'cunt', okay?"

"So what?" says the Pretty Face, winking at me. "A cunt is a cunt is a

231

cunt!"

"*You're* a cunt!"

"I *have* a cunt! I'm not a cunt!"

"Your cunt *smells*!"

"My cunt *emits*! It emits the aromas of *life*! My cunt *is* life!"

"Your cunt is a hole!"

"My cunt is the Mother of *all* Cunts!"

"You're nothing more than a life-support system for your silly cunt!"

"Yes," answers the Pretty Face, coyly, "but *what* a cunt!"

"Shut up!" hollers Bosco. "Both of you just shut up!"

Inkhead laughs. He whips his head from side to side, bouncing his jet-black curls, then sticks his tongue out at all of us.

"You're so weird!" says the Pretty Face.

"*My most honored citizens,*" the King begins. "*I'm afraid I must inform you of a most serious matter. There are not enough funds to finance several of our glorious military expeditions, so food pellet rations will again have to be cut. Now, I know that—*"

"I fucking knew it!" yells the Pretty Face. She starts to turn off the TV but I stop her.

"Not yet. There's an execution following. We need to be able to describe it in detail to get our attendance cards signed, remember?"

"Oh, I forgot. Did you see the last one?"

"No," I answer. "I was on my way back from picking up my food pellet coupons."

We live on the seventy-fourth floor of Building #339 in Zone 52 of City Z. Each building is 100 stories tall, and has four one-bedroom apartments on each floor. We're quite fortunate because our building is one of the outer buildings, and we live on the side of the building next to the out-facing side, which means we have a sideways view of the desolate plains and empty, bombed-out hills beyond.

Everyone is in the Army. Whether we're needed or not depends on a gigantic rotating schedule. I have just finished a year on the Montana front.

Hopefully, and barring any new outbreaks of fighting, I can enjoy a year or two of freedom from military activities. Those unfit for military duty are given jobs in food production, hospitals, the funeral industry, and of course, outside sales. Sales involve the distribution of government-sponsored products and purchasing is mandatory.

We are allotted 100 New Dollars per week, along with five food pellet coupons. We're required to donate 40 New Dollars back to the government and present ruling King. The rest goes to city maintenance. We are also required to attend public executions as part of our "Citizenship Loyalty" training.

There have been seven public executions so far this week: one fanatic who lobbied for the immediate execution of the King, four homeless panhandlers, and two repeat offenders who refused to purchase items from salesmen. I had only gotten six of these executions signed off my card, so I was a bit nervous. Forgery has been next to impossible since the ultra-scanners were put into use. An incomplete card means a hefty fine, and quite possibly a lengthy series of interrogations in the Palace dungeon.

♋

We're hanging around the apartment later that afternoon, just smoking and watching the tube. We stay in the apartment most of the time. The streets are too hostile, what with all the roving gangs of high-pressure salesman. As stated, if confronted by a salesman one is obligated to purchase something no matter what. Wally Wooten is a salesman, but as his roommates we fall into a special category.

We tend to hang out in the living room watching TV, fucking, or smoking cigarettes and playing strip poker. We always keep a watchful eye on the bedroom door, however. We like to keep tabs on Wally's comings and goings actually, and especially since this "mother" thing. He is very careful not to let anyone see into the bedroom, and always locks it carefully whether he is going out or just going to the bathroom. We originally thought his "mother" was really sick maybe, or perhaps has some disfiguring disease.

Just then the bedroom door opens and Wally appears, dressed for work. He is wearing a pair of lime green corduroy pants and pink T-shirt. His long brown hair is fastened into twin ponytails, and his piercing blue eyes scan the room like an electronic device. He puts his finger to his lips as he closes and locks the door.

"She's asleep," he whispers. "Don't disturb her."

"She's already fuckin' disturbed," says Bosco, tucking his black T-shirt into his blue pin-striped jeans. "Why don't you just—"

"Not so loud!" hisses Wally. "What th'fuck you tryin' t'do?"

"I think maybe I want a little of it, if the truth be known," grins Bosco, rubbing his groin. His own long blond hair is tied back in a single ponytail. "I can almost smell it!"

"You're fucked up, man," says Wally. "She's my mother."

"Then I'm the King's only son," announces Bosco.

I look over at the Pretty Face. She catches my eye and smiles sweetly.

***

A few nights later we're all gathered quietly around the door to the bedroom. Wally has creatively stuffed the keyhole with wet toilet tissue, but Inkhead has been slowly and meticulously poking and prodding at it with an ice pick. It isn't long before a tiny hole appears. A hole we don't dare make any larger lest we be discovered. We take turns of course, peering into the bedroom, and the sight that greets us is rather interesting needless to say.

The Pretty Face sees Wally Wooten standing at the foot of the bed, totally naked, with a hard-on, flapping his hands like some large featherless bird. "He has a very small penis," she whispers. "I knew it! I knew that was the reason he never let me touch him or see him naked with the light on!"

I see a woman, presumably "Mrs. Wooten," on the bed with her legs in the air, spread wide apart. I can't see her face. She has thick tufts of black pubic hair, sliced in half by the angry red glistening slash of her inner sex.

"Non-regulation pubic hair," I whisper.

Inkhead takes over and sees Wally parading about the room, still flapping his arms before finally arriving back at the foot of the bed, where he suddenly launches himself into the air and lands, still erect, atop "Mrs. Wooten," who instantly and without any hesitation whatsoever wraps her legs around him and begins pumping for all she is worth.

"Whoa," whispers Inkhead, squinting. "Too much, man! His own mother! Too fucking much!"

Bosco is too late to see anything. They have by then covered themselves with blankets.

"Fuck!" he says softly.

♋

The next afternoon we're again sitting around the living room, doing nothing, when there comes a loud knocking at the front door. We all jump nervously. The only visitors we ever receive are the building captain, the police, or any number of salesmen. I look through the peephole, then turn and shake my head.

"A weird little man," I say. "He looks like he tunes pianos, but he's probably another salesman."

Bosco gets up from his folding beach chair and looks through as well.

"He's got a thick bundle of official-looking papers under his arm, plus a big sample case. He's definitely a salesman. Let's just ignore him."

"We're required by law to let him in to display his wares," says Inkhead.

"Fuck him and his official-looking papers!" Bosco says. "I say we ignore him!"

"Yeah...if we're not home, he can't do anything."

"Okay," says Inkhead, deferring to Bosco. "Is it agreed, then?"

"What if he's from the Association of Concerned Citizens?" I ask. "We could be fined for not letting him in and answering his questions."

"Fuck it!" says Inkhead. "All he could do is report us to the Bureau of Known Faces. That could take years before anything got done. Is it agreed we ignore him?"

"Agreed," we all say in unison.

"Wait!" says the Pretty Face. "I've got an idea! Let's knock back!"

"Knock back?" I say. "You mean fuck with him?"

"Yes!"

"But he'll know someone's home...then we're fucked!"

"Not if he can't prove it," says Bosco. "I get to be first!"

The loud knocking comes at the door again. Five forceful thumps with a closed fist. This time Bosco answers with five equally forceful thumps, then looks through the peephole.

"He's looking a bit perplexed," says Bosco. "Yes, I believe we've succeeded in rocking his tiny world."

"Let me try," says the Pretty Face. She raps softly, waits a few seconds, then raps again. "What's he doing now?"

"Nothing," says Bosco. "He—wait! He's...I think he's gonna—"

Several loud thumps come at the door, followed by muffled shouts.

"What did he say?" asks Inkhead.

"He says he has an eight inch dick and would like to make violent love to the Pretty Face!"

"Really?" squeals the Pretty Face. She pushes Bosco aside, stands on tiptoe and gazes through the peephole. "Oh, pooh! He's just a tiny man! He probably has a tiny pookie too."

"That he is," I chuckle, "and that he may."

"He can't really fuck me, can he?" asks the Pretty Face. "I mean not without an official permit, right?"

"Possibly," says Inkhead, the most knowledgeable concerning public law. "It depends on if his paperwork is in order...and salesmen do receive special gratuities sometimes."

The door to the bedroom opens and Wally steps out. He wears a pair of baggy green wool trousers with a hooded maroon pullover sweatshirt. As usual, he is careful not to let anyone see into the room. He clicks the knob lock, then takes out his key and locks both deadbolts.

"What's up?" he asks, turning around to face us.

"How's your cunt?" asks the Pretty Face.

Wally stares at her coldly.

"Haven't we discussed this already?" he asks.

Another series of loud knocks come at the door.

"There's a little salesman at the front door," says Inkhead, picking lint off his black shirt, "who would like to fuck the Pretty Face with his eight inch dick."

"Really?" says Wally. "You'll have to let him in, you know."

"Hush!" says the Pretty Face, blushing. "I think he should be invited in to fuck *her!*" She steps past Wally to the bedroom door and knocks on it loudly. "Mother!" she yells.

"Who is it?" says a muffled female voice.

"Hey!" shouts Wally, grabbing the Pretty Face by the arm. "Get away from there!"

"Let her go!" I shout, bristling. Wally backs off, startled. He knows I'll beat him to a pulp with very little hesitation.

Another series of loud thumps come at the front door, followed by more muffled shouting.

"Who is it?" repeats the voice behind the bedroom door.

"God*damn* it!" says Wally to the Pretty Face. "Do you see what you've done!?"

"No," answers the Pretty Face, smiling. "What *have* I done?"

♋

Early the next morning the bedroom door opens and Wally Wooten steps out, once again adorned for work. He wears a beige turtle-neck pullover and lavender slacks with sharp creases. A gold chain hangs from his neck, with a large medallion dangling at the end. A lit cigarette is wedged into the corner of his mouth. He glances at us without saying anything, then bolts the bedroom door.

"Well?" says the Pretty Face. "Get any on ya?"

"Don't start!" says Wally curtly. He strides through the living room to the front door. Bosco stands up and blocks his path.

"Hold it," he says.

"What's the idea?" says Wally, a bit nervous.

"Nothing," says Bosco, patting Wally's shirt and fingering the medallion. "You look a little disheveled, that's all. We want you to look your best when you hit the street."

"I look fine!" says Wally. "Stand aside!"

"Okay," says Bosco, grinning. "Whatever you say."

Wally glares around at us, then opens the front door and leaves. He slams the door behind him.

Bosco smiles, then holds up Wally's signed execution card.

"Here," he says, handing it to me. "It won't be much of a problem to change the name at the top. It's easier than trying to forge it."

♋

City Z consists of 1000 identical 100 story buildings built in a gigantic triangle, with four-lane streets running between each building. At the very center is the Palace of Management, where the King lives and the Assembly meets. We rarely go down to the streets unless there's a mandatory execution. It's just too weird.

There are five people assigned to each apartment. Four men and one woman. As there is an extreme shortage of women, the lone woman has to service all four men.

♋

The Pretty Face stands naked in the living room, smoking a cigarette and doing knee-bends. As is required, her red pubic hair has been shaved into a sharply defined triangle in honor of the city as well as devotion to the King. Bosco, also naked, is sitting cross-legged on the floor in front of the television, playing with himself while watching a pro-government propaganda film depicting our glorious military. Bosco has been nervous lately as he feels sure a fresh tour of military duty is approaching.

I am curled up on the floor near the kitchen, monitoring the progress of a huge roach that is slowly making its way up the far wall. I'm fully clothed, wearing a pair of Inkhead's black overalls and a sea green wife beater I borrowed from Bosco.

Bosco begins to moan slightly, then much louder. Thousands of identically-clad government troops goose-step across the screen. Bosco's face twists up in a grimace.

"*Witness your supreme forces...*" drones the TV.

"Oohh!" Bosco shouts. The Pretty Face quickly sinks to her knees before him and engulfs his swollen penis with her full lips. Her throat begins contracting as she drinks from his jetting fountain. A vein pulses visibly in his neck. A highly-decorated general now stands on a tall platform saluting the endless streams of marching soldiers. They all have fixed bayonets. The roach is hesitating at the top near the ceiling.

"*In honorable battle...*" speaks the TV.

A key is thrust into the front door. It twists around and a moment later the door swings open allowing Inkhead to enter the room. He is unfit for military duty and works three days per week at one of the city mortuaries. He's an apprentice embalmer and always wears black.

"Hello, kids," he says. "How's every little thing, hmm?"

"*Our gallant fighting troops in action...*" offers the TV.

"You smell like embalming fluid," says the Pretty Face, wrinkling her nose. Semen dribbles down onto her chin.

"I taste even better!" replies Inkhead. He tosses his head back and forth, shaking his black curls.

Hundreds of jet fighters are whizzing across the TV screen now. A red, white, and yellow emblem is superimposed behind them. Bosco sits dazed, his penis withering. A glob of semen clings to the tip.

"*The bombing of Montana, and how it affected...*" shouts the TV.

"I hear we're in for more food pellet cuts," says Inkhead.

"We heard," I say.

The bedroom door opens and Wally steps out. He is dressed in red plaid slacks with a coffee-colored polyester long-sleeved shirt. He quickly shuts the door and bolts it.

"Mother is napping," he announces. "She requests that no unnecessary noise be made for the next two to six hours." There is a dark stain around the zipper of his pants, which is a little better than half-way down.

"We'll certainly take that into consideration," I shout. "Shut up, everyone!"

"I see your winkie!" says Inkhead, pointing at Wally's crotch.

"*Consider a full-time career in...*" wails the TV.

"Hey!" says Wally, reddening. He quickly zips up his pants. "I'm serious now."

"Screw you!" says the Pretty Face. "We should report you to the Bureau of Known Faces. You know we're only supposed to have five people in the apartment."

"I don't think so, babe," he retorts wickedly, once again composed. "If you inform on me, the Bureau will just have all of us killed. You know as well as I do that they don't give a fuck. They'll just clean out the apartment and fill it with five more citizens."

"He's right," says Inkhead.

The roach has made the decision to cross the ceiling. It's about two feet out into the middle of the room, just above Wally's head, when I interrupt and point at it.

"Oh, good God!" shrieks Wally, pressing himself up against the wall. "A roach! Kill it, Bosco! Kill it now!"

"He's certainly a big fellow, isn't he?" I say, watching the roach.

"Kill it, Bosco! Please!"

"My yes," says Bosco. "The biggest in quite a while, don't you think?"

"As our ruthless army conquers the hordes of..." pukes the TV.

I'm lying on my back staring at the ceiling when the bedroom door slowly creaks open and a dark-haired woman peers out. My heart thuds violently as I realize I'm seeing Wally's "mother" for the very first time. Her dark eyes dart to and fro as she looks suspiciously about the room. She then begins to sniff the air. She appears to be in her late forties. Orange lipstick is smeared all over her mouth, and one of her false eyelashes has slipped and is now clinging vertically from her left eye. When she sees me, her face twists into a weird sneer and she pushes the door the rest of the way open. She's wearing this pink furry bathrobe which she does her best to hold together with one blue-veined, claw-like hand, but not enough the prevent one of her enormous breasts, complete with erect pink nipple, from poking its way out. Her hair, though a thick and luxurious black, is extremely disheveled, and her eyes look screwed up, vacant.

"Wally?" she whines. Her voice is a bit slurred, thin and nasally. I can see the outline of a pack of super-long cigarettes in the robe's lower front pocket. She smells a little like rubbing alcohol.

Xanax? I wonder.

"Where's my Wally?" she asks. "Where's my blue-eyed boy-toy?" She grins at me, and I catch the brief glimmer of what I think might be a wink.

"He's out selling cheap watches and government-endorsed funeral plans, Mrs.-uh...Wooten," I say. "May I be of some assistance?"

"You can come on in and grease my wheels," she smirks. "I'm a little squeaky. What's your name, honey?"

"Dick," I answer.

"Dick, eh?" she slurs. "Well, that's certainly a coincidence. I've been lookin' for you all of my life, know what I mean?"

"Are you sure you're okay, Mrs. Wooten?"

"I *am* Mrs. Wooten!"

She lurches suddenly out into the living room and over to the front window where she whips open the drapes, allowing the bright sunlight to fill the dark room. Grinning broadly, she bursts into song:

"The bone in the pie! The bone in the pie! The bone, the bone, the bone in the piiieeeee!!!"

"Mrs. Wooten?"

"I *am* Mrs. Wooten!" she says.

"I know," I reply.

"I am Missuss Woooottten," she sings in a deep breathy voice.

"I know," I repeat.

She turns back to face me, then slowly opens her furry pink robe. Then the front door opens and Inkhead, Bosco, and the Pretty Face enter.

"Well, well, well," says Bosco, licking his lips. Inkhead is grinning like a fool. The Pretty Face begins to laugh.

"A party cunt!" she says, gleefully.

Mrs. Wooten looks a bit confused.

We all close in on her.

Inkhead pins her arms behind her.

The Pretty Face pulls open the pink robe.

Bosco gets the leather restraints from the closet.

I'm first.

⊙

"She's dead, goddammit!" says Inkhead, pacing back and forth in the

241

living room. "She's fucking dead and so are we! What are we gonna do?"

"You mean what's Wally gonna do, right?" I ask.

"Fuck! How could you be so stupid, Bosco?" says Inkhead. "You put the straps on too tight! You knew you were strangling her! You knew she wouldn't be able to take it!"

"Hey, don't put it all on me!" says Bosco, running a nervous hand through his long blond hair. "She looked like she was enjoyin' it! You were right here too! Why didn't you do something?"

"What the fuck are we gonna do?" repeats Inkhead.

"We're gonna have to dump her, that's what," I say. "Get that tan-colored blanket from the closet."

♋

The bedroom door is wide open when Wally gets back to the apartment. He enters, a smirk covering his face, then notices the body on the floor.

"Mother!" he shrieks.

"Shut up!" says Inkhead.

We all jump on him. We never liked him that much anyway.

♋

The body has to be disposed of, that's for sure. We stand around nervously in the living room, staring down at her. It isn't a good situation. Bosco lights a cigarette and begins pacing. He takes several quick drags. Smoke billows all around him.

"What the fuck!" he says. "I can't believe it! I just can't believe it!"

"Look," I say. "What's done is done. We gotta just get rid of her."

"What about you-know-who?" Inkhead gestures toward the bedroom where Wally Wooten is presently tied up. "What about that?"

"To hell with him, too!" I say. "If they discover that more than five people live here, we're screwed anyway, and you know as well as I do that they don't waste a lot of time. We gotta drop her. Bosco, gimme a cigarette, will ya?"

"Fuck it! I say we dump him, too!" says Bosco, tilting his head toward the bedroom. "That sheep!" He pulls a cigarette from his pack and tosses it to me.

"Throw her off the roof?" says the Pretty Face. "Just throw her off the roof?"

242

"Something like that," I say. I light the cigarette and blow more smoke out into the air. "True, we'll have to do it in broad daylight, probably later today since we're not allowed out of the apartment after nightfall, but it's not impossible. There are 400 apartments in this building, and 2,000 residents. It will take them years to even get close to figuring it out. People get tossed off buildings all the time. Of course they don't publicize it much, but we all know it happens."

"Maybe we could pass it off as a suicide," offers Inkhead. "They won't look as closely, will they?"

"No," says Bosco, shaking his head. "They'll do an autopsy and figure out that she was strangled. No, suicide's out, and another thing...most suicides don't bother to go to the top floor unless they live on one of the lower ones and want a guaranteed kill. She's not registered to live here, so if we toss her out our own window they'll know something's up and we'll be fucked anyway. They can tell how far the body's fallen you know, through some kind of aerodynamic test or something. They'll be able to narrow it down to within a few floors anyway."

"Yeah, I guess you're right," says the Pretty Face. "It's imperative that she's never traced back to this apartment, no matter what."

"You know what happens to suicides that live?" says Inkhead, scratching his curly black hair. "They wind up in the isolation ward of the city hospital. They keep them in these dark tanks, floating in liquid nutronium, with surgically-implanted tubes feeding them. They spend the remainder of their lives there...although sometimes they farm out the body parts."

"Really?" says Bosco. He takes another nervous drag off his cigarette.

"Yeah. They pipe in this weird 20th century, avant-garde electronic music too. Stockhausen and stuff like that. 24 hours a day."

"Ooh, no thanks," says the Pretty Face.

♋

An hour later we have her on the roof, near the edge and covered with the tan-colored blanket. It closely matches the color of the rooftop. We don't have much time because of the gunships. Bosco figured out that one passes over the top of our building every three minutes on the average. They have twin, side-mounted .50 caliber machine guns. Two live gunners. Robot pilot. All computer-aimed, lock-on-target stuff. They don't fuck around in the least.

"Quickly!" hisses Inkhead. "I hear rotors!"

We all duck into the maintenance shed in the center of the roof. Bosco lights a cigarette and takes a deep nervous drag. The sounds of the helicopter get progressively louder. If the maintenance man or building captain surprises us, he'll have to go over too.

"Don't leave the butt up here," I caution. "They could trace it."

"Right," says Bosco. He crushes it against the bottom of his shoe and sticks the butt into the top pocket of his shirt.

Through a crack in the doorway, I watch a black shape skimming just above the rooftops of distant buildings and getting larger. A few seconds later the huge gunship whizzes by, its double rotors furiously chopping the air, then is gone. I catch a quick glimpse of the side gunner. He is peering into his computerized auto-mated vision-scope. A black helmet covers his head.

"Now!" I say as the gunship diminishes.

We dash back out onto the roof and yank the blanket from the body, then Inkhead, Bosco, and I heft it up and carry it to the edge.

100 stories is very high up. I get pretty queasy looking over the side. None of the buildings have retaining walls or anything like that. I can see that the others are very frightened, and wonder if my own eyes reflect the same fear.

"I *am* Mrs. Wooten!" says a soft voice.

"Shit!" hollers Inkhead, startled. "She's fuckin' alive!" We look at her face. Her eyes are open. She's smiling, still heavily drugged as Wally must have kept her. We hesitate next to the edge.

"What now?" asks Inkhead. "Another helicopter will be flying over soon."

"We proceed as planned," says Bosco. "She's too doped up to feel much, and besides...it's way too late!"

"You're right," agrees Inkhead. "We need to deal with it. It's definitely too late."

"Okay," I say. "Ready?"

"I," says a weak voice, "am Mrs. *Wooo*tten! I *am* Mrs. Woooooten!"

"1-2-3 go!"

We heave her over. The winds catch her and she begins spinning around rapidly, then flipping end over end, quickly diminishing as she plummets downward. Her bright pink robe flaps about her like a set of useless wings. When she's about halfway down, we turn and hurry back to the rooftop doorway. Inkhead grabs the blanket, folding it as he follows us. His jet-black curls bob all about his head.

We take the stairs even though it's slower. The elevators have cameras and their movement is timed and monitored. It takes us eleven and a half minutes to get back to the 74th floor. We could already hear the sirens. As we dart through the stairwell doorway, I see a small figure down the hall in front of another apartment. It's the tiny salesman from a day or so earlier. He looks up at us, then quickly bolts down the hall toward the opposite stairwell. I wonder if the others also saw him. The sirens are getting louder as we enter our apartment and close and lock the door behind us. The Pretty Face has a card game already set up. She has also lit several cigarettes and placed them in different ashtrays. We quickly assume our positions.

"The little man," I say, gasping for breath from my exertion. "The one from the other day. He was in the hall. He saw us."

"What little man?" asks Bosco.

"The salesman we fucked with."

"God*damn*!" says Inkhead. "They usually don't bother people as long as they buy, but if they're fucked with...oh, shit! The fucker probably isn't wasting any time turning us in!"

Within half an hour we hear the sound of booted feet in the hallway.

"Here they come!" whispers Bosco. "What do we do?"

"I don't know," I whisper back. "Maybe it's just a routine check. Maybe the fucker kept his mouth shut."

"No," says the Pretty Face, terrified. "They don't have *that* many soldiers. He ratted us out! He ratted us out!"

We hear the apartment door opposite ours being broken down, followed by short bursts of machine gun fire and screams. The apartment across from ours is becoming vacant.

They're closing in.

The Unauthorized Woman

Bosco, Inkhead, and the Pretty Face are all huddled near the front door listening. Inkhead catches my eye and motions for silence.

We hear muffled words, then something heavy being dragged out into the hallway from the apartment. More footsteps follow. I hear the rattle of heavy chains amidst crying, and know the survivors are being taken into custody. I think I catch the word "interrogation," among the indistinguishable whisperings. A few minutes later they're gone. We know not to go out into the hallway for a while.

"We lucked out! He got the wrong apartment!" whispers Inkhead. "Maybe the tenants across the hall fucked with him, too!"

"We'll be next, I'm sure," mumbles Bosco fearfully.

The Pretty Face comes over to me and takes me in her arms. We slip into the bedroom, where Wally Wooten is gagged and hog-tied on the floor, and make love as quietly as we can.

I kick Wally viciously in the ribs after we're finished. He can't scream because he's been gagged, but his eyes bug out angrily.

We figure that they're through searching the apartment opposite ours, so the Pretty Face and I decide to hide there 'til morning. Once the police figure out they got the wrong apartment, it's a cinch they'll soon be back. Locked and loaded. Bosco thinks we should all stick together and leave as soon as possible. He and Inkhead are tossing a few things into bags. One can hide for quite a while if he or she keeps moving during the day. It's also rumored that one can live in the subway tunnels at night. I decided we ought to split up, meet them later.

The Pretty Face and I quietly open the bullet-riddled door and go in. The place has been ransacked, but there are warm blankets. We have some food pellets too. We sleep.

In the middle of the night we hear loud shouting across the hall, followed by machinegun fire. We listen as they ransack the apartment. Inkhead and Bosco left hours earlier so hopefully they're safe. It doesn't take them long to find Wally Wooten hog-tied on the bedroom floor. As soon as the gag is removed we can hear him screaming our names, denouncing us as traitors to the government. Several loud shots cut his screaming off rather abruptly.

The Pretty Face and I stay in the vacant apartment across the hall until morning. There are dried bloodstains on the carpets. There are bullet holes in the walls. For some reason the police never come back over there. We know there isn't much time, though.

♋

We stand on the edge, the Pretty Face and I. We know it will only be a matter of moments before they break through the rooftop doorway. She loves me, I know that now. All those looks she'd given me were really love. I know that now. I think of the long hours of torture/interrogation that lay ahead of us if we're captured. I think of her screams in the torture room. I look in her eyes. She's crying. Why does it have to be like this? We were lovers long before we were in love.

"I'm the unauthorized woman," she says. "I always was."

"I know," I answer. "I know."

I look over the edge. My head swims and I feel dizzy. The street far below is filled with police, military troops, and curious onlookers. Wind ruffles our hair. She clings to me. She loves me. I know that now. There's no place for us here. No place at all. They've reached the door to the roof and are pounding furiously at it with the butts of their weapons.

I smile bravely and take her hand.

She reaches up and wipes a tear from my eye.

We jump.

About the Contributors

Abigail Parsley has published a number of short stories that have appeared in such venues as *End of the Line*, *Cthulhu Sex Magazine*, and *Horror Between the Sheets* among others. Despite being best known for her works that evoke a gentler feminine aspect of horror, she enjoys continuously browbeating her alter ego, **Michael Amorel**, into literary submission. She thanks the Goddess for her lovely son.

Michael Amorel has published a number of short stories that have appeared in such venues as *Monster's Ink*, *The Dream People*, *Demons and Shadows II* and *End of the Line* among others. Despite regular trips to various institutions, he enjoys murdering the works of his alter ego, Abigail Parsley. In addition, he is the founder and head editor of *Cthulhu Sex Magazine*.

Brandi Bell lives in San Diego and currently teaches at Grossmont College, for the Institute of Reading Development, and for the Upward Bound program. She has published widely, both on line and in print, is a former editor of *Fiction International Magazine*, and has taught at San Diego State University. Brandi writes mostly in the vein of sexual politics while waiting for a heart transplant of the emotional kind.

Wendy Brewer lives in Maryland with her three boys. She has been published in various online and print magazines. Her ebook, Beyond *Damnation*, can be found at http://www.double-dragon-ebooks.com/single.asp?isbn=1-55404-081-7&genre=Supernatural/Horror She can be reached by email at: WriterLdy@aol.com

edited by John Edward Lawson

Kevin L. Donihe's novel *Shall We Gather at the Garden?* was released in 2001 by Eraserhead Press. A co-authored book (with Carlton Mellick III) will be released in 2005. Kevin's short fiction has appeared in over 140 publications in ten countries. Venues include *The Mammoth Book of Legal Thrillers*, *Flesh and Blood*, *Chiaroscuro*, *The Café Irreal*, *Poe's Progeny*, *Retort Magazine*, *Bathtub Gin*, *Star*Line*, *Electric Velocipede*, *Book of Dark Wisdom*, *Cthulhu Sex*, and others. He also edits *Bare Bone*, a story from which was reprinted in *The Mammoth Book of Best New Horror 13*.

Cake Earthhead is an artist and writer whose works have terrorized such websites as *The New Absurdist*, *The Whimsical Icebox*, *Art and Entropy*, and *The Dodsley Pages*. His work can also be seen in the upcoming issue of *The Dream People*, and the anthologies edited by Nancy Jackson, including *Trip the Light Horrific*, *Dream the Dark Majestic*, *Travel to a Time Historic*, *Goremet Cuisine*, and *Mind Scraps*. Additionally, he is currently working on a novel to be titled *Churchboy*.

Efrem Emerson is a caucasion space alien from the Crab Nebula. Some of his short term goals include hooking up with a cute female dwarf, selling Herbalife, and speaking before a group of well-dressed mannequins. He's published short fiction in *Fiction International*, *Dream People*, *Bastard Fiction*, and Raw Dog's *Sick* anthology.

J.M. Heluk ives in a hundred-year-old, restored NJ farmhouse aptly named, Midnight Acres. The author has shared pages with such horror icons as Jack Ketchum, Poppy Z. Brite, Joe R. Lansdale and others, and has been published in several anthologies. J. M. Heluk firmly believes the saddest part of life is death, for the pleasure of writing will never be had again. This is for you, Monty. Live well.

Michael Hemmingson lives in Ocean Beach, a part of San Diego, CA. His most recent books are *Expelled from Eden: A William T. Vollmann Reader*, *The Rose of Heaven*, *House of Dreams Books I*, *II*, and *III* and

Tempting Disaster

Melody: The Las Vegas Quartet Book I.

Born in Mountain Ash in 1963, **Mark Howard Jones** now lives in Cardiff, the capital of Wales. He has had stories published in print and online magazines and anthologies on both sides of the Atlantic. His new chapbook *Night Country* is available from Project Pulp. A previous collection, *Unknown Pleasures* (with Jeffrey Thomas), was published by Dream People Publications in 2003.

John Edward Lawson is an author, editor, and publisher living just outside Washington, DC. He was born in 1974 and enjoys traveling. His poetry collections include *The Horrible* (2005) and *The Scars Are Complimentary* (2002); fiction includes the novel *Last Burn in Hell* (2005) and seven chapbooks. While serving as editor-in-chief of Raw Dog Screaming Press and *The Dream People* webzine, John has also been editor of the anthologies *The Wicked Will Laugh*, *Sick*, and *Of Flesh and Hunger*. Spy on him at www.johnlawson.org.

Dina Lenkovic was born in 1951 in Zagreb, Croatia. To date she has had a number of solo shows in Croatia, Austria and Germany. Her vision of the ballet Swan Lake, images of which were used for one of the posters of a performance by the CNT in 1999, won second place in an international competition of the Soho Fine Arts Institute in New York. She is a member of the UK association The Society for Art of Imagination. In 2000 she won a special commendation from Ernst Fuchs and Philip Rubinov-Jacobson at the exhibition 100 Sacred Visions in Austria's Payerbach. In 2002 she was named artist of the month for October-November by the Society for Art of Imagination for the picture "The City Burning." Her works have also been published in several books of *New Art International* issued by the Book Art Press of New York and in the book *Contemporary Art* published by the Soho Fine Arts Institute.

Simon Logan is the author of the hit underground collection *I-0* (Prime

Books 2002) and the novella *The Decadent Return Of The HiFi Queen And HerEmbryonic Reptile Infection* (Eraserhead Press 2004). Two more collections of his work are in production—*Nothing Is Inflammable* is a collection of industrial fiction and *Rohypnol Brides* is a collection of fetishcore fiction. Both will be published simultaneously in late 2005 by Prime Books. You can find out all you need to know about him on his website www.coldandalone.com

J. Scott Malby ekes out a precarious existence along the cliffs of the spectacular central Oregon coast and seeks his inspiration from the interaction between individuals and their enviornment. This extract is from *Tales of the Lavender Investigative Agency*, a book of short stories in progress.

Ronald Damien Malfi is the author of the novels *The Space Between* and *The Fall of Never*. He floats.

Jessica Markowicz is a futureroticist who believes in Goth and the routine practice of cosmic onanism in the shallows of San Diego. Jessica's enthusiasm for Sci-Fuck has landed her work in *Sick: An Anthology of Illness*, along with other sticky forums.

Carlton Mellick III has published 8 books of postmodern punk horror. He has had over 80 short stories published in magazines, chapbooks, and anthologies, including *The Year's Best Fantasy and Horror 16*. His first published novel, *Satan Burger*, is becoming a cult favorite among fringe lit and alternative culture circles, and has been the #1 bestselling horror novel at Amazon.com. He lives in Portland, OR, and online at www.avantpunk.com.

A self confessed asylum candidate, **Perry McGee** lives in Ohio with his black cat Salem and his albino Burmese Python Butterscotch. His tales of dark fiction and psychological horror appear on such sites as *Darkhalf, House of Pain, The Dream People, The Murder Hole, Horrorfind*, and many others. Anthologies containing his work are *Of Flesh and Hunger, The Other Side of Madness, Things That Sing With Salty Wings*, and Kevin Donihe's strange little book about walruses. Print magazines containing his tales include *Thirteen Stories*, *Cthulhu Sex*, and *Lullaby Hearse*. He was recently apointed editor of rumble e-zine. When he isn't writing lurid tales of insanity, he works construction and drinks beer.

Lance Olsen is author of 15 books of and about innovative fiction, including, most recently, the novel *10:01* (Chiasmus Press), which appears in both print and hypermedia manifestations, as well as hundreds of short stories, essays, reviews, and poems. He lives in the mountains of central Idaho and at www.cafezeitgeist.com

A writer of fiction, poetry, and plays, **Vincent W. Sakowski's** work has appeared around the world in a variety of magazines, e-zines, and anthologies. His plays have been produced at the University of Saskatchewan and in the Fringe Festival. He is the author of the novel: *Some Things are Better Left Unplugged*, an anti-epic tale of the surreal. Recently, his novelette, *It's Beginning to Look a Lot Like Ragnarok*, appeared in the anthology: *Open Space: New Canadian Fantastic Fiction*.

Alec S. Scott (ASS, or AssBackwards to his friends) was recently diagnosed with Texas of the Liver by a doctor named McCracken. Since he had no idea what Texas of the Liver was—and since the name McCracken made him laugh—Alec ignored the analysis, bravely choosing instead to continue his thankless duties as an unpaid observer of Mankind's End (presently in syndication around the globe). He currently resides—as he has for the past eleven years—in Jesus, Louisiana, with his wife, Benay (a.k.a. the first recognized Beta Anomaly), his mother-in-law, Mama, and his black-and-white tomcat, October. He has also been rumored to write a short story, screenplay or two, though he'll deny such allegations when confronted directly.

Craig S. Snyder is an amateur writer and web designer from Columbus, Ohio. His fiction occasionally appears on literary websites and on his own site, *The Mighty Head*. He is one of the editors at *rumble*, a small microfiction e-zine, and posts to a weblog, *Ethereal Code*. His online fiction sometimes appears under the pseudonym "headsfromspace".

Darren Speegle's work has appeared or is forthcoming in such venues as *The Third Alternative*, *Brutarian Quarterly*, *Crimewave*, *ChiZine*, and *Inhuman*. He is the author of two short story collections: *A Dirge for the Temporal*, Raw Dog Screaming Press, 2004; and *Gothic Wine*, Aardwolf Press, 2004.

When not banging his head on the keyboard, Darren enjoys hiking, biking and the great outdoors. Darren lives in Juneau, Alaska, where he is currently at work on his first novel. Visit his website at: www.darrenspeegle.com

Alyssa Sturgill's work has been featured in *Cthulhu Sex*, *The Dream People*, *Crown of Bones* (anthology), *Gothic Fairytales*, *Dream Virus*, *Tempting Disaster* (anthology), *Decompositions*, *A Kick in the Nuts* (anthology), *Girlskin* (chapbook), and assorted less memorable publications. She is the co-editor of *Bloodcookies Webzine*, DJ of its MP3 radio counterpart Bloodcookie Radio, and author of its movie review column, Cinemasochism. She is deeply and psychotically obsessed with obscure cult and horror flicks, and has several rather mind-wrenchingly unpleasant screenplays in the works.

Jeffrey Thomas is the author of the novels *Everybody Scream!* (Raw Dog Screaming Press), *Letters from Hades* (Bedlam Press), *Monstrocity* (Prime) and *Boneland* (Bloodletting Press), and the collections *Honey is Sweeter than Blood*, *AAAIIIEEE!!!*, *Terror Incognita* and *Punktown*, recently re-released in an expanded edition with twice as many stories as the original. A German-language version of *Punktown* features art by H. R. Giger. Thomas' anthology appearances include *A Walk On the Darkside*, *The Thackery T. Lambshead Pocket Guide to Eccentric and Discredited Diseases*, *Leviathan Three* and *Sick*, and he edited the shared-world anthology *Punktown: Third Eye*. He lives in Massachusetts.

Clint Venezuela is an alien from an unknown planet. He enjoys breathing in public, avoiding alcohol and oranges, and the smell of ice white paint. He is fascinated by silverfish and the color black. He suffers from frequent headaches. He enjoys the writing of D. Harlan Wilson.

Christian Westerlund has published fiction in various anthologies and magazines. His graphic novel Angelskin will be available from NBM Publishing in mid 2005. Unfortunately, he can't stand sushi.

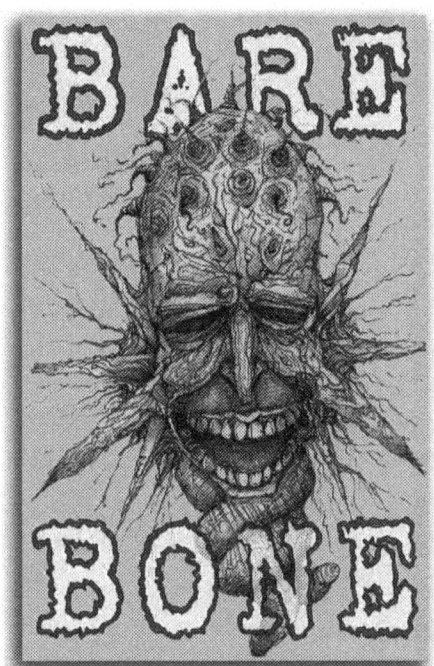

Bare Bone #5, $9.95, 140 pgs
edited by Kevin L. Donihe

Bare Bone #6 continues the spine-tingling tradition of the series featuring the fiction and poetry of today's most exciting authors. From the twisted poetry of Michael Arnzen to the surreal and haunting stories of Darren Speegle and Jeffrey Stadt this issue packs an hallucinatory punch.

"Without inhibition, this selection of tales incorporates everything from the surreal to the frighteningly mundane...The atmosphere in the book produces an almost palpable dementia..." - Horror-Web.com

RAW DOG SCREAMING PRESS

www.rawdogscreaming.com

With a surgeon's skill editor Kevin L. Donihe stitches a diverse collection of fiction and poetry together to bring *Bare Bone* to life. Another Dr. Frankenstein, he assembles the pieces of others, birthing one complete monster to send lurching towards the darkness.

Past stories have received Honorable Mentions in *The Years' Best Fantasy and Horror* and one was reprinted in *The Mammoth Book of Best New Horror #13*. *Bare Bone* is now a bi-annual anthology.

Bare Bone #6, $9.95, 140 pgs
edited by Kevin L. Donihe

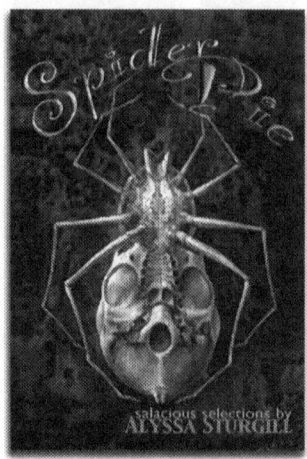

Sick: An Anthology of Illness
Edited by John E. Lawson, $15.95, 208 pgs

The world of publishing has just received its bill of health, and the prognosis isn't pretty. Literary marauders are rising up from the hazardous material bins labeled Horror, Surrealism, & Science Fiction. Here the pen is not merely mightier than the sword; it is a plague heralding the apocalypse for convention, writing a dirge for complacency. These Sick stories are horrendous and hilarious dissections of creative minds on the scalpel's edge.supernatural.

The Fall of Never
by Ronald Damien Malfi, $17.95, 347 pgs

A young woman, long estranged from her family, is forced to return home when her sister is involved in a mysterious accident. After years of suppressing the past she must struggle to remember for her sister's sake. But nothing is as it seems in Spires, her ancestral home, where cold hearts rule the hearth and deadly secrets lurk in the forest. Plunged back into the dream-world of her youth Kelly is faced with the reality of her own role in the tragedies afflicting her family.

Last Burn in Hell
by John Edward Lawson, 150 pgs

Kenrick Brimley is the state prison's official gigolo. From his romance with serial arsonist Leena Manasseh to his lurid angst-affair with a lesbian music diva, from his ascendance as unlikely pop icon to otherwordly encounters, the one constant truth is that he's got no clue what he's doing. As unrelenting as it is original, Last Burn in Hell is John Edward Lawson at his most scorching intensity, serving up sexy satire and postmodern pulp with his trademark day-glow prose.

www.ingramcontent.com/pod-product-compliance
Lightning Source LLC
Chambersburg PA
CBHW050500260626
47157CB00004B/1130